THE BUTTERFLY MURDERS

JEN TALTY

JUPITER PRESS

This book is a work of fiction. Names, characters, places, and incidents are products of the author's imagination or used fictitiously. Any resemblance to actual events or locales or persons living or dead is entirely coincidental.

of the romance grabs you emotionally and the suspense keeps you sitting on the edge of your chair. Great characters, great writing, and a believable plot that can be a warning to all of us."
Desiree Holt, USA Today Bestseller

"*Dark Water* delivers an engaging portrait of wounded hearts as the memorable characters take you on a healing journey of love. A mysterious death brings danger and intrigue into the drama, while sultry passions brew into a believable plot that melts the reader's heart. Jen Talty pens an entertaining romance that grips the heart as the colorful and dangerous story unfolds into a chilling ending." *Night Owl Reviews*

"This is not the typical love story, nor is it the typical mystery. The characters are well rounded and interesting." *You Gotta Read Reviews*

"*Murder in Paradise Bay* is a fast-paced romantic thriller with plenty of twists and turns to keep you guessing until the end. You won't want to miss this one..." *USA Today bestselling author Janice Maynard*

BOOK DESCRIPTION

Special Agent Kara Martin swore she'd never return to Rochester, the town steeped in memories of her parents' brutal murders. For thirteen years, she's buried the past and built a career chasing justice. But when a congressman's teenage daughter is savagely killed, Kara is thrust back into the place she's tried to forget—and into the path of the man whose heart she once shattered.

Detective Shane Rogers has endured his own tragedies: the loss of his wife and the near loss of his son to a rare heart condition. Now, with his son thriving after a life-saving transplant, Shane has reclaimed his passion for solving crimes. His first case back—a grisly murder—throws him face-to-face with Kara, his first love and the woman who broke his heart.

As Kara and Shane race to catch a killer targeting transplant recipients, they're forced to confront their shared past and a rising tide of emotions they thought were buried. Each new murder reveals a chilling pattern, as the killer harvests organs mirroring the ones the victims had received.

When Shane's son is kidnapped, the case takes a horrifying turn, and the clock begins ticking. Can Kara and Shane stop the killer before the boy becomes the next victim?

NOTE FROM THE AUTHOR

There is an old saying in writing that every author has that one project that is "the book of their heart". This would be mine. This book has taken many forms and has been re-written a few times. While it has more suspense than any other book I've ever written, I wove the romance into the hunt for a serial killer, which is just the kind of romance my readers have come to love. It's a reunion story, which I LOVE, and Shane and Kara have spent many years in my mind and heart as I thought about and wrote this book. I hope you enjoy!

To Deb Diez. Thanks for always making me laugh. I couldn't ask for a better best friend!

FOR MOST PEOPLE, the start of a New Year brought with it a New Year's Resolution. Homicide Detective Shane Rogers never believed in them. But he did hope for a fresh start after two years filled with illness and death.

The decision to go back to work on New Year's Day seemed like the perfect way to ease into a new beginning, except Shane had forgotten one crucial detail: murderers don't take the day off.

He stepped from his vehicle and ran a hand through his unruly, thick black hair that was a little longer than a cops typical cut, falling to the top of his collar. His son had told him he was just too old and nowhere near cool enough to pull off the look. Scratching the back of his neck, fingers brushing against the strands, he decided to keep the longer hair. He was starting his life over. Might as well have a new look.

He brushed his hand across the Glock securely clipped to his belt. A sudden rush of heat pounded in the center of his chest. The crisp night air burned his lungs.

He moved passed a small crowd that had gathered behind a police barricade manned by some of the city's finest. He flashed his badge, holding it tighter than usual, keeping his hand steady.

"Sign in," the uniformed officer said.

Shane did as instructed, knowing it was procedure for every crime scene and anyone who dared cross the line would have to file a report. Snow floated gently to the ground, adding to the eight inches that had collected in the last couple of days. The weatherman said it wasn't going to ease up, but get worse, which wouldn't help with the crime scene because the fresh flakes were covering potentially important evidence.

Bright red and yellow lights flashed across the sky as a half dozen police cars, an ambulance, the medical examiner's car, and two fire trucks, lined the road. The side street was on the outskirts of the city, just west of the Genesee River. A couple of local news crews had set up their equipment on the far side of the street, all hoping to be the first to break the news. Thus far, all they'd been told was that a body had been found. Nothing about the victim being a fourteen-year-old girl. Nothing about the fact that Congressman Cleary was the father of the deceased.

Shane looked at the names on the list. His partner,

Will Jones, had signed in, along with two other uniformed officers, Dr. Eric Green, who was the local medical examiner, and his assistant, as well as the police department's forensics team.

"Were you the first responder?" Shane asked the officer as he forced himself to focus on the crime scene.

"No. He's at the front door. I arrived five minutes after and taped off the area."

"Thanks," Shane said.

The cracked wooden steps dipped under his weight as he made his way up the porch and into the house. The building was ice-cold, and he had left his driving gloves in the car. He clasped his hands together, rubbing vigorously, and then stuffed them into his pockets.

Wires dangled from the ceiling and popped out of the wall sockets. Graffiti and a few pornographic images covered the walls. "You the first responder?" he asked a uniformed officer standing by the doorway.

He nodded. "As soon as I saw the body, I called homicide."

"Notice anything I should know about now?" Shane asked.

"I was more concerned with making sure the crime scene was secure and dealing with the adolescents who called it in," the officer said. "Body's upstairs. Last room on the right."

Shane kept his steps slow and methodical. The

sounds around him were no longer distinct, merely muffled noises that echoed in the recesses of his mind. *White noise*, they called it. It helped him stay sharp. His mind churned over everything he knew about this case so far.

Which wasn't much.

He took the stairs one at a time, trying to get a feel for the place. Every homicide crime scene had a texture to it. Even though the body was found upstairs, all the rooms could contain clues that may lead them in the right direction. He looked at every detail as he made his way to the back bedroom, noting the trash and needles left behind from crack users. This house had seen its fair share of crimes before this murder.

His partner stepped into the hallway. "Shane," Jones said. "Over here."

Shane was the only guy he knew on the force who was called by his first name, but only because of a clerical error where it was noted his first name was Roger and his last name Shane. By the time he'd had it corrected, he was already known as just 'Shane'.

Jones wore the typical black pleated slacks, white shirt, and dark sport coat that every detective kept in his closet. "Are you ready for this?" Jones questioned.

Shane nodded, although he wasn't entirely confident. "What do we have, exactly?" A surge of urgency raged through him like a wave crashing against the sand. His heart beat so fast his hands shook. Just nerves. A normal reaction to being away from homicide for nearly a year. As soon as he got into the swing of the investigation, it would be like riding a bike.

"I've never seen anything quite like this," Jones said, running his fingers through his hair. "The bastard literally carved out her eyes."

Shane inched his way into the room and immediately fixated on the lifeless body sprawled out on the cold, bare floor with eight small candles around her body. One near the top of the head. One at the feet. And three on each side of the body. It appeared only the one by her head had been lit.

Despite the nausea, his mind snapped into focus. He eased closer, slipping the latex gloves Jones had handed him over his hands.

The girl's eyelids sank into the holes where her eyeballs had once been. A person's eyes could be the gateway into their soul, letting the world see them for who they really were. Even in death, the eyes seemed to hold onto the person's last thought, or visual, or sound. This victim had none of that.

Small teardrops had been drawn on the girl's cheeks. Her mouth had been covered with duct tape. Shane noted it was from the tail end of the tape, as the cardboard had been flipped up on the right side of the victim's mouth.

The young girl's hands were tied above her head with a thin rope. Her skin had turned purple from livor mortis, her hands blue and her arms lined with dark bruises. Shane concentrated on the knot. Just your regular double knot. Nothing special.

"Let me through!" a male voice shouted. "I'll have your badge."

Shane glanced between his partner and the door as two police officers tried to restrain Congressman Cleary as he tried to push his way into the room. Jones and two members of the forensics team blocked the view of the body.

"You can't go in there, sir," the uniformed officer said. "You're contaminating the crime scene."

Shane took five quick steps toward the door. "Congressman," he said in a level voice. "I'm going to need you to step outside."

"I need to know if that's my daughter!" Cleary's eyes were bloodshot. His breath reeked of alcohol, yet it still took two cops to hold him back. "Let me in, Detective."

Shane could understand the man's need, but this wasn't the time or place. Not when forensics was still dealing with her naked, bound body. Even if the initial investigation of the crime scene had been completed and the body covered, it still wouldn't be the right place for a father to view his child, making it the last memory etched in the man's head, haunting him for the rest of his life.

"Let us do our jobs," Shane said. "Your presence puts everything we do under fire when we catch who did this and go for a conviction. As a former D.A., I think you can understand the implications of you being here."

Cleary's nostrils flared as his chest puffed in and out.

"We'll get someone to take you home," Shane said. "Go be with your family."

"I can drive myself."

Shane shook his head, then said to one of the officers, "Make sure he gets home."

"I'm calling Captain Morrell. He'll let me stay. Be part of the investigation." Cleary squinted, pursing his lips in a tight line.

"You do that," Shane said. "Outside. If my captain calls and clears it with me, I'll let you in. All right?"

Cleary quickly turned and stomped off down the hallway, the two officers following swiftly behind.

Shane turned his attention to the victim once again. He swallowed as he let his gaze lower to the rest of the body. The killer had stripped her of her clothes, leaving them piled neatly on the floor near the door. The lower parts of her body were dark purple-black, a condition called lividity, and normal in the decaying process. It was impossible not to think about his son, Kevin. It had only been six months since his son lay in a hospital bed, just days from death before a heart miraculously had become available, giving his son a second chance at life.

"Cleary being in this house has already put our

investigation at risk," Jones said, standing next to Shane.

"If his name isn't on the log book, it's going to be worse," Shane said.

The girl's ankles were crossed and bound with a run-of-the-mill thin rope and loose knot, but it appeared some of skin had been rubbed raw.

Bending to one knee, Shane studied the lines and circles on the victim's discolored skin. The markings looked as if they had been made from a marker of some sort.

"Any reason to think it's someone other than Congressman Cleary's daughter, Emily?" Jones asked.

"She looks identical to the picture they gave us and..." Shane forced out a few short breaths. "The clothes and jacket match the description Mrs. Clearly left to the letter, right down to the brand of the parka. She's the only missing child in the area."

Jones stood there, hands on hips, blinking his eyes rapidly. During most investigations, he'd remain stoic and philosophical. He didn't have children. Probably never would. That was because his younger sister had half a dozen, one of whom had been killed in a mass shooting at a mall a few years back.

"Any sign of sexual assault?" Shane reached into his coat pocket and fingered his cell phone. The need to hear his son's voice was too strong to ignore.

Dr. r Eric Green, the M.E., glanced up. "I won't speculate."

"Was there a ransom note?" Shane asked Jones. "Any indication on why someone would want to hurt the Congressman or his family? Has the Congressman been threatened lately?"

"Not that we know of."

"Smells like bleach," Shane said. "I don't see any blood. You'd think cutting out the eyes, there'd be a lot of blood."

"Crime scene techs will check for blood with Luminal," Jones said.

Shane stepped to the other side of the body. "It makes sense the scene would be clean since the killer took the time to fold the clothes, indicating he cared."

"Look at her hair, too," Jones said.

It looked soft and smooth. Recently styled. Shane bet there wasn't a single tangle in her long golden locks. "What do you make of the drawings on her body?"

"Message of some kind, maybe," Jones said. "Took pictures on my phone. Want to run it through some databases by morning. See if it gives us a lead. I've asked a few people what they think the design could be and I've gotten different answers."

"Looks sort of like a butterfly if you stand over the body." There was a long single line down the center of her chest. It reminded Shane of his son's scar. "But looking at it sideways, it looks like a mirror image."

Jones stepped to the other side. "I go for the

9

butterfly based on the patterns and drawings inside what would be the wings."

"Me too," Shane said. "Hey, Doc, do we know anything about how the eyes were removed?"

"A sharp object." Green glanced up with an arched brow. "I'll let you know when I know more."

Shane ditched his gloves, stuffing them into a plastic bag, and then pulled out his notebook. He ran his fingers over the leather cover before flipping it open, a habit he developed on his first day as a police officer. He tapped his pen against the paper before scribbling the word *eyes*. He also made notes of his first impression of the crime scene, noting the layout and position of the body. He tried to re-create the images the killer had drawn on the body, hoping it would trigger something, but so far, nothing. He shoved the pad back into his pocket. He'd compare them with the written reports later.

Jones stared at the body, hands in his pockets, head tilted. "Why the eyes?"

It was a rhetorical question, but Shane answered anyway. "Could represent how the killer thinks the victim viewed him. Some say the eyes are the gateway to a person's soul."

"What about the black market?" Jones asked. "Remember that case where the funeral homes were removing bones and replacing them with PVC piping?"

"I do," Shane said. "They were selling the bone marrow on the black market."

"They could also be a trophy," Jones said. "Remember that one guy in Buffalo who took finger-nails? That was weird."

"Weird is being polite. One more question, Doc," Shane said. "Was she alive when the killer took the eyes?"

"Not going to speculate on that either," Green said. "I'll let you know when I know." It was his standard response, no matter the question.

Shane swallowed the bile that was lodged in the back of his throat. He prayed the young girl didn't suffer too much. No murder was ever easy, but a child? There were no words. He stepped away from the girl and scanned the room. He checked his notes to see if what he saw differed from his first impressions, but so far, the only thing that stood out was a distinct smell of bleach, antiseptic, and vanilla, which he assumed was from the candles. "Kids found her, right?" Shane asked.

"Yep," Jones said. "All minors. Came here with some beer to party. They're in the patrol cars, waiting for parents. They were pretty shaken up, but still can't rule them out."

"That's rough," Shane said. "But we've seen teenagers do some pretty insane things. Any drugs?"

"No," Jones said. "First responder indicated that his gut says they found her here. Not going to be an easy memory to erase."

"You don't un-see something like this." Shane watched the forensics team snap a few more pictures.

With each flash of light, he mentally stored his own version of the scene in his brain. He moved around the room, trying to get a feel from every possible angle.

"What have the kids said so far, if anything?" Shane asked.

"They told the officer they came to party. Had a thirty-pack. Fifteen were already finished, so they were well into their party since it was only the four of them."

"Why'd they come upstairs?"

"First responder said two of them wanted privacy."

"Teenage drunk sex." Shane took a few moments to walk the perimeter of the room, searching for another way in or out. "Only one candle lit. Maybe the kids interrupted the killer after he'd killed the girl, but before he could finish lighting the candles. If that's the case, where did he go?" Shane stopped at the doorway, looking for a place a person could hide. There were two other bedrooms with closets, and a small bathroom. "What about footprints in the snow? Any patterns indicating someone jumped out of one of these windows?" Shane noted that in the front room anyone could have climbed out a window, onto the porch roof, and jumped from there.

"Footprints all over the place," Jones said. "But with this constant snowfall, it is hard to figure out who's who and where they went."

"So, either the killer hid in another room until the kids ran and called us, or..." Shane let his words trail off. "Where did the kids go before we got here?"

"Down to the 7-Eleven just two blocks away." Jones stepped aside, letting the medics roll in the gurney. "The 7-Eleven attendant said they came in screaming and crying and he could barely understand them."

Shane was still trying to absorb the surroundings as the medical examiner wrapped a body bag around the young girl.

Shane's phone buzzed. He looked at the screen. "It's the captain."

"You've always been his favorite," Jones chided.

"Hello?" Shane put it on speaker.

"Heard you had a visitor," Captain Terrence Morrell said. He and Shane had butted heads a few times, but not where it mattered.

"I'm hoping when I step outside he's long gone."

"He is," Morrell said. "I'm heading to his house now, but he's pretty pissed off."

"I would be, too, if I thought my kid had been murdered," Shane said.

"I get it," Morrell said. "But would you have called the Feds in as a personal favor *before* the body had even been ID'd?"

"Fucking great." Jones rolled his eyes. "Special Agent what's-his-name?"

"No," Morrell barked. "He called the D.C. office and now we're getting two agents from the Violent Crimes Unit, even if the vic isn't his daughter."

"Why?" Shane didn't like the sound of that. He had less of a problem working with the Feds than Jones did, but no one wanted to work with a team of Feds from D.C. "There's no reason to ask the FBI for their help."

"He's a powerful Congressman with sights on the presidency, who already compromised the crime scene. We might need the FBI to placate Cleary and help clean up any mess he might make."

"They're just going to get in our way," Shane said.

"Deal with it," Morrell said. "I want you both at the morgue right after you wrap things up at the crime scene. Cleary is demanding to view the body tonight."

"Wonderful," Shane muttered as he tapped the red button on his phone to end the call. "Let's go talk to the kids before we leave."

Shane pulled into the parking area of the morgue at Strong Memorial Hospital. "Hey, Siri, call Kevin Rogers."

He closed his eyes, trying to forget his last visit to the morgue just a little over a year ago.

"Hey, Dad," Kevin's voice boomed over the speaker of his cell phone. "What's going on?"

"I'm going to be later than I expected," he said. "Just wanted to say goodnight."

"I'll wait up."

"No, you won't," Shane said. "You need your rest."

"Whatever."

Shane tapped his chest. The disappointment in his

son's voice was undeniable. "We'll have a big breakfast in the morning."

"Grandma is making that French toast bake thing, so we can just pop it into the oven in the morning."

"My favorite," Shane said as Jones pulled into the spot next to him. "Got to go, little man."

"I'm not little," Kevin said. "I don't want to be called that anymore."

Shane shook his head. So many things had changed. "Love you." He tapped his phone and stepped from his vehicle, pulling his coat tight as the wind howled.

Captain Morrell met Shane and Jones at the door to the back hallway of the hospital, where the morgue was located. A flash of his wife's body, badly mangled, her face partially smashed in, sent a shiver across his spine as his muscles contracted, shooting pain messages to his brain. He pushed the memory from his mind.

"Cleary and his wife already ID'd the body. It's Emily." Morrell was in his early fifties. Completely grey. About five-ten. A little on the heavy side, but physically fit. Tonight, he looked as though he had aged ten years.

"That sucks," Jones muttered.

"We need to tread very carefully on this one," Morrell said. "Cleary is a well-liked man; not just in the political arena, but locally as well. People are going to want answers and fast."

"Does the press know yet?" Shane asked, taking in a few slow, shallow breaths as they made their way down the long corridor to the waiting room where he could see the Cleary's sitting on something that barely passed as a sofa.

"Not yet," Morrell said. "Cleary's wife says she knows you."

"Alice," Shane said. "We went to the same high school. Couple of years older."

"Then I guess you know Kara Martin as well."

Shane felt his heart swell as he sucked in a harsh breath before letting it out slowly. "What does she have to do with this?" It had been a long time since he'd heard that name.

"She's one of the Feds coming in tomorrow. Local connection. His wife mentioned she recognized the name."

"Yeah, I know her. Knew her. Haven't talked to her in years," Shane said, pushing any memory he had of the woman who broke his heart out of his head. "Anything we need to know before we talk to Cleary and his wife?"

"He's still drunk, so don't push too hard. He can get real mean when under the influence, but get what you can," Morrell said. "I've been here as a friend, trying to remain impartial. I want you to do your jobs, and that means no special treatment, but it also means to remember that Cleary holds a government job..." Morrell paused. "... more importantly, they've just lost a child."

Shane blinked a few times, picturing his son in his

hospital bed. Dry, cracked lips. Body so weak and frail he couldn't lift a small cup to his mouth. Death had only been days away and had he not gotten his new heart, his son would not have survived. Still, nearly losing a child wasn't even remotely close to the actual devastation of having a child murdered. "We understand," he said.

The congressman sat on a short sofa that Shane knew from his own experience to be hard as a rock. Mrs. Cleary leaned into her husband, one arm tightly wrapped around her body. She clutched at his free hand. She looked up as Shane and Jones sat across from them. Her eyes glazed over with emptiness and shock. "These are two of my best detectives," Morrell said, making the rest of the introductions before saying his goodbyes, leaving Shane and Jones alone with the grieving couple.

The congressman's hands noticeably trembled. His bloodshot eyes were moist.

"We're sorry for your loss," Shane's voice cracked, and he cleared his throat. "Most of this is a formality, but you understand procedure. The clock is ticking, and we have to examine every possibility."

Alice cupped her face and moaned.

Mr. Cleary banged a hand on the coffee table. "I want whoever did this to pay," he said, his voice sharp, his tone and inflection indicating anger more than anything else. "Ask your questions and then go find whoever did this to my girl."

"Mrs. Cleary..." Shane started.

She held her husband's hand. Her shoulders shook as she let out a few more sobs of grief.

"I'm so very sorry to have to do this," Shane said as he pulled out his leather notepad, running his fingers over it. "We need all the information we can get so we can find your daughter's killer."

"Then get on with it," Congressman Cleary barked.

Shane wasn't surprised by the congressman's attitude. Everyone dealt with grief differently. He was, however, surprised by Cleary's wrath while holding his wife, who obviously needed his comfort, not his rage. "You said your daughter had gone into the village?"

"She'd been outside building snowmen with her little sister who had gotten cold and came in and said that Emily had gone over to her best friend's house," Mrs. Cleary said, her voice barely audible.

"Did Emily often go off on her own?" Jones asked.

"She's fourteen. She babysits the neighbors. It's not like she can't go places by herself. She's a responsible kid." Mrs. Cleary wiped her eyes.

"Did she often go places without asking?" Shane questioned.

"She'd made the plans the night before," Mrs. Cleary said. "I was surprised she hadn't come in to get her cell phone before she left."

"Why didn't she have it with her when she was playing with her little sister?" Shane asked.

"This is her third one in a year and I wouldn't let

her take it outside to romp around in the snow with for fear she'd lose it, or break it."

"We'd like to take that into evidence. See who she's been talking to. If there's anything out of the ordinary on the device." Shane continued to study the parents. Mrs. Cleary looked as though she might pass out at any moment. Her face was pale, eyes swollen from crying. But it was the emptiness in her gaze that took Shane's breath away.

Congressman Cleary had been the District Attorney when Shane first started as a beat cop and then later as a detective. Cleary was known for making deals to clear his desk and to keep one of the best records in the state. Even if he had a case he knew he could win, he'd always push for a plea. Shane and Jones had one of their first cases reduced to a plea bargain. Cleary had said that some of the collection of evidence was iffy, so he'd given the asshole a deal he just couldn't refuse. The man who sat before Shane today was a far cry from the D.A. Shane remembered.

"We've looked at her phone. No strange numbers. No inappropriate messages," Cleary said. "I don't like what you're insinuating."

"I didn't mean to offend," Shane said. "We'd still like it. She could have been targeted and her phone could help us. We'd also like to go through her room. Would you be willing to sign off on letting us remove anything that could help us?"

Cleary nodded.

"What led you to call the police?" Jones asked.

"I called her friend's house about twenty minutes after her sister came in. She wasn't there, but her friend was. I called a few other friends. Nothing. I waited an hour before I called my husband, who called the police." Mrs. Cleary lowered her head again and began to sob. Congressman Cleary tightened his grip around his wife, tears welling in his eyes.

"Have you noticed anyone hanging around lately?" Jones asked. "Anyone in the neighborhood that doesn't belong here? Anything suspicious at all?"

Mrs. Cleary shook her head. "It's a safe neighbor..." her sobs overtook her words.

"We're very close with our neighbors," Cleary said, his voice tight with emotion. "We organized a search party and looked around the neighborhood and all of Emily's favorite places until we got the news a body had been found."

"We're sorry to have to ask you this, Congressman Cleary," Jones said, "but can you tell us where you were this morning?"

Cleary let out a long breath. "I left the house around eight. Got a cup of coffee and a pastry at the Wegmans on East Avenue. You can check my credit card records. I got to my office downtown no later than nine. My assistant met me there around the same time. I was there until my wife called. She called my cell since the office was technically closed."

"Thanks," Shane said. "We'll need your assistant's name."

"Heather Underman," Cleary said between gritted teeth.

Shane wrote the name in his notebook. "Can you think of anyone who has it in for you? Wants revenge? Anything at all."

"I'm sure I made a few enemies from my days as D.A.," Cleary said. "I can get you a list of all the violent cases I closed. Will take a bit."

"We can get those records," Jones said. "Anything else you think is relevant?"

Cleary shook his head.

"If you think of anything." Shane handed the congressman his card, "give us a call directly. We appreciate you taking the time to talk with us."

"Just find the bastard." Cleary gripped his wife.

"Truly sorry for your loss." Shane stood and followed Jones through the long hallway to the front door without shaking the couple's hands. Once outside, his own body began to tremble. He shook out his hands.

"What do you think?" Jones asked.

"I think I need to get home. I need to see my son. Clear my head and regroup."

"I understand," Jones said.

"Kevin has a doctor's appointment in the morning."

"I'll cover, no worries."

"Thanks."

"What are partners for," Jones said.

Shane got in his car and headed for home. The need to be near his own son was so overwhelming it caused a crushing pain in his chest.

---

*S*hane didn't bother to check to see if he'd closed the door behind him as he bolted into his house. He knew it was well after ten, and Kevin was most likely sound asleep, but he had to see him, even if it was to merely watch his chest rise and fall with each peaceful breath he took.

"Shane," his mother said.

"Give me a minute." He raced through the kitchen, across the carpet runner in the living room and up the stairs, taking them two at a time, only slowing when he was at the top and about three feet from Kevin's bedroom. The door was cracked open just enough for him to stick his head in.

Kevin lay on his side, curled up, hiding under his blanket. A circular light shone from under the thin covers.

Shane cleared his throat.

The light disappeared, but the body mass on the bed hadn't moved.

"I know you're awake," Shane said as he stepped across the room, and then sat on the edge of the bed. The hall light illuminated the room. "I'm glad you like to read, buddy, but it's past your bedtime. You need your rest."

Kevin pulled back the covers. "It's not that late," he said with a scowl. "It's not like I have anything to do tomorrow."

"You've got a doctor's appointment."

"Oh." Kevin tossed his book and flashlight onto the floor next to his bed. His dark hair stood up from the static created by the blanket. His brown eyes darted around the darkened room. "Well, it's not like it's a school night, since you won't let me go back."

Shane shook his head. "Not the time or place to get into this argument. We'll discuss it during sunshine hours."

"No, we won't. You'll just tell me you don't think I'm ready. I feel fine."

Shane leaned over and planted a kiss on his son's forehead. He placed the back of his hand on Kevin's cheek, letting it rest there for a long moment.

Kevin batted his hand away. "I don't have a fever."

"That's good." It wasn't too long ago he remembered worrying that every time his son fell asleep, he might not wake up. He'd given up on the idea that Kevin might ever play sports, much less be able to run around on the playground. Just a few months ago, Kevin couldn't even climb the stairs without getting winded. Now, the doctors were telling him that his life could not only be normal, but that Kevin could do almost anything. Be anything. Shane swallowed.

Cleary's daughter had every possibility snuffed out in a cruel twist that couldn't even be described as Fate. Or God's will. Just an act of senseless violence.

"I want to go back to school," Kevin said, tears welling up in his eyes. "Even Dr. Nads said it was okay."

"I'll think about it."

"That's what you always say." Kevin settled down in his bed and pulled the covers up to his chin. "Goodnight, Dad."

Shane realized he'd just been dismissed, and knew it was best to just let it go for now. "I love you, buddy. Sleep well."

"I love you back."

Well, that was something. Shane slipped from Kevin's bedroom and headed back downstairs to the kitchen, the ache in his heart only slightly pacified. The crime scene had left him with a queasy feeling deep in the pit of his stomach. That wasn't anything new. Every murder did that to him, but this one affected him on a deeper level...and for so many reasons it was hard to pinpoint the cause of his unease. He chalked it up to having been on voluntary administrative duty for so long. That and knowing that Kara Martin was returning to Rochester.

"Where's Kevin's chart?" he asked his mom as he placed his cell phone and keys on the counter. "Was his temperature normal? Did he take his meds?"

"Relax." His mom handed him an open blue folder

with all of Kevin's information. "It's been six months since his surgery. He understands he has to be diligent."

Shane studied the chart which indicated no changes, but he couldn't relax. He had no idea how to ease up when it came to Kevin. It didn't matter how well he'd been doing; his body could always reject the heart. "He's ten and it would be easy for him to forget."

"You make it impossible for anyone to forget." She snagged the folder and tossed it to the kitchen counter.

"That's a good thing."

"No, it's not. He needs normalcy in his life." She narrowed her eyes, glaring at him the same way she had when he was a small boy and had managed to get himself in trouble. It wasn't a look of disappointment, but more of frustration.

"There really isn't anything normal about a ten-year-old boy having a heart transplant a year after his mother died when her car was hit by a drunk driver." He pulled his gun from his belt, checked the safety, and then placed it in the safety box on the shelf in the closet, as he did every night. "Only seventy-eight percent—"

"Don't start tossing statistics out at me. Your son is alive and beating the odds. That's all that matters."

Shane tucked his head in the refrigerator to grab a beer. He really didn't want to hear this lecture again. He'd heard it a million times, in various forms, from everyone in his family. Hell, even Kevin's doctor seemed to enjoy telling Shane to lighten up. Healthy or not, death was always there, waiting and ready.

"Don't ignore me when I'm speaking to you." She firmly shut the refrigerator door, almost smacking his nose. "We are all well aware of the odds, but even Dr. Nads says we should focus on his recovery."

Wasn't that what he was doing? "Watching for signs of rejection is part of his recovery." He took a healthy swig of his beer, leaning against the counter.

"Yes, but you go overboard. You're overbearing, overprotective, and damn right annoying about it all. Kevin shouldn't be stressed out about taking his temperature. It should just be something he does. Same goes for his medicine. The doctor said the whole thing needs to become a part of his daily routine."

He could hear his own voice in his mother's words. He used to be the easygoing one; Janet had been paranoid and fretted over every little thing.

Slowly, Shane took another sip of his beer. He could picture Janet following Kevin around when he first learned how to walk, all worried he'd fall and hit his head and get a concussion. When Kevin had been diagnosed with cardiomyopathy, it had been Janet's worse nightmare come true, but she'd been the one who remained grounded and strong while Shane fell apart. "Speaking of doctors, he's got an appointment in the morning at eight and I've got a tough case. I want to get in early. I know it's late notice, but can you get here at six instead of meeting me at the hospital? I'll be able to make it there for the appointment."

"I can do that. X-ray appointment, right?" his mother asked.

"Yeah. To make sure his breastbones are completely healed. It will probably last about an hour, but I need to go over some paperwork first thing, then leave right from the hospital for a briefing."

"No problem," his mother said as she rubbed her hands on the dish towel then tossed it to the sink. She leaned her hip against the counter and crossed her arms. For most of his life, he'd been told he was the male version of his mother. He had her thick black hair, intense dark eyes, long legs, and the inability to keep his opinions to himself. But one thing he could count on from his mother was not to ask too many questions about whatever happened on the job. She read the papers. Saw the news. She knew what was going on but had respected that Shane never wanted to bring his work home unless he had to.

"When is Theresa moving in? I've been really worried about what you're going to do if and when you got called to work in the middle of the night and you can't reach me and Dad, or your brothers."

That had been something that still weighed heavily on his mind. It was part of the reason he'd stayed away from going back to homicide in the first place, until his sister Anna had called, asking if her daughter could move in because of some housing problem at the University of Rochester. "She'll be here Thursday, but Anna mentioned something about coming in a day or two early to visit you. Didn't she call you?"

"Not yet," his mother said. "It was really nice of you to take her in like that."

"Anna knew I needed help, and I don't think Theresa liked living in the dorms, so it seemed like a good idea at the time."

"Are you having second thoughts?"

He second-guessed everything these days. "I know she's family, but I don't like the idea of leaving Kevin with someone so young. Kevin's needs are special and she's barely twenty."

"You have got to stop this. You're going to make Kevin paranoid about everything and that's no way to live. Besides, you know Theresa wants to go into medicine."

"Come on, Mom. Are you going to tell me you've stopped worrying about all of us? I seem to remember when I first became a cop you'd call my house every day."

"Now that is an exaggeration. I called regularly because, if I didn't, you'd never call me. I still call you regularly. And no, I will never stop worrying about you kids. Or my grandkids. But you know this is different. You're causing stress in his life that he can't afford to deal with."

"No, I'm not."

"Yeah, you are." She held up her hand. "Besides, you need to get a life."

"Oh, no. We are not going down this road again." Two years might be enough for a man to start dating again after losing his wife to a drunk driver, but not for Shane. Not when Kevin's illness had taken a turn for the worse only months later. Even now that Kevin was doing better, Shane still wasn't ready.

"I'm just saying you need to take care of yourself, too."

"I'm doing just fine, thank you very much." Shane shook his head. He was tired of having this conversation.

"You're lonely."

"I'm busy."

"Same thing," she said. "It would be good for you to go out. Meet people. Date even."

"Drop it."

"No," she said as his phone buzzed, the screen lighting up with a second text message from Kara. His mother looked between the phone and him. "Kara Martin? Why is she texting you? When did you start talking to her again? Is there something I should know?"

He'd ignored Kara's first text because he didn't want to deal with her, or the case, until after seeing his son, but he'd put her name and phone number in his contacts, which was why her name was prominently displayed on his screen. Perhaps that had been a mistake. "She's an FBI agent who is going to be working with me on a case. She's letting me know what time she'll be at the precinct tomorrow."

"She's coming to town?"

He nodded.

His mother smiled.

"Don't go getting any ideas," he said.

"Been a long time since you've talked to her. How do you feel about that? About seeing her again?" Leave it to his mother to go right to his feelings.

"It's work. It's not personal. There's nothing to feel." Only, he felt an array of emotions that spanned from anger to excitement.

His mother lifted her chin. "But it is personal, and you're feeling something on that level. I can see it in your eyes."

He kissed his mother's cheek. "Drive home safely and I'll see you in the morning."

Shane watched his mother pull out of the driveway before closing and locking the door. He checked his watch. It wasn't too late to call Kara, but instead he fired off a short text saying he'd call her in the morning and asked what time would be good. He just wasn't ready to hear her voice again.

2

FBI Headquarters, Washington, D.C.

ROUTINE WAS IMPORTANT to Special Agent Kara Martin. Every morning she'd wake up, put on her running clothes, and jump on the treadmill for one hour. Her routine almost never changed, even on weekends. She'd then turn on her coffee maker, and while it percolated she'd shower, then quickly blow dry her long brown hair, then put it up into a ponytail at the nape of her neck. Her makeup consisted of mascara and light brown eyeliner, which matched her eyes. She never bothered with lipstick or face powder.

Her morning ritual started at five and ended at eight when she strolled into the FBI headquarters in

Washington, D.C., except for on Fridays when she stopped at the bakery for her father's favorite doughnut. She'd buy two, putting one in a bag for the security guard at the Federal Building. Then she'd take one bite of the other greasy, glazed fried cake, in her father's memory. She'd hold on to the doughnut all day, taking small bites, usually finishing it by dinnertime.

Her father used to call it the 'Treat O'Friday' and it was just between her and dear old dad. It had been his day to go into work late, and he always spent the morning with Kara. It was their alone time. If heaven were an easy trip, she'd go there every Friday with a dozen doughnuts.

This Friday happened to be the second day of the New Year. Her boss had called her in to discuss being the FBI liaison in a case involving the death of a New York State Congressman's daughter in her hometown of Rochester, New York. A place to which she swore she'd never return.

"Good morning, Sunshine," Stanley, the guard at the metal detector said as she handed him the doughnut. "Oh, how I live for Fridays," he said.

"Me, too."

He never asked why she'd started bringing the doughnut, but she sensed he understood how important it was to her.

"How was your evening?"

"Exceptional." Kara placed her weapon and badge in the tray. Entering the office wasn't any different than going through security at the airport, except the security here was probably better. Definitely nicer. "Have you finished watching *Breaking Bad* yet?"

The guard shook his head. "I did manage two episodes last night. That show is addicting."

Kara stepped through the machine and collected her belongings, including an overnight bag. "Best show ever written. After that, you've got to watch *Bloodline*."

"You really need to get a life," Stanley said.

"Work, great movies, and televisions shows. That's my life."

He shook his head. "Have a great day, Sunshine."

"You, too," she said.

She made her way through the Federal Building and into the Violent Crimes Unit. Her father's murder had sealed her fate in becoming an FBI agent and working specifically with this unit. It had taken her awhile to achieve this goal, but only because she'd nearly screwed up her life when she couldn't get past the pain of her existence.

She tossed her purse into her desk drawer and rolled her overnight bag to the corner of her office before refilling her travel mug with fresh coffee and heading for the conference room. Little information had been forwarded to her regarding this case. The fact that she had no idea how long she'd be in her hometown only added to the nerves of seeing Shane again. No matter how hard she had tried to put him out of her mind, he always managed to invade her thoughts and dreams.

As she entered the conference room she expected to see the entire team, but instead was greeted by her team leader, Special Agent in Charge Austin Cummings, and Special Agent Ben Foster.

After she took her seat, she checked her phone. No messages from Shane. She shouldn't have reached out to him like that.

Foster slid her a file. "So, you know the lead detective," he said as he tapped the folder in front of her. Foster was a year older than Kara and looked more like a hockey player than an FBI agent. He had two distinctive scars on his face: one across the top of his right eye, the other down the left side of his cheek to his mouth. He was also missing one tooth, which he'd said was removed when he got hit in a fight playing junior hockey up in Toronto. Kara was pleased she'd guessed he'd been a hockey player from the start. But the best part about Foster was his dry sense of humor and off-color remarks.

Technically, Foster was Kara's partner. But the team generally traveled together. This time it appeared she and Ben would be flying solo.

"We went to high school together."

"His captain has been informed that you're coming," Cummings said. He sat at the head of the table. He was approaching sixty. His hair was jet-black, obviously dyed, but it was thick, so it didn't look too bad. He was a handsome man, with well-defined features and soft green eyes. He'd been the one to interview her years ago, right out of training. She was lucky to have been assigned to the unit of her choice.

She watched as her boss flipped through the contents of the folder. He shook his head, let out a long sigh, and ran his fingers across his cleanly-shaven chin. "This is a sensitive case. Congressman Cleary made a statement early this morning that puts the Rochester P.D. in a bad light. He doesn't think the missing person's case was handled properly, but we don't want to upset the locals. This is their case. They have lead."

"Not a problem." Kara stared at Foster. He was notorious for ruffling the locals' feathers in ways that fueled the rivalry between local police departments and federal agencies. "Right, Foster? No pushing the buttons of those we're supposed to be supporting."

"That's asking a lot of this old dog," Foster said. "And oftentimes they start it."

"Well, don't finish it," Cummings said. "You two work with the locals, not against them, but play mediator with Clearly."

"We can do that," Foster said.

"I can do that." Kara pointed to Foster. "Not so sure he can. Last time we worked a murder case he got into it with the local Chief of Police. It wasn't pretty."

"Really, I can behave." Foster winked. "Pinky swear."

Kara shook her head.

"Plane is gassed up and ready. Call in if you need anything." Cummings exited the office.

It was at that moment that Kara's cell phone buzzed, Shane's number popping up on her screen. She answered immediately, mouthing to Foster who was on the phone. "Hello?" She slipped from the conference room and headed back to her office to gather her things. "Shane?"

"Hey, Kara." Shane's voice still had that husky timbre she remembered.

Memories of her childhood flooded her mind's eye. Long walks on the beach at Durand Eastman Park. Laughter riding up the chairlift at Bristol Mountain in the dead of winter. Spending the night in his dorm room. His voice alone had been the source of everything she once held dear.

"How are you?" he asked.

"Good," she said. She and Shane had been the 'it' couple in high school. Everyone thought they'd stay together forever. "I'm getting ready to head your way. Should touch down in a couple of hours." She steadied her hand. She had a job to do. What she had with Shane ended fifteen years ago, and should have no bearing on the present.

"You have anything for us?" he asked.

"Not yet," she said. "We've got algorithms trying to match possible connections to open and cold cases, as well as known perps, but the computer hasn't generated anything concrete yet. Could take a few more hours. A lot of databases to cover."

"Did you see the Congressman's press conference?" Shane asked. "He called the press to his house at five. Made the 6AM news."

"No, but I heard about it."

"It's been less than 24 hours and we've got jack shit as far as a lead."

"Any chance there's been a prelim autopsy report?"

"I'm told in the next 24 hours, but the M.E. is going to take his sweet time with this one, crossing every 't', dotting every 'i'. He put a rush on a lot of the lab work, but no one is going to want any mistakes, so even a rush is going to be double-checked."

Kara saw Foster waving at her, so she snagged her overnight bag and her purse and headed out the door. "I've got to go. We'll talk more when I get there."

"It's good to hear your voice again," Shane said. "Been a long time."

"It has." Kara ended the call and took a deep breath. Long time or not, he still affected her on every level.

3

SHANE RACED DOWN THE hospital corridor, running ten minutes late for his son's appointment. But he'd gotten through all the reports filed by the officers who'd been at the crime scene last night. He turned a corner, nearly hitting a woman carrying a basket of flowers. "Sorry," he said as he passed.

He pushed open the door to the transplant wing of Strong, a place he'd become intimate with. He knew every doctor and nurse, as well as all the administrative staff.

"Good morning," a nurse he'd never seen before said.

"Hi." He looked around but didn't see his son or mother. "My son, Kevin, and his grandmother—"

"Are you by chance Shane Rogers?" The nurse

looked to be in her mid-thirties, maybe a few years older than Shane.

He nodded.

"Your son just went down to X-ray."

"I'll head there."

"You'll end up missing them," she said. "Can I get you some coffee?"

He let out a long breath. "All right. Thanks." He knew the most important part of today's visit was after the X-ray, when they sat down and talked to the doctor about the results, but it didn't make him feel any better that he didn't get to see Kevin before the simple test. "You must be new," Shane said.

"I worked in the ER for a few years. Got burned out, so I asked for a transfer up here." She handed him the coffee. "Your son is adorable, and quite good at card tricks," she said.

"Thanks," he said, appreciating the woman's kind words.

"However," she hesitated, "did you know he's carrying a pocketknife? Not that there's anything wrong with that, per se, just thought I'd ask."

"I know." Shane's chest tightened. He hated being tough on his son, but he'd told him a million times there was a time and place for the knife, and the hospital wasn't one of them. "He's not supposed to have it on him when he leaves the house. Thanks for letting me know."

"You're welcome." She smiled sweetly.

"What exam room?"

"Four," she said. "Nice to meet you."

"You, too." He hit the button to the automatic doors and entered a long corridor filled with other patients having various tests. This is what he called the nice side of the wing. It's where there were happy tears. Patients living their lives when death had been imminent just a few short months ago.

He pulled back the curtain to room number four.

"Look who made it," Dr. Nads said as she stepped into the room behind him.

"X-ray done yet?"

"It is," Dr. Nads said. "Kevin wanted to give a little magic show to the staff."

The last present Janet had bought him was a book of magic tricks. Since her death he'd become obsessed with magic, and if Shane was being honest with himself the tricks made it feel like Janet was still with them in some small way.

"I wanted a chance to talk to you privately."

Shane didn't like the sound of that. "Okay."

"He's doing great, physically," Dr. Nads said. She wore the standard white lab coat over blue scrubs. Her light brown hair fell short of her shoulders. She wore little to no makeup, which she didn't need anyway. "His breastbone is completely closed, which was the purpose of this visit. His heart rate is normal. I did draw some blood today. I won't have the results until later, but I suspect that will all be normal, too."

"Then why the private convo?"

"I know this has been a difficult couple of years for you, but your constant obsessing—"

"I'm worried about my son's recovery and you're making me nervous."

"Your constant worry is starting to affect Kevin in a negative way. He worries you're going to baby him for the rest of his life."

"I think I resent that," he said. "I'm following doctor's orders." Shane had been doing everything exactly the way he'd been told. He followed the recovery program to the letter.

"I know, and you're doing a wonderful job. His body is recovering nicely. However, I'm more concerned with his emotional and social growth right now. Has he been playing with other kids? Being as normal as possible is a key factor in terms of lifelong success."

"We go to the support groups. He has a few friends there. He texts and plays video games with them."

"What about other kids who haven't had a transplant? Other kids who aren't in his therapy sessions or in rehab with him?"

"He spends a lot of time with his cousins."

"Don't get me wrong, I think your family is fantastic and a great support system. But I can't stress enough the need for Kevin to feel normal. He was so happy that you went back to being a detective, doing what you love to do. And I see that has had a positive effect on him. But he needs to go back to what he's good at, and that's being a kid. It's time for him to go to school."

"Look, I think he needs more time to adjust. I just went back to work full-time and I'm involved with a tough case. Our lives have changed enough. I can't afford to be worried about Kevin in a situation I can't control, and there are too many things that could go wrong in school."

"Like what?"

"He could have signs of rejection, but the school nurse might think it's just a stomachache and ignore it."

Dr. Nads actually had the nerve to crack a smile.

"He could fall down the stairs," Shane added, realizing he was overreacting and that there was no way he could control every aspect of his son's life.

"He could fall down the stairs at home right in front of you. And as far as the school nurse is concerned, she'll be informed about his condition and would notify you and me if he even spiked a slight fever, which could happen while at home with the tutor, and could just be an ear infection or stomach bug. These things do happen."

"What about gym class? He shouldn't be doing things like football, or lacrosse, or—"

"I'll provide a list of safe activities he'd be able to participate in, but as he grows bigger and stronger he will be able to participate in things you never thought possible for him six months ago."

"You've got an answer for everything, don't you?" He didn't feel like arguing anymore because, deep down, he knew she was right. "I don't want to throw a lot of changes at him all at once."

"I understand, but your return to work and him going back to school are two changes that are going to be good for the both of you. If you sign all the paperwork, I'll make sure I talk with his teachers, the nurse, the principal, and anyone else you think necessary. But if he doesn't start living again, then his new heart is going to feel that in other ways."

He ran his hand through his hair. "It's hard not to focus on all the things that could go wrong."

She closed her eyes for a moment and nodded. "I know. I think the strong relationship you have with Kevin and the rest of your family, has really helped him with the early parts of this recovery. However, it's time for you to step back and let him start to take over his treatment. He can take his own temperature, do his exercises, especially now that you won't always be there. He's ready and he wants the responsibility."

"Do you think he can handle it?"

"He might be young, but it's no different than teaching him how to brush his teeth. At first, you do it for him. Then you observe, making sure he does it right. Then you ask him if he's brushed; if he hasn't you give him the evil eye and he goes and does it until it becomes habit."

"I feel like you're over-simplifying things."

"You need to understand that by giving him the responsibility he's going to own it, and in the long run it's going to make him feel good about himself. That's a huge part of his recovery."

"But what if he forgets his meds? Or doesn't pay attention to his temperature? This could be a life-threatening mistake."

"You're not giving your son enough credit. First, he knows what he's been through. Second, I'm not suggesting that you walk away, never to discuss it again. I'm merely suggesting that you make it more his responsibility than yours. Give him gentle reminders. At the end of the day, ask him about his temperature chart. Have him show you what he's documented, instead of you taking it and writing it down. To over-simplify, treat it like homework. He does it, you check it."

"That's all easier said than done. You're basically asking me not to worry."

"There's something else you need to consider in all this." Dr. Nads stood and walked over to him, placing her firm hand on his shoulder. "Kevin is worried about you."

"Did he say that?"

"He's worried you won't ever have a normal life for yourself."

"I'm doing the best I can."

"And you're doing a great job. Kevin should be here shortly, and I know you need to get to work." Dr. Nads smiled. "One step at a time. Take things slow. Let's start with him going to school and settling in with your niece. I already put her on all the forms and I'll meet with her on Wednesday. From what I've heard, she's going to be great with Kevin."

"Okay. School it is," Shane heard himself say, but wanted to take the words back as soon as they left his lips.

THE SUSPECT'S DAUGHTER

4

SHANE PULLED THE YELLOW sticky note off his computer screen that summoned him to the conference room. He gathered all the paperwork that had piled up on his desk over the last hour and a half and did his best to push his personal life to the back of his mind. As much as it warmed his heart to see his son so excited about going back to school, Shane had to find a way to put all those thoughts in a box for now and concentrate on the Cleary case.

"Everything go okay with Kevin and the doctor?" Jones asked as soon as Shane stepped into the conference room.

Shane nodded. He took the open seat next to Jones. "What did I miss?" The doctor was right about one thing, worrying about Kevin every second of every day didn't do anything but make Shane nuts.

"A few more reports came in. I put copies in the folder. Not much new was added since you breezed past me in the parking lot earlier this morning."

Shane tapped his finger on the folder in front of him. "I've skimmed the new ones."

"I hope you have a handle on all this, because the captain should be back any minute and he's not in a good mood."

Shane opened the folder and leafed through to where he'd left off, and started reading, trying to mentally organize everything in his mind.

"How do you feel about Kara coming into town?" Jones only knew of Kara and Shane's history because of one drunken night shortly after Shane's wife had died. He'd been feeling like life didn't want him to be in love and happy. He had no idea what he'd told Jones that night about Kara, and he wasn't sure he ever wanted to know.

"My relationship with her was a long time ago."

"She hot?"

"She was back then." Shane had often thought of Kara in both good and bad ways. She'd broken his heart, and now that she was coming back he realized it had never completely healed over the years.

"If she's still hot, mind?" Jones asked.

"You're asking me if I mind if you hit on my ex-girl-friend?" Shane knew Jones was trying to lighten the mood, especially since Jones was in an on-again-off-again relationship, but still.

"Pretty much," Jones said.

"Yeah. I mind." Shane was a little surprised by how quickly and harshly he made that statement. Then again, who wasn't sentimental about their first love? Their first everything.

"Are we up to speed?" Morrell asked as he appeared at the door.

"Getting there," Shane said.

"Did you read about Cleary's life as a District Attorney?" the captain asked. He moved to the front of the room and positioned himself behind the podium, where he sat down on a tall stool, just like he'd do if he were addressing the entire department.

"He was the D.A. when I first made detective. We've crossed paths a few times." Shane flipped through the pages. "Why?"

"Near the end of his time at the D.A.'s office he prosecuted a case where a young man, barely eighteen, John Rodney, was accused of breaking and entering a neighbor's house. The neighbor, Rick Haughton, caught the kid in the kitchen and called the cops. He said the boy had been harassing his teenage daughter, Lisa. Haughton demanded they do something about it. Cleary wasn't going to take the case to trial, so it was negotiated down to a misdemeanor with probation, community service, and mandatory counseling." The captain paused for a moment. "Case closed, until about six months later when Rodney breaks into the

Haughton house again, strung-out on drugs, and rapes the daughter."

"I remember that case." Shane swapped a glance with Jones. They'd both just made detective and had been paired together. It wasn't a homicide case, but he remembered the frustration of the lead officers who had fought to have Rodney face the maximum time in prison.

"Then you'll remember that Haughton's daughter killed herself a few months later. Days after her death Haughton shows up at a party, looking for Cleary who just resigned as D.A. and is now the good Congressman. Haughton was drunk and babbled all sorts of threats, one of which was to make sure that Cleary understood exactly what it was like to lose a child. To make him pay for his inability to put criminals behind bars. A restraining order was filed and that was the last time we know they crossed paths."

"Did Cleary think to tell the officers in missing persons about Haughton?" Shane asked.

"No. But that was before the note," Morrell said.

"What note?" Shane thumbed through the files in front of him, not finding anything about a note.

"When Cleary opened his newspaper this morning there was a note inside from Haughton," Morrell said.

"When was the note found?" Jones asked. Obviously, this was news to him as well.

"About twenty minutes ago."

"What did the note say?" Shane asked.

"How does it feel?" Morrell responded.

"That's it?" Jones questioned. "How do we know it was from Haughton?"

"Because he signed it," the captain said. "Cleary called me this morning, flipping out, demanding an arrest."

"I hope you mentioned that his little stunt with the press conference could have affected the case negatively."

"I mentioned that," Morrell said. "But I also told him we'd get a search warrant and bring Haughton in." Morrell handed Shane some paperwork. "Bring him in," he said. "We can hold him for 24 hours. Not sure if Special Agents Martin and Foster will meet you there, or here. But no push-back about the Feds being here. Got it, Jones?"

Jones nodded.

"Captain," Shane said. "What about the eyes? If it's Haughton, why would he remove the eyes?"

"I have no idea," Morrell said. "But you better find out before Cleary does something really drastic."

"Giving a press conference was drastic," Shane mumbled.

"Well, then, let's solve this case. If we don't soon, it's my ass on the line with the Chief. I don't think you two want that shit storm."

"Why'd you leave the note?" Shane shifted in the metal chair as he sat across the table from Haughton in the interrogation room. The florescent lights flickered in unison with Shane's headache. They'd been at it for half an hour now and had gotten nothing of use out of Haughton.

And no word from Kara.

"I told you." Haughton looked like an eighty-year-old, his face etched in deep lines, though he was only fifty-eight. "I'm glad he's getting a dose of his own medicine. I'm glad he has to experience the agony that has been my life since my little girl died. I feel bad about his daughter's death, I really do. But I don't have any sympathy for what he's going through." Haughton narrowed his eyes, almost daring Shane to challenge his conflicting emotions. He carried a world of hurt behind his pale blue eyes.

"So, you killed his daughter to seek revenge," Jones said. He'd positioned himself by the door, leaning casually against the wall, checking out his fingernails.

"No. I didn't kill her. I don't wish any child dead. But it's hard not be a little glad that he now understands what I've been going through. To feel what it's like to lose the most precious thing in your world. I will admit I wanted him to see things through a different set of eyes. I wished it. But I would never kill an innocent child. That's the truth."

"What do you mean," Shane asked "'through a different set of eyes'?" The first time through the questioning, Haughton never once mentioned anything about eyes.

Haughton slumped back in his chair. "Walk in my shoes for a minute."

"Not a minute," Jones said. "His daughter is dead. He'll be walking in those shoes for the rest of his life. And you gave him those shoes when you abducted and murdered his little girl."

"I didn't kill his daughter. I would never do that."

"But you're glad she's dead," Shane said. "You even said so."

"No…I said I'm glad he has to feel the pain…never did I say I was happy an innocent child had died."

"To me, that has to mean you're glad she's dead," Shane said. "How else could he feel that way?"

"I didn't kill her." Haughton closed his mouth tight.

"All right." Shane decided to pull out a couple images of Emily's body. As he slid two images across the table Haughton gasped, then dropped his head to his hands.

"I swear, I didn't do that. I would never hurt a child. Never." Haughton sobbed into his hands, avoiding the images. Shane tucked them back into the file. There had been no smirk pulled across Haughton's lips. The groan seemed to come deep from the man's gut. That said, many killers couldn't view their victims, especially when they felt remorse.

"Where were you yesterday?" Jones asked

"At home, alone most of the day."

"Can anyone verify that?" Jones asked.

Haughton shook his head. "I think I'll ask for a lawyer now."

"Just makes you look guilty," Shane said.

"You've already decided I'm guilty," Haughton replied. "I'll need a public defender."

"Suit yourself." Jones jerked opened the door. It screeched across the hard floor. "We'll call one right now."

Shane rubbed his temples as he stepped from the interrogation room, shutting the door behind him. Whoever created florescent lights had to be into torture of some kind, because Shane had never been under one that didn't flicker.

"What do you think?" Jones stood in the hallway, hands on his hips.

"I don't know. The comment he made about the eyes and Cleary getting what he deserves is kind of hard to ignore, but I think I believe him when he says he didn't kill her."

Shane rolled everything Haughton had said in the interview around in his brain. It wasn't so much Haughton's denial over killing Emily that Shane believed, but the sheer honesty that shone from his eyes when he spoke of his disgust for Cleary. But when he briefly glanced at the pictures of Emily, Shane saw Haughton's disgust turn to pure sadness and heartache.

He'd seen that look on himself when Kevin had been diagnosed. And in his son's eyes the moment Shane had to tell him his mother had died. But still, Haughton had motive. A strong one.

Jones ran his fingers down his long chin, a habit he developed when he'd taken two weeks' vacation and grown a beard. "What he says is contradictory and he feels like Cleary might as well have raped and killed his own daughter. He wants Cleary to suffer. Readily admits it. But what about the kid, John Rodney, who actually raped Haughton's daughter? I mean, Haughton doesn't seem too concerned with him, you know? Doesn't seem to be any payback for him."

"He's in prison. Maybe Haughton feels like he's already paying?" To Shane, Haughton had nothing to lose... having already lost his daughter, then his wife to divorce. It made perfect sense on every level but one: Shane's gut level.

But a gut feeling needed to be proven; even when at his best, his gut could be wrong.

"I don't know," Jones said. "Haughton thinks the rape could have, should have, been prevented, therefore he didn't do his job. He holds Cleary personally responsible for his daughter's suicide."

"Yeah, but he denies killing the Cleary girl and owns up to everything else. Why would he do that?"

"To mess with us. To fuck with Cleary. Make him suffer more somehow."

"Maybe." Shane's phone vibrated. He glanced at it. A

text from Kara letting him know she'd be landing in ten minutes, which meant in approximately thirty minutes he'd be face to face with the woman who broke his heart at the ripe old age of twenty.

---

*T*he moment the FBI jet skidded to a stop at the Greater Rochester International Airport, Kara started to fidget. Being nervous was not a feeling she welcomed.

"Jesus, it's cold out here," Foster said as they got into a Suburban that had been dropped off for them. "And what's with all these piles of snow?"

"Welcome to Rottenchester," Kara said, giving him the evil eye as he took the driver's seat. Driving would give her something to focus on instead of the uncomfortable awkwardness she felt being in the same city as Shane, "where there are two seasons: Winter and Construction. We get two weeks of summer in July, if we're lucky."

"I see why you left this place behind. It's like one giant dark cloud. Where to?"

"Why don't you let me drive? I know the area, also I don't trust that you can handle the snow."

"Whatever floats your boat," Foster said, getting out of the car and jogging around the front.

Kara just climbed over the armrest, her prim and proper days long gone. "I don't have a boat to float."

Foster laughed. "How about whatever makes the river flow."

"Har har, funny guy." She checked her watch, then her phone. "Shane and his partner already picked up the suspect and questioned him. Let's head to the precinct."

"How well do you know the detective?"

The roads were freshly plowed, with only a thin layer of snow, but as soon as she hit the gas the back end of the SUV skidded on black ice. Piles of the white stuff mixed with dirt and salt, at least five feet high, lined the streets. "We met in preschool and grew up together. We were best friends for years until we started dating. He took me to prom and then we spent two years at SUNY Albany before I transferred to Georgetown." She used to love the winter here. She and Shane would jump into his old beat-up pick-up and fishtail the entire way to Bristol Mountain to spend the day skiing. It was mostly man-made snow and not the best skiing experience. But it was close. And she and Shane did it every chance they could.

"Why'd you break up?" Foster said.

"Long story." She pulled the SUV into the 51st Precinct and parked, slamming the gear shift a little too hard into 'Park'. Shaking her hands, she struggled to push the memories she'd been trying to forget for years. Some good. Some not so good. She pushed open the doors and inhaled a deep, long breath, then let it out slowly as she and Foster approached the main desk. She held her badge up, making sure she gripped it tightly to keep her hand from trembling. "Agents Martin and Foster to see Detective Shane Rogers."

"Welcome," the desk officer said. "Homicide is on the third floor. Let me take you to the conference room."

The precinct was much like any other police station, with a long counter between the waiting room and main reception area. She stood at the door until she heard a loud buzz before it swung open, rattling slightly. Her heart hammered against her chest. Her palms were damp and clammy. Every case got to her on a physical level, but not every case had her ex-boyfriend as the lead detective.

"Follow me," the desk officer said as he led them through a small corridor to the elevator.

The building smelled of coffee, and not good coffee. More like three-day-old coffee grounds someone decided to reuse. Men in suits and ties sat at various desks in the center of the main room. She didn't see Shane, which only increased her pulse.

The desk officer opened the door to a conference room and let her and Foster pass. "The detectives will be with you shortly."

"You're being awfully quiet," she said to Foster, who leaned against the wall near the door. "I've been waiting for a smart-ass remark."

"I told you I could behave," Foster said. "Figured

since you know this detective and it's your hometown, I probably shouldn't antagonize anyone."

"Thanks." She sat down on one of the hard metal chairs, but then stood and started to pace. Her mind raced out of control. She held the case file in one hand while she tried to read the words on the page, but to no avail. She was about to come face to face with Shane Rogers. A man she'd once loved. A man she'd wanted to marry. Have children with. But he did that with someone else.

"You okay?" Foster asked.

"Yeah," she said. "Just tired."

"You're acting like you're more wired than tired."

Foster was right, she was completely wired. Worse, she was unfocused. She was about to excuse herself to the ladies' room when Shane sauntered in, his hands casually in the pockets of his dark blue trousers. Her gaze caught his and she couldn't breathe for a moment. She just stood there. Staring.

"I'm Shane," he said, breaking eye contact with her and extending his hand to Foster. "And this is my partner, Jones," he said, gesturing to the slightly shorter man with dark hair and blue eyes.

Letting the air out of her lungs as slowly as she could she stared at Shane, who looked almost exactly like the last time she'd seen him. He might have a few new wrinkles around his copper eyes, but other than that he had the same muscular build. The same sexy smile. His pants still hung on his trim waist and she bet his body was still ripped.

This train of thought was going to have to stop.

"Hello, Shane," she said, in as strong of a voice as she could muster, holding out her hand.

"Long time no see." Shane took her hand in a firm shake, holding it a little longer than appropriate.

An electric pulse soared through her body. He smiled, but it didn't ease the awkwardness between them.

"Been thirteen years, I think." Reluctantly she pulled her hand from his, immediately feeling the coldness of the room.

"About that," Shane said. "You look good."

"So, do you."

"Before we go any further," Foster said, "we'd like to make clear it we're here because the higher-ups feel it will help prevent Cleary from going off half-cocked with the press like he did yesterday. We're not here to take over or get in the way, but to help in any way we can."

Kara noticed Jones cracked his knuckles at the same time Foster did. Not necessarily a good sign as the two men eyed each other.

"Good to know," Jones said.

"We've questioned Haughton," Shane said. "He admits to writing the note and leaving it at Cleary's house. But he denies killing Emily. He's lawyered up, but cooperating. Search warrant of his house has been granted and is being executed as we speak. Our second team is supervising. So far nothing."

"Can we have the names of the detectives on the second team?" Kara asked.

"Detectives Pollock and Benster," Shane said. "They will be backing us up until we've put the case to bed."

"We just got the preliminary autopsy report." Jones handed Kara a copy. "The M.E. believes her eyes were taken out before she died of strangulation."

"That's messed up," Kara muttered.

"You can say that again." Foster rubbed his eyes.

"M.E. said whoever cut out her eyes did so with a skilled hand and small blade. At first glance, it looked like a medical scalpel. Got forensics on that. Also waiting for the toxicology report. We've got a rush on it," Jones said.

"How long are you planning on holding Haughton?" Foster asked.

"The full twenty-four, as we're stretching out the search warrants," Shane said. "But unless we find something we're going to have to let him go by tomorrow at noon, and that's going to make Cleary very unhappy."

"I watched a tape of his press conference." Kara sat down next to Foster as they thumbed through everything the detectives had given them. "You know we went to school with his wife, don't you?"

"Yeah," Shane said. "She's in bad shape. I think she blames herself."

"You think Haughton did this?" Kara turned to

looked over her shoulder, staring up at Shane. He leaned against the wall, hands in his pockets, his fixed stare directly on her. "It's possible."

"Any other suspects?" Kara asked, swallowing the tension that engulfed the room.

"Nothing, but the ritualistic aspect has us digging into cold cases," Shane said, then offered a slight smile.

"We've pulled three cold cases from New York that deal with mutilation. I brought copies for everyone," Foster said. "I suggest you make yourselves familiar with those cases and see if there's any pattern. We'll also be checking the religious angle."

Kara eyed Foster, letting him know his tone was antagonistic, before turning back to the files. "Our tech analyst is running the markings that were drawn on the body," Kara said.

"We think it's a butterfly," Jones said.

"Do we know if the victim had a thing for butterflies?" Kara asked.

"We don't," Shane said, his voice echoing off the concrete walls. "But we do have permission to search and take things from Emily's room."

"Maybe Foster and I should do that," Kara said. "Only because of Cleary's aversion to his local police department. Any idea why that is?"

"As D.A., he was notorious for plea bargaining," Jones said. "He plea bargained more cases than any other D.A. in the state of New York. He didn't like going to trial and encouraged all his A.D.A.s to offer whatever they could to keep their record the best in the state. It often pissed us off and he, in general, butted heads with a lot of cops."

The door squeaked open and a uniformed officer stepped in.

"Congressman Cleary is here," the officer said. "He wants to have a word with the federal agents."

"Speak of the devil," Shane said. "Do you want to talk with him?"

"I'd like to have a little more time to go over everything before I sit down with him," Kara admitted.

"You should know Cleary's intoxicated," the officer said. "He's tossing insults and threats about having half of us fired if we stand in his way of talking with the FBI. Might be a good idea to placate him."

"I'd have to agree," Shane said. "Considering he's the one who brought you here, blowing him off now could create a distraction in the case we just don't need."

"Wonderful." Kara stood, brushing the front of her slacks before taking off her blazer and putting it on the chair. "We're happy to speak to him."

"Get a car ready to take him home," Shane added. "And someone to drive his car back to his place. But be discreet."

The officer nodded.

There was a long awkward silence as they waited. It was difficult for Kara not to continue to glance in Shane's direction. He'd once been the center of her life.

Looking at him now filled her heart with a world of regret.

Cleary finally entered the conference room. He was a tall man, about six-one, but the strong stench of whiskey was more notable than his haggard appearance.

"Congressman Cleary—"

Cleary interrupted Kara. "I heard Haughton is here. You better have arrested that son of a bitch."

"He's in our custody," Shane said. "We're still interrogating him."

"I wasn't talking to you." Cleary stepped into Kara's personal space. She didn't back down, though she nearly gagged from the alcohol assaulting her nostrils. "I was asking her. You're FBI, right?"

"Special Agent Kara Martin," she said. "I haven't had the chance—"

"Did the bastard confess?" Cleary inched a tad closer. His hands were on his hips, legs shoulder-width apart.

Kara cocked her head slightly backward, but held her stance.

"Not yet." Shane stepped closer, standing perpendicular to her. "You know how this works."

Kara knew she was going to have to give the man something to calm him down. "He's confessed to putting the note in your newspaper, and search warrants are being executed."

"By the locals?" Cleary yelled. "I can't tell you how

many cases I was forced to plea out because of lack-adaisical police work. I don't want them heading up this case."

"We're working together," Kara said. "I've been informed you've given us permission to search Emily's room. I'd like to do that sooner rather than later."

"Fine," Cleary said. "But only when my other children aren't there."

"We need to do it today," Kara said. "We can only hold Haughton for twenty-four hours. Time is of the essence."

"All right," Cleary said. "In an hour?"

"How about we go back with you," Kara said. "I promise it won't take too long."

"That's fine." Cleary's demeanor appeared to calm down a tad. "But," he pointed a finger at Shane, "that man had better not walk out of this station unless it's in handcuffs to County to await trial."

"We're looking at all the evidence," Jones said. "I understand you want—"

"You don't understand shit," Cleary hissed. "You've got the killer in your custody. That bastard murdered my baby girl!"

"Congressman," Shane said in a stern, but caring, voice. "I can't even pretend to understand what you're going through right now. I have a son. He's ten and he just recently had a heart transplant. I can't wrap my brain around the idea of losing him, though I almost did. We're doing everything we can. The FBI has brought us similar cases, and while we're searching Haughton's place for evidence we're also going to check these other leads. You know we have to."

Kara swallowed. She knew he'd moved on, but she hadn't known his son had had a heart transplant.

Shane's words seemed to pacify Clearly, but not his resolve. "I know he did it. I'll give you the twenty- four hours, but let this be a warning that if you don't make an arrest by then, there will be hell to pay."

"Let us do our jobs," Shane said in a calm and soothing voice, the timbre much like she remembered.

Cleary nodded.

"We'll be by shortly to go through Emily's room. Please tell your wife, in case she's not there when we arrive, that Kara Martin says hello, and give her my condolences. We went to high school together." Kara wanted the Congressman to know she had a personal stake in this case. She thought it might ease his mind, though Shane had been much more effective.

"You're from around here?" Cleary asked. His bloodshot eyes looked dry as he blinked a few times.

"I grew up in Pittsford, a couple of streets from your wife," Kara said.

"Martin?" Cleary rubbed the stubble on his chin. "Your parents were mur…"

"Yes," Kara said. No need opening that wound any further. She held out her card. "Feel free to call me day or night. My partner and I will be in the area until this case is solved."

Jones quickly ushered Cleary out.

"Go with him," Kara said to Foster, who stepped out of the conference room.

"I'm going to make a radical suggestion," Shane said.

"And what is that?" Kara asked.

"Let's work in teams. One local. One Fed," Shane said. "You and me. Foster and Jones."

"I don't think that's such a good idea; Foster doesn't always play nice in the sandbox."

"I got that impression," Shane said. "Neither does Jones, which is why I think it's a good idea."

Kara didn't know if Shane wanted to spend time with her, or if he actually thought Jones and Foster teaming up was a good idea, but she did agree that working one local with one Fed was a good idea. "All right. We can give that a go, but if our partners go at it we need to change that up right quick."

"Agreed," Shane said. "We can go question Cleary's assistant before we go to his house. Let Foster and Jones question Haughton and his lawyer."

Kara laughed. "Those two, with the chest pounding antics, just might work in an interrogation."

Shane smiled. "Jones is really good."

Kara stood. Shane held the door open for her with one hand, files tucked under his arm.

"After you," he said.

Always the gentleman. Some things never changed.

5

ARA HATED THE IDEA of someone else driving, a control issue she'd developed after she'd broken up with Shane. Besides, she much preferred the SUV to Shane's sedan, but she'd lost the coin toss fair and square.

"What do we know about Heather Underman?" Kara asked. She stared out the window, watching the large dollops of snow hit the glass and then melt from the heat of the car. It snowed in D.C., but nothing like this. For a second, she thought she'd missed the fluffy flakes.

"She's worked for Cleary since his days in the D.A.'s office."

"What did she do there?"

"A clerk," Shane said. "When Cleary ran for office, she worked on his campaign, and then became his personal assistant."

"That's convenient." And cliché, but there were truisms in clichés. "What else? How old is she?"

"In her mid-thirties. About our age." Shane kept both hands on the steering wheel.

Not once did he glance over at Kara, which bothered her. "She's essentially his alibi."

"Yep." Shane maneuvered the vehicle into a parking spot in front of a single-family home off Park Avenue. He leapt from the car and raced around the front before she had a chance to unbuckle.

And he hadn't changed as he reached in, taking her hand in his.

"Always the gentleman."

"Old habits die hard," he said.

"What? No kiss on the hand?"

He tilted his head. "If you insist." He pressed his lips against her cold hand. When he released her, he smiled.

"I don't like the circumstances, but it is good to see you," she said. And she meant it. There might be a lot of unresolved issues between them. They may always be unresolved, but seeing him wasn't as difficult as she thought it would be.

"It's good to see you, too," he said, though he wasn't as convincing. He stuffed his hands into his pockets and started walking toward the house. "How do you want to play this?"

"I don't want to play it. Just let her tell us where she was on Thursday. Go from there."

"Works for me." Shane rang the doorbell then turned his back, hands still in his pockets. The Shane she remembered was outgoing and often a bit on the loud and obnoxious side. This Shane was different. He was quiet. Reserved.

"Yes?" A pretty brunette with legs that went on forever answered the door. She wore skinny jeans, and a tight sweater with a V-neck that showed off her cleavage.

"Are you Heather Underman?" Kara flashed her badge.

"Yes?"

"I'm Special Agent Martin. This is Detective Rogers. Can we ask you a few questions about last Thursday?"

"Sure," Heather said. "Come on in."

Kara followed her through a small foyer and into the living room. There was a dark brown leather sofa against the outside wall, with a big picture window behind it. Two matching chairs with ottomans were on the other side. The back wall had what Kara thought could be an expensive painting. Or a very good knockoff of one. She also noted that there were a lot of upscale Mackenzie Child products around the room.

"Can I get you anything?" Heather asked.

"No thanks," Shane said. "We don't want to take up too much of your time."

Kara sat on the sofa, Shane to her right. Heather sat in the chair across from them. She fiddled with her fingers, an obvious sign of being nervous. "What did you do last Thursday?" Kara asked.

"It was New Year's Day, but Congressman Cleary asked me to come in to go over some paperwork."

"Do you often work holidays?" Shane asked.

"Sometimes." Heather had crossed and recrossed her legs five times in the last three minutes.

"Anyone else go into the office that day?" Kara asked.

Heather shook her head.

"Do you have to sign in anywhere in your building?" Kara asked.

Heather nodded.

"So, when we check the logs, it will show both you and the Congressman signed in between..." Kara let her voice trail off.

"Look," Heather said. "I was with the Congressman, but it wasn't at the office. He was here. I can't lie to you about that, but considering everything he and his family are going through right now, can't we just go with we were at the office?"

"Not unless there is a witness other than you and the Congressman that can verify your whereabouts," Kara said.

"You've got to be kidding. You think the Congressman, or I had something to do with Emily's death?"

"Can't rule anything out just yet," Shane said. "How long have you been having an affair with Congressman Cleary?"

"Six years," Heather admitted. "It works for us. I don't want to ever get married, deal with a husband, or have children. He doesn't want to leave his wife or kids." Her shoulders slumped slightly.

Kara was a tad surprised that Shane jumped to the affair so quickly, but it stunned her how readily Heather acknowledged the affair. "Have you and the Congressman discussed being honest about where you were on Thursday?" Kara asked.

Heather nodded. "He would have preferred I didn't admit to him being here. He wanted me to lie, but I know that would be worse, especially if you checked the log, and not just for me, but for him. He was here with me, all morning until his wife called. But I'm begging you not to tell Alice. I might be the other woman, but I don't want him all to myself. He has a life with her and his kids and what they're going through is just horrible. I don't want to be the person who makes it worse."

"Not our place to judge," Kara said. "And we won't advertise it, but this conversation will be in our report."

"What about work?" Shane asked. "Any problems on the Hill? Arguing with any of his constituents? Strange calls? Fights with any of his staff? Anything out of the ordinary at all?"

"No," Heather said. "I mean, there's always office gossip, and he can be a bit of an asshole sometimes, but everyone mostly likes him."

"Are you sure?" Kara asked. "Even the smallest of

arguments can be something deeper. So, if there's someone he's in constant conflict with, please let us know."

"Not that I can think of."

"We appreciate your time," Shane said as he stood. "Call us if you think of anything that might help us catch whoever killed Emily."

"Will do," Heather said.

Kara followed Shane out to the car. The snow had turned to freezing rain. "You get the feeling she's hiding something?"

"Oh yeah," Shane said. "When Cleary was D.A., most detectives secretly wished he'd slip and break his neck the way he handled most of the cases that came across his desk. No way is he that well-liked."

"*D*o you think Alice Cleary knows her husband is cheating on her?" Shane asked as he pulled his vehicle into the Cleary's' driveway.

"Heather Underman doesn't think she knows."

"Not what I asked," Shane said. Once he put the car in park, he raced around the car once again to open the door for Kara. It was a running joke between the two of them back when they were dating. He'd been a jock his entire life. He could be rude and crude, and what his friends would call socially unacceptable to the human race. But his freshman year, when he and Kara got serious, his father had a long chat with him about how to treat a lady. And Kara was a lady in every sense of the word. Sure, she was a tomboy and could keep up with him in any sport, but she was all woman, even back then. Shane's father told him the secret to a lasting love life was the little things.

He'd done all those things and she'd still left him.

He opened the passenger door, took her hand, and instinctively kissed it. "Habit," he said.

"You do that with all the ladies?"

"No," he admitted. "Just seemed like the right thing to do with you."

"You got so teased by everyone for that."

"Yeah, well, I had the hottest girl in school. And doing things like that got me into your pants."

She laughed. It was a soft laugh. Easy. Sweet. "You're still a bit of an egotistical pig."

"I was never a pig," he said.

Quickly, they walked to the front door, freezing rain pelting them in the face. Cleary jerked opened the door before they could even ring the bell. He must have been watching for them. "You've got twenty minutes," he said. His breath still reeked of whiskey. He swayed and stumbled a bit, the glass in his hand spilling dark liquid on his shirt.

Shane and Kara followed him through the foyer, up the stairs. Cleary stopped at the first door. "I haven't been able to go in there since we found out." He stepped back. "I'll be right here while you do whatever it is you need to do."

Shane pushed open the door and immediately he noticed the freshly made bed. Not a single toy or piece of clothing or anything on the floor. A far cry from what his son's room looked like. There wasn't a single poster of any pop star or teen idol on the walls. Instead, there were a few decorative pieces that matched the white wood trundle bed with a matching desk and vanity. The bedspread was a deep purple. The curtains matched.

Kara sat down at the desk and rifled through the drawers. She glanced at Shane and pointed inside one. A couple of folders were neatly stacked inside. The center drawer held pens and pencils, all in containers.

Shane made his way to the closet and pulled open the double doors. Cleanest closet he'd ever seen, with clothes carefully hung on plastic hangers. Shoes were in a couple of different hanging storage racks. Not a single object lined the floor. There were a couple of boxes on the top shelf. He pulled them down and brought them over to the bed. Kara placed a few items she'd found on the bed as well, then looked out into the hallway. "He must have gone into his room or something," Kara whispered. "This does not look like a teenage girl's room."

"When you were fourteen, you had posters of some guy from that TV show you loved. Drove me nuts. You thought he was so hot. Kind of hard to compete with."

"Yeah, well, you had a thing for Jennifer Aniston."

"Still do," he said. "Look at this." He waved a book. "Found a few notes hidden inside." He pulled them out and started reading to himself. "These are more like journal entries." On the page, Emily wrote a lot about boys and things she'd done with them. Also, about drinking for the first time. "She was pretty worldly for a fourteen-year-old." Shane showed it to Kara before taking a picture of it. "We need to take this, but not sure…" he flipped it over. "Hold that thought." He tapped at a drawing of a butterfly. "Not really like the drawing on the body, but maybe there's a connection to the killer and butterflies."

"I've got the paperwork, so all he has to do is sign it for us to take anything we find in her room," Kara said as she tossed a few more notebooks onto the bed. "More journals. They were under a couple of large books in the desk. Descriptions of sexual acts and she names this guy, Doug McCauley. She really likes to doodle. Ladybugs, butterflies, cupids, and I think that looks like a bong."

"It does." Shane went for the closet again and started looking through pants pockets.

"What are you doing?"

"Where did you hide your stash when you were a kid?"

"I never had a stash, and the only time I got high was with you at our Junior Ball."

"Yeah, that didn't end well." Shane didn't find

anything. "She's a little young for that kind of risky behavior."

"Not really," Kara said. "Remember when we were fourteen."

"We weren't doing what she describes. Some of what she describes I've never done."

"Let's get Cleary to sign off and ask him about this Doug kid."

Shane followed Kara out of the bedroom and into the hallway, enjoying the sway of her hips. A little curvier than he remembered, but her ass still looked firm and squeezable.

"Congressman Cleary?" Kara called.

"Downstairs," Cleary said, now standing at the bottom of the stairs with a fresh glass of whiskey on the rocks. "Did you find anything?" He swayed and slurred his words.

"We found some journals." Shane took the steps quickly, then stood two feet from Cleary. The smell of alcohol was so strong it smelled more like pure ethyl.

"Journals?" Cleary questioned. "She kept a journal?"

"Looks like a diary. We'd like to read it and have our analyst go through it, looking for any clues as to what happened to your daughter," Kara said. "If you could please sign this, we can take the journals into evidence."

Cleary took a sip of his drink, stumbling backward, and bumped into the table in the foyer. "If you think it will help." Cleary took the paper, putting it on the table, and scribbled his signature before waving his hand dismissively. "My wife will be home soon and I'd rather the two of you not be here." His tone had gone from anger and rage to utter sadness and defeat.

"Do you know a young man by the name of Doug McCauley?" Kara asked.

Cleary opened his mouth, then paused, glancing at the ceiling before answering. "I can't say that I do. Why?"

"Emily writes of him in her diaries," Shane said. "Could you ask your wife about the name?"

"Sure." Cleary pinched the bridge of his nose.

"I take it you have a cleaning lady or service?" Kara asked.

"My wife handles all that, but yeah. I think they come two or three times a week."

"Do you know when they were here last?" Kara asked.

"I have no idea."

"Could you get that information for us?" Kara asked.

"Ssuure," Clearly slurred out the single word.

"We spoke with Heather Underman a little while ago." Shane knew it probably wasn't the greatest time to let Cleary know, considering his condition, but if he didn't inform the congressman, it would most likely cause a different set of problems down the road.

Cleary drew his lips in a tight line, glaring at Shane.

"She informed us you were at her house that morning," Shane said. "We can't leave that out of our report, and it will make it difficult to completely rule the two of you out as—"

"You're an asshole." Cleary poked Shane in the chest.

He wanted to respond with a shove, but instead he fisted his hands and held his ground. "I don't care who you're sleeping with, I only care how it affects finding *your* daughter's killer, so I respectfully suggest you think long and hard about what's really important here."

"I didn't like you as a beat cop, and I like you less now," Cleary said. "Get out of my house."

"Thank you for your time," Shane said, jaw clenched. "We'll see ourselves out."

The wind howled as Shane and Kara ran to the car, their bodies pelted with large, cold drops of wet snow. For a moment Shane thought about not opening the car door. He was falling into an easy, comfortable, and completely too familiar pattern with Kara. But it just wasn't in his nature, so he walked with her to the passenger side and helped her in. He tried to tell himself that he was just being a gentleman, which he was, as he did this for his wife. But he didn't do it for everyone. Certainly not fellow female officers.

"I'm impressed with how you held your cool with him," Kara said.

He rubbed his chest. "I wanted to haul off and hit him square in the nose, but he's so wasted I'm not even sure he'll remember half of what happened this evening."

"Emily's room was way too neat," Kara said as he started the vehicle and backed up.

"Makes me wonder if they cleaned it after she was found."

"But why would they do that?" Kara had turned sideways, her gaze catching his. "What are they hiding? What don't they want us to know?"

That was a good question. One Shane had no answer for.

It was well into the dinner hour. Jones had texted they were getting nowhere with Haughton and the second team was going to pick up the questioning. Time to call it a day. "Where can I drop you?"

"Mind taking me back to the precinct? Foster is going to wait for me."

"Not a problem," he said. "We're going to have to let Haughton go by noon tomorrow."

"We'll deal with that tomorrow."

The ride to the precinct was done in silence, which was nice because he had a splitting headache, though the sound of her voice might have eased that tension. Then again, it might have distracted him to the point where he'd be one of the cars in the ditch.

He rolled to a stop in front of the station.

"Please don't get out of the car. I can open the door myself."

He nodded. "I'm enjoying working with you. You're a good agent."

"Thanks. The feeling is mutual."

He watched her step from the car, pulling her blazer over her head as she raced to the double doors. She turned and waved, then disappeared. He let out a long sigh. It was going to be a long couple of days, with her under his skin in more ways than one.

6

SHANE ROLLED INTO THE Holiday Inn Express, astounded that Kara had been waiting for him at the entrance of the hotel. He figured he'd have to text her he was there and wait a few minutes. He smiled and waved, a little stunned how his skin warmed at the sight of her. She wore fitted jeans that showed off every luscious curve. Under her fleece jacket, she sported a black turtleneck. Memories of kissing her neck, just below her earlobe, which drove her nuts, brought a little hot shiver to his body. Her hair was pulled back in a ponytail and he wanted to yank out the band and let her long hair fall over her shoulders. He refrained from hugging her when she plopped herself down in the front seat. The ride to Shane's favorite coffee shop was filled with small talk and a big dose of tension.

At least on his part.

It seemed odd to him that he felt no guilt over his attraction to Kara. Not that he'd ever really been attracted to any woman other than his wife, but he thought this should feel like cheating.

But instead, it felt like Janet was looking down on him and smiling. Almost giving him her blessing at starting his life over, which was even stranger considering Kara was the woman sitting next to him, making him want things he thought he'd never be able to have again.

"This is new," Kara said as she stepped into the coffee house.

"Opened up about ten years ago. There's one in the village of Pittsford as well." He took in a big whiff of the bitter coffee laced with sweet, sugary scents.

The line was ten people deep, and most of the tables and sofas were taken. "Go find a seat and I'll get us coffee."

"Mocha for me. Large. Loaded with everything."

"Got it."

Shane had always loved a good coffee shop. The kind where there were big soft chairs to sit in. It wasn't so much the intoxicating mixture of strong coffee and various pastries, but the way everyone inside seemed to stop for a moment, relax and possibly read, or simply have a conversation with an old friend. After his wife died, he'd often come here to feel as though he was a part of something, though he sat alone. Drank his coffee alone. And he felt alone, but it gave him something to do. A place to step away from the utter loneliness he felt when Janet died. Months later this shop became a place where he could clear his head, so he could go back to the hospital and be a good father to his sick son.

Now it was a simple reminder of how he got to this place in time.

He slipped his change into his pocket, took the two tall cups, and then navigated through the crowd to the table in the back corner where Kara waited for him. She stirred up so many emotions, both good and bad. What weighed heavily on his mind was that he thought he didn't need closure with Kara. He'd gotten over her and had a wonderful wife and son. A good life where she was a distant memory.

But now that she was back in his life? Nothing about their romance or subsequent break-up was distant.

She smiled at him as she wrapped her fingers around the cup. He settled himself into the chair across from her and sipped the scalding liquid, careful not to burn his tongue. He wanted to reach out and touch her. Hold her in his arms again. Feel her soft skin and listen to her breathe. But at the same time, he still had a pang of hurt and twinge of anger that forced him to keep a safe distance.

"So, we know Cleary is having an affair," Kara said. "And he was with her that morning, but nothing else that can corroborate their alibi."

"Probably feels guilty as hell he was with his mistress instead of being at home that day."

"I would think so." Kara nodded as she tucked a small piece of dark brown hair that had fallen out of her ponytail, behind her ear. He remembered how soft her hair was, and he'd always enjoyed running his fingers through it. "I can't imagine a girl Emily's age could have a room so clean and free of all things youthful."

"Almost felt like a guest room."

"The room just felt cold." Kara pursed her lips and blew into her thick paper mug.

"One never knows what goes on behind closed doors," Shane said. "Besides, remember what a neat-freak my sister was? Well, she still is. Drives her kids nuts. Theresa, her daughter who is living with me, will tell you that if she even walked out of her room to use the bathroom before making her bed in the morning, Anna would have a cow."

"So, you think they're just compulsive when it comes to having everything perfect?"

"Their entire house is like that. It's like no one really l lives there. All for show."

"That says a lot about a person," Kara said. "When appearance matters more to them than reality or even people."

"I suppose," Shane said. "You get the memo that Haughton was released a few hours ago?'

"Foster told me."

"What do you know about how Cleary handled the Haughton case?" Shane asked, keeping the conversation to business, ignoring the urge to kiss her. Just once. Get it out of his system.

"It was barely a case and Haughton's daughter was no angel. She'd been busted with drugs, and while her sexual history wouldn't be admissible in a court of law it would have been brought up somehow, putting her in a very bad light with a jury. Cleary had to know his best bet to get the case off his desk was to offer a decent plea. That's what he did. Ended badly, but we both know he had no way of knowing that Rodney would escalate to rape."

"According to Cleary, and cell phone text records, Rodney had been verbally abusing the Haughton girl for months. From what I read, I can see how easily it could escalate," Shane said.

"I'm not disagreeing, but Rodney didn't have a record, and the text messages didn't come into evidence until the rape. As a matter of fact, the records state that the texts weren't even mentioned in the first offense." Her fingers cupped her paper mug as she held it close to her lips, blowing and taking a small sip.

"Haughton is adamant that he showed Cleary the texts," Shane said. "I understand the break-in was Rodney's first offense, but looking at the reports I think Cleary brushed the sexual harassment under the table because he didn't have a strong enough case. I understand that, but he could have gone harsher on the plea."

"There is another reason a D.A. would push for a plea in a case like this," Kara said. "Often, Haughton's daughter responded to those texts, and she wasn't always telling the boy to stop. One could argue she encouraged the dirty talk to continue."

"Doesn't justify rape."

"Do you really believe Haughton could have killed Emily? Carved out her eyes?" Kara asked.

"I wouldn't put murder past a grieving father," Shane said. "But the eyes, the drawings, and the candles feel too ritualistic, something I can't get past."

"Did you get to read through the cases I sent over?"

He sipped his coffee, mentally pulling up the files. "The one in Albany, where the killer cut off all the fingers, but they were never able to nail their only suspect."

"The suspect was the victim's stepbrother. We've got a field officer interviewing him now."

"Okay," Shane said, "but that was in Albany. Why come to Rochester? Why Emily?"

"He was flagged for the butterfly tat on his back."

"Doesn't look anything like what we saw on the body."

"But it's a lead," she said. "The young man murdered in Rhode Island also had a butterfly tatt."

"Emily didn't have a tattoo." Shane enjoyed a little

too much the easy back and forth he had with Kara. Their ability to talk through a case together was something that normally developed over the course of working with one another.

"That's true," she said. "What did you think about the Boston case I sent you?"

Shane swallowed as he remembered the images. A young man found in his home. He'd been bound and gagged, and the killer had ripped open the victim's gut. It was messy, and his intestines were sprawled all over the bed. "The only one that feels remotely like our case is the one in Boston."

"Agreed," Kara said. "But no candles. No drawings on the body. Eyes still in the head."

"The design on Emily's body freaked me out at first," Shane admitted, though he couldn't fathom why he randomly spit out the statement.

"Why?"

"My son has a scar all the way down the middle of his chest from his heart transplant." Shane traced a finger down his own chest.

"I can understand why that would bother you." Kara leaned in, setting her coffee on the table, reaching out and gently touching his hand before retreating.

"What do you make of all the markings?" he asked, her touch lingering on his skin.

She leaned back in the chair, crossing her legs. "We sent that back to our tech analyst who is searching for other images like that and what they could possibly mean. As soon as she has a hit, I'll let you know."

He noticed Kara's gaze kept darting from him to her coffee. She used to do that when she had a question she was uncomfortable asking.

"What's on your mind?" he asked.

"A lot of things. Mostly the case..." she paused. "... but also, some personal things."

"What kind of personal?"

"When was your son's surgery?"

"A little over six months ago," Shane said. "This is my first case back since spending a year on administrative duty."

"Is he your only child?"

"Yes," Shane said.

"What's your wife like?" she asked.

"My wife died two years ago, in a car accident." It was impossible to hide the tremble in his voice.

"Jesus," she muttered. "I'm so sorry."

"Thanks." Shane had learned long ago that the universal 'I'm sorry' was the only thing people could say, because often there were no words. It was the only time 'sorry' was used to be empathetic versus apologetic.

"What's your son's name?"

Shane felt the smile tug at his lips as he proudly puffed out his chest. "Kevin. He's a real pistol. He's a brain like his mother. He's been out for a year between being sick and the surgery, and just went back to school this week. He's very excited about it."

"He sounds like a fighter, just like his father," she said. "When they told you after you broke your leg you'd never ski again, oh my Lord, you were going to prove them wrong."

"Not only did I prove them wrong, but I never missed any part of the next season. I did, however, develop an aversion to motorcycles." He laughed at the memory. He'd been fourteen, and Kara, and he had just started dating if you could call walking her home every day and stealing a few kisses under the bleachers dating. Actually, their romance started in grammar school. From the day he met Kara Martin, she'd been the love of his life.

"I thought your father was going to break your other leg."

Shane smiled. "Took me all summer to pay off the damage I did to that bike and Mr. Henderson's garage. You know, he still lives there, and every time I go to my parents' house he waves his finger at me, then points to his door, telling me it's never been the same."

"Not sure which motorcycle incident was worse."

"Oh no," Shane said. "You're supposed to take that to your grave." He stood, knowing this conversation was headed in a direction where he might ask her why she'd left him. He wasn't ready for her answer. "Let's go check out that crime scene. It starts to get dark around four-thirty, so we only have about an hour of sunlight."

He offered his hand. She looked up at him with her dark brown eyes, her lips turned upward in a slight smile. Instinctively, he laced his fingers through hers. He squeezed her hand, then untangled their fingers. "Sorry. I don't know why I did that."

"It's okay."

They drove in silence the rest of the way to the house where Emily's body had been found. When Kara sat in the car for a few extra minutes, he realized this was only blocks away from where her parents had been murdered. He reached his hand into the car, taking hers, feeling the slight tremble. "We've got all the photos. We can leave."

"I'm good." She squeezed his hand, then let it go. "It's good for me to be here."

The Kara he remembered was stubborn. And proud. He'd learned in all the years she'd been his best friend and his girlfriend that she was her own person, capable of making her own decisions, and she was stronger than anyone he'd ever met.

This Kara was just as strong, but she had a softness and a sense of loneliness that tugged at his heart. He gently placed his hand on the small of her back and led her toward the house.

Snow had covered the steps, but the crime scene tape was still intact. He followed her up the stairs. She stood in the bedroom where Emily had been found. She took out a pad of paper and started writing things down. Shane pulled out his own notebook, running his fingers over the top. He'd never forgotten that Kara had given him the pad their last Christmas together.

"The one candle that had been lit barely had any wax that gathered at the bottom, so it wasn't lit long. You can see it was there." Shane pointed to the floor. "There were three candles on each side of the body, and then one at the head, and one at the feet. All vanilla-scented. The lab found that some came from BrightLite, but others came from Yankee Candle, and one candle they still aren't sure about. Might have been homemade or one from a trinket store of some kind."

"Okay, so eyes are in the head. Maybe the other candles weren't supposed to be lit." Kara looked around the room. "The report noted no visible signs of blood."

"The CSI unit saw it on the floorboards with Fluorescein screening." Shane swallowed hard. "In the right eye socket the M.E. found glue."

"Glue?"

Shane pulled out his phone and pulled up the last email he'd gotten. "Yeah. Glue. And parts of the eye socket had been cauterized."

"We've seen killers who can't stand the sight of blood. Others are obsessed with it. One case I worked the killer would drain the victims of their blood, then have sex with the corpses."

"That's one I've never seen," Shane said.

"One I wish I'd never seen," Kara said. "Back to Emily. Why here? What makes this place so special?"

"At least a dozen houses on this street alone are either condemned or abandoned."

"So, a great place for drug dealers, users, prostitutes, and killers." There was no mistaking the harshness and anger in Kara's voice. He suspected it was more than the case that had gotten under her skin.

"My guess is this was a place of convenience, but one the killer had to know about."

"Who owns this place?" Kara asked.

"Technically the city," Shane said. "Most condemned buildings in this area are owned by the city, and I heard some will be demolished come spring."

"Get a listing of owners for the last ten years."

"You really think we need to go back that far?" Shane held his phone to his ear, waiting for the desk officer to answer.

"Might as well," Kara said.

Shane quickly gave the desk officer the information then put his phone into his pocket. "It's freezing in here." He checked his watch. It was getting into the dinner hour and he knew he needed to get home to see his son, at least for a few hours. "Do you want me to drive you to the... take you to the street where your parents were murdered?"

Kara shook her head. "No. I don't want to go there now. Maybe after this case is over. I don't want to cloud my judgment."

Shane could relate to that. "Where can I drop you?" he asked, but before she could answer, his phone rang.

"It's Jones." He pressed the phone to his ear, motioning for Kara to follow him down the stairs and back into the warm car. "What's up?"

"We got another murder," Jones said. "And I'm pretty sure... no, I'm damn sure it's the same killer."

7

KARA SUCKED IN A BREATH as they pulled up in front of a house on Field Street near Clinton Avenue. Not the best part of the city, but certainly not the worst. Two city police cars, one Monroe County Sheriff's car, the CSI unit, a few unmarked cars, and a fire truck were already at the scene.

Kara followed Shane up the creaky steps of a house that looked like it had seen better days. They both signed the log, knowing they'd have to file a report. She glanced around the small foyer, noting the number of people in the room who also had to file a report, which she'd end up having to read. "We really need to reduce the number of people inside the crime scene."

"Agreed," Shane said. "I'll get my captain to send out a memo."

The house had been broken up into three apartments. One upstairs and two downstairs. "I'm going to go talk to Foster," she said, holding a hand over her nose. The smell of rotting flesh hung in the air like a cloud of thick smoke.

"I'm heading to where the body was found," Shane said.

"I'll be there shortly." Her eyes burned from the stench as she made her way across what appeared to be a living room.

"Tell me what we've got," she said to Foster, whose face looked as green as she felt.

"Male. Twenty-one, according to his driver's license."

"Why does Jones think it's the same killer?"

"Eight candles. All vanilla-scented. But this time all of them had been lit. The body was found bound, gagged, and naked."

"Eyes missing?"

Foster shook his head. "But the medical examiner says there appears to be knife wounds in the victim's back."

"What's the connection to the Cleary case?"

"Other than the candles? Nothing. The body is badly decomposed, so we don't know if there were any drawings."

"Did you see the notes and journal entries Shane and I found?" Kara asked.

"I did. Pretty heavy stuff for a fourteen-year-old. The boy she wrote about is eighteen, and if what she stated is true, he could be facing statutory rape charges."

"I noticed every page had a butterfly on it, and I still think the markings on the victim look more like a butterfly than anything else." Kara had no idea how Jones could stand there without covering his mouth. Even with the cold air seeping in through the front door, the smell was worse than rotting eggs mixed with used hockey equipment that had been sitting in a hot car, baking for days.

"I concur," Jones said.

"We rechecked Emily's phone." Kara tried not to swallow. The taste of death was worse than tar. "The boy's number doesn't come up."

"Kids delete that shit all the time, especially if they don't want their parents to know."

"Need to get the phone records of Doug, the boy Emily writes about, and have a little chat with him."

"Not we," Foster said. "Shane can interview him. He has a son and understands kids. He gives the impression of being a caring and understanding kind of guy. Not to mention he's more even-keeled than the rest of us."

"I'm sure that can be arranged." Kara pulled her turtleneck up over her mouth and nose. She held her breath as she made her way past a few street cops and into the kitchen. Shane stopped her in the doorway. He looked her square in the eye, pausing for a moment, as if searching for something in her gaze. Or maybe trying to tell her something. "We can't let Cleary know there's a connection," Shane said. "I called both my captain and the chief and they agree. We have to keep a lid on many of the similarities. My second team is here. They're talking with some of the neighbors."

"I'd like to meet Detectives Pollock and Benster."

"I'll make sure I introduce you before we leave," Shane said. "There are enough similarities to Emily's case to connect the two. Forensics will gather up the wax and see if we can match it to Emily's crime scene. It will be interesting to see where these candles come from. The Lab's putting a rush on it."

Kara nodded. "So, do you think the killer was able to finish the ritual? If it was indeed a ritual?" she asked, wondering what on earth those candles meant.

"Not sure," Shane said.

"How many deaths has this city had so far this year?"

"Five," Shane said. "This is number six. All but this one and Emily's were either domestic or drug related."

"We need to find out if Haughton has any connection to this victim, and if he has a thing for candles and butterflies," Kara said. "That song "Butterfly Kisses" is now stuck in my head."

"I know what you mean." Shane looked away. "Janet used to give butterfly kisses to Kevin every night before bed."

"So, did my dad when I was little." Kara's mind flooded with fond memories of her father. "Butterflies can mean so many different things. But we're not sure the drawing on Emily's body was a butterfly, and we don't know if this Doug kid she talks about in the journals likes butterflies."

"We're just going to have to go ask," Shane said. "The sooner the better."

"I think we might want to question the ex-Mrs. Haughton as well. She might have some insight to Haughton that connects him to both cases."

"Thought of that, too," Shane said. "Tomorrow is Sunday; should be able to catch her at home."

"I can handle it if you want to take the day off." Kara stepped around Shane to get a better look at the crime scene. She took out her notepad and did her best to ignore the death that loomed over them. She'd never been good with dead bodies. She didn't know anyone who was, except for medical examiners, coroners, and funeral home directors. Those people weren't normal. It took a special person to want to cut into a dead body, or prepare one to be seen by family members. It was something she never quite understood. And never wanted to. Then again, they probably thought being an FBI agent wasn't normal.

"No days off for a while," Shane said.

She sucked in a breath as she scanned the body, which was belly-down, face turned to the side. Arms over his head, tied together with duct tape. That was different than the Cleary girl, who had been tied with rope, though over her mouth the killer had used duct tape. His legs were also held together with duct tape at the ankles. There were two open wounds on both sides of his lower back. "Any idea how long he's been dead?" She knew the question had been asked, but no harm in asking again.

The M.E. didn't look in her direction, but answered the question. "I can only estimate at this point as being over a week, based on the decomposition, but I can't be sure."

"Fair enough." Kara looked around the kitchen in search of clues. Anything that might tell her something about the victim. She always started with the victim. She truly believed the dead could still communicate if only the investigator cared enough to listen. To get to know the victim.

The kitchen sink was filled with dishes. There were crumbs left out on the counter in front of an ancient toaster. The kitchen floor, however, was clean. Spotless, actually. A sharp contrast to the rest of the apartment.

"The name on the driver's license is Gregory Donagen," Shane said, standing behind her, his hand on the small of her back, his thumb gently rubbing, as if he sensed her need for comfort. "The tenants of the other two apartments in the building say he was a student at the U of R, studying medicine."

"So, what does a student at the U of R have to do

with Cleary or his daughter? How is he connected to Haughton or our new suspect, Doug?" The questions that filtered through her mind came at her at high speed, and she couldn't keep up with her own brain.

"Damned if I know," Shane said, tugging at her arm. "Detectives Pollock and Benster have the other tenants in the backyard, ready to be interviewed. I don't know about you, but I need some fresh air."

"Hell yeah," she said. As soon as they left the building, they were bombarded with shouts from news crews asking for a statement. "This is your investigation. Your call."

"I don't make statements." Shane kept his hand firmly wrapped around her arm. His other hand waved off the reporters. "I've never made one in my career and I don't plan on starting now," he said.

Two men stood on the driveway near the back of the house. They both wore fleece coats with Rochester PD on the back. One was well over six-feet, and the other was closer to Shane's height at five-eleven.

"This is Pollock and Benson," Shane said. "This is Special Agent Martin."

"Call me Kara," she said, stretching her hand out.

"The other downstairs apartment is rented by another student," Pollack said. He was the taller of the two and well-muscled. He had blond hair and blue eyes. Young-looking. Maybe in his mid-twenties, which would be young for a detective.

"Same major?" Kara asked.

"No. This one is education," Benster said. He had to be closer to mid-thirties. He was broad and bald. Reminded Kara of Kojak. "The two young girls live in the upstairs apartment. One is probably a hooker. Says she's a dancer. We don't have many nightclubs around here. The one we do have; the dancers are hookers. The other is a hairdresser."

"That's an eclectic group." Kara felt the snow wiggle its way into her shoes, hitting her socks. The heat from her foot melted the snow, which would only turn to ice in a matter of half an hour, or less.

"None of them seem to be friends," Benster said. "Except the two girls."

"Got the sense," Pollock continued, "that the education major isn't thrilled with any of his neighbors."

"Good to know," Kara said. "Divide and conquer?" she asked Shane.

"I'll take the girls."

"Ah, no," she said. "You've got the young man. I've got the girls."

"Yes, ma'am," Shane said, then headed to the young man who was standing in the backyard, leaning against the tree. The girls were also in the backyard, but they were by the garage, huddled together, wrapped in a couple of blankets. "Hello," Kara said. "Mind answering a few questions for me?" Kara opted not to introduce herself, though she made her weapon visible. There was enough speculation about why the FBI was involved. They didn't need more.

The girls were both blondes, but one had fine straight hair, shoulder-length. She was on the chubby side, probably the hairdresser. The other had thick, wavy hair that was waist-length. She was tall and skinny, so Kara assumed she was the dancer.

"Did you know the victim well?"

Both girls looked at each other and then shrugged. The taller one said, "Not well, but he always said hello. A couple of times we sat out on the front porch and talked, but not often."

"I work nights," the other one said. "I'm a dancer. Going to make it on Broadway."

So, Kara's assumption about who was who had been wrong. Never assume. "Good for you," Kara said. It was always worth validating a witness. "What can you tell me about the victim? Did he have a lot of friends over?"

The girls shook their heads, then the dancer said, "We never really saw him with anyone. He was kind of private, you know?"

"I offered to cut his hair," the other girl said. "But he said no. He was happy with the guy he went to, who, by the way, did a horrible job."

Kara's fingers were turning white as she scribbled in her notepad. "I understand it was one of you who called about an odor?"

"Yeah," the hairdresser said. "That was me. I banged and banged on the door, but he never came. Thought he went to go visit family and left food out. Or that maybe it was some weird experiment. He's done that before. Once he started a small fire in his living room. We had to have the fire department over. The landlord was so pissed that we thought for sure he'd toss him out, but he didn't."

"Do you know what started the fire? Maybe candles?"

"A small propane thing, I guess," the hairdresser said. "He told us later he was doing a lab for school. So, because of that, I decided to give it another day on the odor thing, figuring it would just go away. But it just got worse. So, I called a few hours ago, when I got home."

"What about the other tenant?" Kara nodded toward Shane and the young man who lived in the building.

"He's been gone for the winter break. Guess his family lives in Utica or something. He got back today, just as we were calling. Totally wigged out when he entered the foyer area we all share. He had some chick with him who got upset over the smell and where he lived, and left."

That's convenient, Kara thought.

"Does anyone in the building use candles or incense?"

The girls shook their heads.

"What about butterflies? Do you know if Gregory liked butterflies?"

They looked at each other and shrugged. "Who doesn't like butterflies," the hairdresser said. "Are there some weird poisonous butterflies now in Rochester? I've heard there are some in, like, the rain forest or something and, you know, all these new diseases are showing up in mosquitoes and shit."

"No, nothing like that," Kara said. "We noticed he had a picture of a butterfly in his room." That was a bit of a stretch. There had been a book on insects in the family room and the cover had a butterfly on it. One way to broach the subject. "Ever hear the victim fighting with anyone? Did he fight with you? The other tenant?"

"He was quiet. And weird. Nice enough to us, but we don't know anything about his social life."

"Would you mind giving me all your contact information? Just in case we have more questions. We can use all the help we can get. Don't want this happening to anyone else."

"Sure," the dancer said.

"Are we safe?" the hairdresser asked. "I mean, was he murdered?"

"We don't know yet," Kara said. She didn't want to freak the girls out, but there was a killer on the loose. A killer they didn't understand. Not yet anyway. "I do suggest you find another place to stay for the next few nights and use the buddy system. Always check in with each with other. And if you think of anything, call this guy." Kara wrote Shane's name down along with the precinct number, then ripped it out of her notepad. Kara heard a ruckus in the front yard and looked over her shoulder. The medical examiner was loading the body into his vehicle. The news crews were shouting all sorts of questions. They weren't getting any answers.

"And please, don't talk to the reporters. It will only make our jobs harder."

The girls nodded. "Can we go?"

"Yes." She watched the girls scurry to a small beat-up hatchback, jumping in and avoiding the reporters as they drove away.

Kara met Shane by his unmarked car. The same car they had come in. He folded his notepad and tucked it inside his coat pocket.

"I can't believe you still have that."

"I've been using it ever since I became a cop. Someone once told me I needed one if I was going to be a good detective." He shrugged. "Have you noticed how our partners are behaving toward one another?"

"I've never seen Foster with a man crush before."

Shane laughed. "Jones took Foster to get a Garbage Plate before they followed up on Haughton. Normally, Jones would be doing his best to ditch the Feds."

"Foster has never shared a meal with a local," she said. "Are those gross things still a big thing here?"

Shane nodded. "Want to go get one?"

"God, no. I've always hated those. Made me sick to my stomach."

"Yeah, it wasn't good drunk food for you."

She smiled at the not-so-wonderful memory of

puking behind a local dive. She checked her watch. "I think we have time to interview the young man in Emily's diary."

"Let's do it," Shane said. "Then I want to go through everything we've gathered so far."

"Me too," she said.

"Why don't we do it together? You can come back to my place. Jones and Foster can report back to us there."

"What about your son? Don't think this would be a good topic for him to be around."

"He's sleeping at my folks' house tonight. I spoke with him briefly. He understands I'm working a big case." Shane shook his head. "He's excited that I went back to work, and he always enjoys a night at the grandparents, where they let him stay up late and eat as much ice cream as he wants."

"It has to be hard being a single dad."

"Sometimes, but my niece is moving in with me. Which reminds me, I need to call her. She's a student at U of R and maybe she knows something."

"Where is she now?"

"In Albany, where my sister Anna lives now."

"Your family always intimidated me."

"I know," he said. "But they loved you."

The words hung in the air for a long moment. She stared at her feet, unsure of what to say, knowing that they probably hated her now.

"Come on," he said. "We're both turning into icicles out here." He opened the car door and smiled.

But it didn't make her feel any better about the past.

———

Shane turned on to Rand Place in the Village of Pittsford and parked on the street in front of the McCauley residency. The house was blue, with a detached single-car garage. Currently, two vehicles were parked in the driveway. An old beat-up Jeep and a newer model CRV. A porch with seven steps, freshly shoveled, led up to the front door. He and Kara climbed their way to the top, then Shane rang the doorbell.

"Yes?" A woman with brown, shoulder-length hair with a single streak of gray on one side, answered the door.

"Mrs. McCauley?" Shane held out his badge. "I'm Detective Shane Rogers. This is Special Agent Kara Martin. We'd like to have a word with your son."

"Why?" Her eyes went wide. "Is he in trouble?"

"We need to ask him some questions about Emily Cleary. The young girl who was—"

"We know who she is," Mrs. McCauley said, her eyes narrowing.

"Can we please come in?" Kara asked.

"Who's at the door?" a deep voice barked, then a tall man with an untamed beard appeared. "What do you want?" He looked Shane up and down, stopping to glance at the badge Shane pulled out again.

"We need to talk with your son," Shane said. "About Emily Cleary."

"Christ," Mr. McCauley said, then turned. "Doug, get your ass down here!" Mr. McCauley pushed open the door. "Take a seat in the sunroom."

Shane exchanges glances with Kara as they made their way to the front room, which wasn't well insulated. The furniture was dated, and the couch sagged as Shane sat down, making sure he had a good view of the foyer. A young man wearing low-hanging jeans and a black sweatshirt, sporting a buzz cut, scuffed into the room.

"This is my son, Doug," Mrs. McCauley said. "You tell them you haven't seen that Cleary girl since we found out she was only fourteen when her father showed up."

Shane exchanged a glance with Kara, who arched a brow.

"When did you speak with the congressman?" Kara asked.

"A couple of months ago," Mrs. McCauley said. "He followed our son home after dropping Emily off at the corner of her street. He yelled horrible things at Doug, but once I heard her age we made sure he understood she was off-limits."

"Have you heard from him since?" Kara asked.

"No," Mrs. McCauley answered for her son.

"So, Emily was your girlfriend?" Shane asked.

Doug shrugged. "We were friends,"

Mr. McCauley stepped onto the porch, but didn't sit down. "My son had nothing to do with what happened to that girl."

"Doug," Kara started, "when was the last time you saw her?"

"A few weeks ago," he said.

"What?" Mr. McCauley shouted. "We told you to stop seeing her. That girl could get you in some serious trouble."

"She showed up here after school, all upset over something. Asked if I'd give her a ride home." Doug shook his head. "What was I supposed to do, let her walk home? She was crying. Upset over her dad and what an asshole he was being."

"What do you mean?" Kara asked.

"He wouldn't let her do anything. Go anywhere," Doug said. "He basically kept her a prisoner."

"How did you meet her?" Shane continued.

"Last summer at the Museum and Science Center. We both took a class there."

Shane studied Doug's face. When he talked of Emily, his right eye twitched and he constantly picked at his fingernails. "I have a thing for insects. So did she."

"Why insects?" Shane asked.

"He's always been really good at science," Mrs. McCauley said proudly. "He's won a few science contests. Even has a full scholarship to college because of it."

"That's cool," Shane said. "So, you and Emily shared a passion for insects. Like butterflies?"

"She was fascinated by butterflies," Doug said. "More like obsessed with them and ladybugs."

Shane couldn't tell if it was difficult for Doug to repress a smile at the memory, or if he was smirking.

"How long did you hang out before her father intervened?" Shane asked.

"A couple of months," he said.

"You text with her?" Kara asked.

"Sure," Doug shrugged.

"We'll need to see your phone," Kara said.

"No, you don't," Mr. McCauley said. "I know my son's rights and you need some kind of search warrant for that."

"We'd rather not go through the red tape," Shane said, then turned his attention back to Doug. "Is there something on the phone you don't want us to see?"

"No," Doug said, "but I'm not giving it to you unless it's some kind of law."

"Did you text her the day she died?" Shane asked.

Doug shifted on the sofa, looking down at his feet. "No."

"Agent Martin here was my girlfriend all through school. We didn't have access to texting back then like you do now, so we used to pass notes to each other."

"So?" Doug scrunched his nose, and looked at Shane as if he had five heads.

So much for winning the boy over. "I'm just saying that we don't care that much about the context of the texting, but more the time frame of them."

"We said no," Mr. McCauley said. "Anything else?"

"Where were you the day Emily disappeared?" Kara asked.

"We spent the day with family in Toronto," Mrs. McCauley said. "We're sorry about what happened to her, but t Doug had nothing to do with it."

"We'd like to speak with Doug alone," Shane said.

"Not going to happen." Mr. McCauley crossed his arms.

"Eighteen is an adult," Kara said. "We don't need you present to talk to him."

"This is my house," Mr. McCauley said. "And we have an entire family that can vouch for where our son was on the day that girl died. My son did nothing wrong. I'd like you to leave now."

"Doug," Shane said, ignoring the father, "did you have sex with Emily?"

"No!"

"Please leave," Mr. McCauley said. "We've told you everything we know. If you want a list of our family members' names, our EZ-Pass records, where we got gas, whatever, we'll give it to you. But the short-lived friendship my son had with Emily has nothing to do with her murder."

Shane knew they weren't going to get anywhere with the parents around, but he also knew that they didn't have enough to take Doug in for any kind of questioning. Not yet anyway. "Last chance to give us access to the phone voluntarily. Otherwise, we *will* be back with a warrant, and I'd recommend not deleting anything because it won't help your son at all."

Mr. McCauley stepped aside. "I'll see you to the door."

"We'll see ourselves out," Kara said.

Shane held her arm as they descended the steps, heading toward the car. "They most definitely were having sex."

"Why did you bring up us writing notes?" Kara asked as she slipped into the passenger seat. "That seemed a little weird and out of the blue."

Shane laughed. "I thought it might win me some points with the kid. Get him to open up, seeing as I still actually have some of the notes you wrote me." He slammed the car into gear and pulled away from the curb.

"You've got to be kidding me."

"Sadly, no. My mother had them all in a box when she cleaned out my room. She gave them to me when I bought my current house, along with my first tooth, hair from my first haircut, and a shit load of other nostalgic items. My mother never got rid of much." Shane had taken all those boxes and put them over the garage, never opening them. Now he wanted to go through all of them.

He glanced toward Kara at the stop sign at the corner of Main Street in Pittsford and Monroe Avenue, heading toward Brighton. She stared out the window, not looking his way at all. He could drop her off at her hotel as they drove right past it, but for some reason this personal trip down memory lane was exactly what he felt like he needed.

Or maybe he was just a glutton for punishment.

8

*J*T WAS WELL INTO the midnight hour. Shane's eyes burned from hours of sitting at his dining room table, staring at files. He closed his laptop. It was rare he'd bring his work home, but that was before Janet had died. Now that he was a single dad, that rule might need some adjustment. "We're getting nowhere. The second team couldn't find any connection to the previous owners of the house Emily was found in. The few prints we have are from the kids who found her. We still need to talk to the local distributors of Yankee Candle and I have a list of all trinket stores in the area that sell candles, along with Bright-Lite Consultants."

"You can buy candles online, too. What about the rope and tape?"

"Rope can be bought just about anywhere. I suppose Amazon as well. The tape, however, is a cheap brand.

Not carried at Home Depot or Lowe's, but carried at places like Kmart, Target, and small local hardware stores." He paused for a moment. "And I guess online, too."

"CSI says whoever tied the rope around Emily's hands and feet was left-handed. Did you notice if Doug was left-handed?"

"He is," Shane said.

Kara looked up over her computer screen. "I've got fifteen cases nationwide that have fingers or toes or other body parts missing, but nothing with candles. I've got another dozen cases where the crime scenes lacked blood from the victims. But no candles. I've got a few religious whack jobs who were into human sacrifice and all sorts of weird practices. But I don't have one single case that has anything to do with candles...and butterflies."

"I can't find any connection between Gregory and Emily. Nothing about the designs on Emily's body either, except for the butterflies that she drew."

"Got our technical analyst working on that. She's amazing and can dig up anything on anyone, match any pattern. The things she finds often amazes me."

"Good to know," Shane said. "One thing I thought was, maybe Gregory knew Haughton's daughter, but that seems to be a dead end. Gregory's parents live in Florida. Foster said they were coming back tomorrow, so we can talk to them then. Maybe they knew the McCauley's."

"I'll add that to our long list of things to ask them."

"We both need some rest." Shane put his hand on the top of her screen. "Shut it down for now. We'll regroup in the morning."

"I'll call a cab."

"Like hell," Shane said.

"I'm not letting you drive me to the hotel at this hour, or in this weather."

"Didn't plan on it," he said. "You can stay here. I've got my niece's room all set up. You can sleep in there." He pointed to the window. "At least another foot has fallen just in the last few hours. The roads are going to be a mess."

"Shane, I—"

"I've got plenty of room. You can wear something of mine to sleep in. We can go to the hotel bright and early, so you can grab a change of clothes."

"I don't want to impose."

"You're not," he said, closing her computer for her. "I'll make you some hot cocoa."

"You remember."

"I remember a lot of things," he said softly.

She looked up at him with her milk-chocolate-brown eyes, her long brown hair falling out of its ponytail. The last time he'd seen her they were twenty. It seemed like a lifetime ago, yet, looking at her now, it felt like just yesterday that she walked out of his life.

It was crazy she could still stir these emotions

inside him. The love he once felt. The pain of her leaving. The confusion of silence.

"Perhaps we should discuss the past." Kara had perched herself on the breakfast bar in his small u-shaped kitchen. "We're working together, and who knows how long this case will last, and I feel tension between us that can't be helping us solve these murders."

He put two mugs into the microwave and hit the start button twice. "I have no problem working with you."

"We do seem to work well together. We've been able to put aside our past for the most part, but it's lurking and it will reach up and bite us in a negative way if we don't address it."

Shane let out a long sigh as he scooped the cocoa out of the can and plopped it into the hot water. "I don't know what to do with all these memories," he admitted. "It took a long time to get over you."

"But you did. You got married. Had a family."

He nodded. "I met Janet the semester I went back to SUNY Albany, alone. She'd transferred in from a local community college. We were on-again-off-again in the beginning, mostly because she got tired of competing with the ghost of Kara, but about a year after you left I finally accepted you weren't coming back and I moved on. With Janet." He sipped the cocoa, collecting his thoughts. The anger he felt when he realized Kara was never returning bubbled to the surface. "You really hurt me. I mean crushed me. If it wasn't for Janet and her patience, I don't think I could have gone on. I really did love her. She accepted you were a part of my past and that on some level the memory of you would always be with me." He paused for a moment, glancing at Kara, who sat tall on the counter, eyes on him. "Why?"

"Why what?" she asked.

"I showed up at your dorm, so we could follow each other home for the summer, both our cars packed full. I hadn't even gotten out of the car when you approached and said you didn't have a home and wouldn't be returning to Rochester."

"You know my parents' house had closed a few months before that."

"And I thought you were rash in selling it after your parents died."

"They were murdered," she said softly. "I couldn't live in that house anymore."

"My parents offered to let you to live with us for as long as you needed."

"I couldn't go back," she said in a voice filled with conviction. "Everything in Rochester reminded me of my parents and, at the time, their murderer hadn't been brought to justice. The mere thought of going back made me sick."

"So, why not talk to me? All you did for most of our sophomore year was push me away. You were constantly fighting with me." Shane had tried to be patient and understanding. He certainly understood she was going through a difficult time. But she didn't have to do it alone.

"I could list a dozen reasons," she said. "I couldn't… I'm not sure I can explain it in a way that you can understand."

"Try. You owe me that."

"I followed you off to college when my parents wanted me to go locally. Their only child. I left them. And they died."

"That wasn't your fault."

"I know that," she said. "But I was barely twenty when they were murdered. All of a sudden, I was responsible for my family home. My parents' belongings. Money. I felt trapped in this weird universe. You were always there for me, but at the time I didn't want anyone. I was in a world of pity and I couldn't stand being a burden to anyone."

"You were never a burden." Shane swallowed.

"But I felt that way," she said. "It was like I was all alone."

"But that's not true. You had me." He slammed his mug onto the counter, hot cocoa splashing out of the mug. "But that wasn't enough, was it?"

"It wasn't like that," she said in a calm voice as she took a napkin and wiped up his mess "It was too much. The kindness of your family. The way you stood by me through it all. It was overwhelming. I loved you so much."

"You had a funny way of showing it."

"You and my parents were my world. I lost them and then I lost myself. I hated what I did to you, but I couldn't face you. I didn't feel like I deserved you. I worried you'd up and die on me, too."

"That's just fucking stupid."

"I know. But it doesn't change how I felt," she said. "I have a question for you."

"What?"

"Why didn't you ever chase me to Georgetown?"

"I did," he said. "I found your address and showed up, only to find you with some guy."

"What guy?"

"I don't know," he said. "It was September and you were walking together as you came out of your dorm. I figured you had moved on already. It was devastating."

"In September? It took me years to get over you as well," she said. "I don't know who you saw me with, but I wasn't able to date anyone until after I graduated, and even then, most of my relationships didn't turn out well."

"Would you have talked to me if I had approached you back then?"

"I have no idea."

He appreciated her honesty. "So, this is the first time back since your parents died?"

She shook her head. "I came back to Rochester the Christmas after I transferred to Georgetown. I came to see you."

"What?"

"I pulled into your parents' neighborhood on Christmas Eve. I didn't know if I was going to go to the door or not, but then I saw you with who must have been your wife, walking hand in hand. I'd be a bitch if I had showed up then. Then I read you got married."

"I guess we both gave up," Shane said. "What about you? Ever get married? Boyfriend?"

She shook her head. "I married my job. It's all that I am. I really am sorry for what happened. What I did to you."

"I'm sorry, too." He reached across the counter and touched her hand. Her eyes met his. No denying there was still a spark, but Shane couldn't even think about that right now. "I'm glad we talked."

She smiled. It wasn't a big smile, but it was something, and it made him feel better. He had his answers; her life hadn't been a walk in the park either. "We both need sleep. Come on. I'll show you to your room."

9

SHANE STRETCHED HIS LEGS, lifting them and resting them on his desk at the precinct, leaning back in his chair. He never liked working Sundays, but during an active homicide it was necessary. The bullpen was quiet. Of the ten desks in the room only a couple detectives were in the office; they were heads-down, working on something. Shane crumpled a piece of paper and tossed it into the air, catching it as it came barreling down toward his face.

"I can't believe you still do that," Kara said.

He hadn't heard her approach. She'd always been good at sneaking up behind him. "Old habits die hard."

"You keep saying that." She sat on the edge of his desk. "What did you come up with?"

"Spent hours interviewing people from different candle companies." He'd just finished filing the last of his paperwork and was now reading everyone else's reports. He quickly glanced at his watch. It was pushing five o'clock. "Didn't uncover much."

"That doesn't sound like fun," she said. "Douglas McCauley's alibi checks out."

"Never doubted that," he said. "No word on the warrant for Doug's phone."

"Not sure that will go through now that he's been ruled out," she said. "Foster and Jones interviewed Gregory's parents, and no connection to the McCauley's."

"Yeah, I got that report. Also, I reread some of the journal entries from Emily. Nearly made me blush, the language coming from a fourteen-year-old girl."

"It was descriptive," she said. "Cleary is angry we let Haughton go. Called me a few choice names. I hope he doesn't have friends with the CIA. The last thing we need is more agents to get into pissing matches with."

"I'm worried about Cleary." Shane continued to toss the paper into the air and catch it, each time tossing it a little higher. He could keep this up for hours. It was how he thought things through. "He's got a real hard-on for Haughton, but I can't imagine what he'll do when he reads his daughter's journal. Even you and I didn't know half that stuff at her age, and we knew some stuff."

"That we did," she said. "Foster and I interviewed a couple of her friends and their parents today. She was sexting other young boys, sending naked pictures, though we have no proof of this."

Shane caught the crumpled paper and tossed it at Kara. It landed on her nose.

"Real mature," she said.

"You used to have better reflexes."

"You used to at least say, 'Hey catch', before tossing it at me." She bent over, picking up the paper, then leaned against the desk again. Deep down, Shane was finding it more and more difficult to keep his emotions in check when it came to Kara. They'd always had a natural flirtatious nature between them and it was getting stronger. And he liked it. Perhaps a little too much.

"Remember in middle school when I first kissed you?" she asked.

"Oh yeah." That was a memory he'd never forget. It was not only his first kiss, but he hadn't seen it coming. "I was pissed."

"Why was that? You seemed to like it well enough."

"Because I had our first kiss all planned out. How I would do it. I'd been planning it for days. You kind of ruined the moment."

"You wouldn't speak to me at all in person after that for weeks."

"I was embarrassed," he said. "I was twelve. It was cool to have a girlfriend, but honestly, the guys all picked on me. They basically told me I was pussy-whipped."

"You were."

"Right." He laughed. "We easily transitioned back to being friends."

"Except for making out in the movies."

"Yeah, those were the days," Shane said. It wasn't until the kissing became heaving petting right before the start of their freshman year that Kara decided, if she was going to let him feel her up, they were going to be exclusive. He nearly laughed at her since they'd been exclusive forever. "Why the trip down memory lane?"

"I was just thinking about Emily and Doug and what else they might not have told anyone. We always said we officially started dating our freshman year, but we had our own secret romance all through middle school. It was just easier for both of us to pretend we were friends... but as they say now, we were friends with benefits."

"I would have liked more benefits than I got," Shane said. "That whacko chick who was your best friend in middle school used to always tell me what a tease you were, and she'd do better. She was a class- A bitch."

"She still is. I saw her a few years ago," Kara said, laughing. "She had the biggest crush on you. That's why she stopped being my friend. I told her if I ever saw her flirting with you again I'd put Nair in her shampoo."

"I had that convo with a few of my friends, but it was more like I'd kick the shit out of them."

"We're getting side-tracked," she said. "We kept our

relationship a secret, pretending to be friends, mean-
while we had make-out—."

"We did a lot of kissing, but sadly I never got passed
second base until our sophomore year, and we never
talked or did the things Emily described until we were
closer to seventeen, and even then, nothing like what
she describes. That reads more like a script for a porno,
not a romance." Shane snagged the crumpled ball and
started tossing it into the air.

"In some of her journals it says Doug, other entries
it says *he*. I just wonder if *he* isn't someone else. Some
other older guy, like Gregory."

"Okay. I'll buy Emily could have been playing the
field at fourteen. You girls are so aggressive."

"Better than being passive-aggressive like you boys,
but really. Think about it. What if she had a thing going
with Gregory? I mean, the girl could pass for eighteen
on any given day," Kara said.

"Then why kill Emily? Makes more sense to kill the
competition," Shane said, but it wasn't really a
question.

"Let's remember that Gregory was most likely
killed before Emily. So, it is entirely possible that
Doug did kill the competition, but then Emily finds
out or is upset because she really liked Gregory
better."

"Gregory was ten years older than Emily," Shane
said.

"She wouldn't care. She probably wanted an older

126

man. Both Gregory and Doug were the shy, quiet type. Both into science."

Shane dropped his feet to the floor and pushed a piece of paper in Kara's direction. "But none of this uncovers any leads or even gives us much of a direction."

"Yeah, we don't have much of anything," Kara said.

Shane looked across the bullpen as Pollock and Benster entered. "Got the report back on the fingerprints at the Gregory scene," Pollack said as he tossed the report onto Shane's desk. "There was one set we can't match. Ran it through every database and came up short."

"Send it to my analyst," Kara said.

"Thanks for doing this on a Sunday," Shane said. "Go home. We'll regroup tomorrow."

"Just wanted you to have that," Benster said. "See you tomorrow." He waved, turning his back.

Shane continued tossing his wadded paper.

"My team leader is sending Foster and me to check out two possible religious connections outside of this area. We leave tomorrow afternoon."

"Going to ditch me again?" The moment the words left his lips he regretted them. "I didn't mean that," he said.

"I can honestly say I'll be back."

Shane laughed. "Guess we've come a long way in a few short days."

"Yep," she said.

"Breakfast tomorrow before you leave?" he asked.

"Only if it's the greasy spoon on the canal."

"I'll pick you up at eight."

"I'll be ready," she said.

Shane watched her walked through the bullpen, her hips swaying slightly. He sighed. He might have gotten over her years ago, but now that she was back…he was still hung up on her.

10

"I'M SO GLAD THIS is exactly as I remember." Kara smiled as she sat down at the table at the best greasy spoon on Schoen Place, overlooking the canal. There hadn't been any booths left, and they were lucky to even get a table since the restaurant was packed. "Everything looks so different everywhere else, but not this place."

"You look the same." Shane flashed a boyish grin and winked. He had always been a unique character. A gentleman, mostly, though he had a bit of the devil in him, always flirting. Back in the day, he'd only flirt with her. It always made her feel special. Still did. Only now, she wondered who else was receiving a good dose of Shane's charm.

"Very kind of you to say."

"No, it's true. I mean, sure, you've aged some, but

you really do look exactly like I remember. Still the prettiest woman in the room."

"And you're still a smooth talker." She tucked her hair behind her ears.

"Had to be," he said. "No one could call you easy and it took a long time to get into your—"

She held up her hand. "I don't know if that's a compliment or not," she said.

The waitress came by and they both ordered coffee, French toast, and eggs, with well-done bacon.

As the waitress poured the steaming dark liquid in their mugs, Kara looked out the window, across the street to the drained canal. She always thought it strange they lowered the level in the winter. The sun tried to pop through the clouds. People were out strolling or running down the canal path in their winter workout clothes. "The M.E. said—"

"I don't want to talk about the case," Shane said. "Not this morning. We'll have plenty of time before you leave this afternoon."

"What do you want to talk about, then?" Kara took a sip of her coffee, fighting the urge to rub her foot against his firm calf like she used to do in the high school cafeteria.

"Anything but the case," he said. "I had dreams about it last night."

"So did I. It's been all-consuming."

"I have moments of reprieve with Kevin," he said. "But this morning was different. I dropped him off at school." Shane toyed with the spoon, swirling his coffee, obviously pondering something that weighed heavy on his shoulders. "I watched as Kevin walked into the elementary school, turning and waving at me with a huge smile, and it reminded me that someone had to die so he could live."

She reached across the table and touched his hand. His fingers lifted, closing around hers.

"It's not like I haven't always known that," he continued. "We've been through all sorts of counseling. Therapy. Group sessions. Talked with people whose loved ones had donated their organs. When Janet died, they held her on life support for an hour. It was an easy decision for me to agree to have all her organs harvested."

"She wasn't a donor?"

"We kept saying we'd get around to putting that on our licenses, but never did. But I didn't think twice about signing those papers. It's what she would have wanted." He tilted his head and locked gazes with Kara. "Someone out there is walking around with Janet's heart."

"Does that bother you?"

"No," he said. "It gives meaning to her death. Only, Kevin really misses her and sometimes he'll rub his scar. He doesn't think I'm looking, but I can tell he's wondering about where it came from... who had to die so he could live."

"I would think it's hard for a small boy to deal with."

Shane held her hand with both of his, stroking her skin with his fingertips. "Christ," he said. "How did we got on this topic? I wanted to talk about something light. Fun. Not deep and emotional shit like organ donation or depressing like the case."

The waitress showed up with their food and Kara had to pull her hand away. Immediately she felt cold and disconnected. While the waitress poured more coffee, she buttered her French toast and poured syrup all over it, the eggs, and her bacon, enjoying the aroma of cinnamon and coffee. Just as she dug her fork into a large bite of eggs, Shane touched her hand.

"Thank you for listening."

"Any time." She smiled. "Now can I eat my eggs, because I'm starving, and I haven't had a good greasy spoon breakfast in years," she said, sensing his need to move onto another conversation.

He laughed. "How you managed to stay so thin with the way you eat has always amazed me."

"I'm not as skinny as I used to be," she said between bites of the best breakfast known to man. The eggs were fluffy. The bacon perfectly over-cooked, and the French toast was to die for with its crisp crunchy outside and moist inside.

"I did notice your ass got a little bigger." He winked.

She held her fork mid-air, her mouth hanging open, narrowing her eyes. "Seriously? You needed to tell me that?"

"Hey, I'm a guy. I notice things like that."

"Of course you do."

"Breasts look a little bigger, too."

She tossed her napkin at him. "That was your one complaint."

"I never complained about your breasts. I only agreed that they were small. And I think I added the word perky. Perky is good." He held his fork in the air as if to toast her before he shoved it into his mouth.

His tongue darted out and licked his full lips. It was impossible not to stare. Some people ate like pigs. Made weird noises and talked with a mouth full of food. Not attractive at all. But the way Shane was handling his French toast this morning was quite seductive. Downright sensual. She wanted to pour syrup all over him and… nope. Not going there.

She pushed her plate aside, leaving only a few bites behind. She could feel her stomach press against her slacks. She also found herself looking down at her breasts. Gravity works. Not as perky as they used to be. She hadn't thought about what she looked like in years. Didn't care much. She took care of herself because she did care that she looked professional, and exercise had always been a big part of her daily routine, but to impress a man? Not in a long time. It had been going on three years since her last relationship. Now *that* was depressing.

"You look deep in thought." Shane waved the waitress over, pointing at his empty coffee mug.

"Thinking about gravity."

"Trust me, they don't look like they're sagging from my vantage point. I'd be glad to cop a feel and let you know."

She burst out laughing. "Dream on."

"I guess that means I'm not getting a handful today."

"This conversation went south really quick," she said.

"Actually, north, but we can head sou—"

"Just stop," she said. Though she really wanted to keep the teasing going. This kind of stuff in the past would always lead to some heavy petting. But she wasn't seventeen anymore, and making out in a cop car wouldn't be appropriate. Besides, it was just banter between old friends. Nothing more.

"We had a lot of good times," he said, then, "I'd like you to meet my son."

She swallowed her breath. That was a quick switch in the conversation that she wasn't prepared for. She'd seen pictures of Kevin. Cute kid. Looked more like his mother than his father, but she could see a lot of Shane in the pictures in his home. "Maybe when I come back."

"That's not a no."

There was not a single valid reason for her to say no. Telling Shane that meeting his son would only remind her of what she'd given up would be hurtful, and not just to Shane. "When I get back."

"My mom wants to see you, as well."

"I'm not ready for that," she said. "I doubt anyone in your family would want to see me again."

"Not true," he said

The waitress came over with their bill, thankfully ending that topic.

Shane tossed the tip onto the table, then took her by the hand, leading her to the cash register. "Still don't take credit cards," he said. "Can you believe that?"

"I saw an ATM in the back."

"I've had to use it a couple of times," he said as he paid the bill.

The crisp air hit her face as she stepped through the door, but the sun had a warming effect. Still chilly, but not ice-cold like it was the other day. She reached out to open the car door, but Shane took her arm in his hand and turned her away from the vehicle, pressing her ass against the cold metal. He ran both his hands slowly up and down her arms. Tenderly. Her breath was labored. His right hand slid up her neck, brushing her hair back. They stood there for a long moment, staring at each other. She searched his eyes for the passion she once saw, but she got confusion instead.

"Shane—"

He pressed his finger against her lips. "I've wanted to do this since I first saw you at the station. I thought when you walked into that room you'd be a memory. But instead, everything I felt for you came crashing back." He brushed his thumb across her lips. "I was still angry, and I wanted to know why. But mostly I wanted to kiss you." He pressed his moist, warm lips against hers, cupping the back of her neck with one hand, the other sliding under her coat, across her side, then holding the small of her back. His thumb caressed in little circles below the spot he knew would make her arch into him.

Unable to pry her mouth from his, she slipped her tongue between his lips and he welcomed the deepened kiss with a groan. Their tongues entangled in a dance they'd done so many times, but there was a newness to it. A reason to keep it slow and controlled.

He slid his hand up the small of her back, hitting the ticklish spot. She arched into him, pressing against his long, muscular body. Her arms wrapped around his shoulders. His hand was now just under her arm, heading toward her breast.

She pulled back. "People are watching."

He looked around, taking a step back, then opened the door for her. "Guess we'll have to see if gravity has taken its toll another time."

She wasn't sure there should be another time, but figured they'd talk about this when she returned to town, after they'd both had a chance to cool off from a very nice trip into the past.

---

*S*hane finished reading the M.E.'s report on Gregory's death, which added a new twist to the case. It appeared that Gregory had a kidney transplant in the last year. Why would anyone take an already donated kidney? It made no sense. He shoved the report to the side and focused on the box sitting on his dining room table. He'd pulled it down yesterday and now it taunted him. Daring him to open it and relive his past.

A sharp knock came at the door.

He'd forgotten his brother, Dave, was working on a site nearby and mentioned he might stop by.

"Place looks good," Dave said as he entered the house. "But you've got some trim that needs work on the front windows. I can take care of that in the spring."

"I'd appreciate it. Beer?" Shane asked.

"I'd love one." Dave was older than Shane by eight years. The twins, Mike and Anna, were six years older. Shane was the baby, and spent much of his youth as the only child in the house. But both his brothers lived close by, and Anna didn't move out of Pittsford until shortly after Kevin was born. Despite their age differences, they were all very close.

"Where are the little man and Theresa?"

"Library," Shane said. "Hate to admit it, but Mom was right. It's nice having Theresa here. She's so much like her mother it's scary."

"She's a good egg," Dave said. "Why do you have a box labeled 'Kara' on your table?" Dave wasn't one to beat around the bush. It was mostly a good trait, but it had gotten him into trouble a time or two.

"Mom gave it to me when they cleared out the attic.

When I moved out, I think I left all that stuff behind, hoping she'd toss it."

"Mom doesn't throw much away," Dave said. "And, so you know, for the record and all, that Mom asked me to check up on you."

"Why? What's she worried about?"

Dave pointed to the box. "She's worried about how you're handling Kara being back, and going through a box of old memories of her, well, it could be therapeutic or it could be something else."

"I had forgotten about the box until I saw Kara."

"So, how is that working out? Being around her?" Dave asked.

"Who's asking? You or Mom?"

"Me," Dave said. "If it's good, I'll report back to Mom. Not so good, I'll tell her you're doing fine."

Shane laughed. "It's been interesting." He leaned against the kitchen counter, looking into the dining room, staring at the box. Before she'd returned, things were finally settling into something that resembled normal, but she changed all that. "We work well together, but the case we're working is a tough one."

"The congressman's kid?"

"Yeah. And another recent murder, but not exactly sure how they're tied together," Shane said. "And that's not public knowledge."

"Nothing you do ever is." Dave sat down at the breakfast bar. "You like working with Kara?"

"I do," Shane admitted. "She's professional. Smart.

Really good at her job. Working with her is easy. Maybe too easy."

"From what I remember of Kara, she was always a hell of a lot smarter than you."

"She studied. I didn't." But his brother was right. Even if Shane had put a good effort in his schoolwork, she'd still be smarter about some things. "We've got a good rhythm with work. She and I have partnered up, and Jones has been working with her partner. I thought it would be weird, but it's like we've been working together for years."

Dave leaned back on the stool, folding his arms across his chest. "Have you and Kara talked? Talked about why she just left you without any real reason?" Dave had always been a good one to work things out with. When Kara had left, he spoke to him about it more than his other siblings. Dave was the least emotional in the family.

Shane nodded. "I can understand why she didn't want to come back to Rochester. Her parents' murder…" he paused, scratching the side of his face. "It was so brutal and random. She tried to be brave and strong, but there were nights I'd wake up in my dorm, and she'd be curled in a ball on my desk chair, crying. Nothing I did calmed her down. If I'm being honest I didn't know how to help her, and while she kept pushing me away I was also stepping back from her."

"You were young," Dave said. "It was a lot to handle."

"Not the point." Shane could see the mistakes he'd made and, while she'd been the one who decided to leave, he hadn't done much to stop her. "She came home to see me a few months after she left."

Dave arched a brow. "You never told me that."

"I didn't know until the other day. She saw me with Janet. Figured I had moved on. That had to have hurt her as much as she hurt me."

"You saw her with another man."

Shane shook his head. "I saw her walking down the same path with some guy. They weren't talking or touching. I was too scared of being rejected and I chickened out of approaching her. She saw Janet and me holding hands, and thought that it wouldn't be right of her to try to walk back into my life. That's very different."

"How do you feel about that?" Dave asked.

"I don't know. The time that Kara is describing was the first time I brought Janet home to meet the family, but we were still struggling because my feelings for Kara were so raw, and Janet and I were more off than we were on. After we went back to school, we broke up for a couple of months. I don't know what would have happened if I had seen Kara then, and thinking about that scenario is one big mind-fuck with all the what-ifs." Shane slowly sipped his beer. "It's only been two years since Janet died and, yet, I find myself having such strong feelings for Kara."

"You loved Janet," Dave said. Of all his siblings, he

was the most in tune with Shane. "And you loved Kara. I imagine this would be difficult for you."

"I feel guilty that I don't feel guilty."

"Janet would want you to move on, and she actually knew and understood what Kara meant to you."

"That doesn't make this any easier. I have to think about Kevin as well."

"You're a good father. You're not going to do anything that would hurt Kevin. You need to stop beating yourself up for wanting to live again."

"But I'm acting like a horny teenager." Shane got two more beers from the fridge, setting one down next to his brother. "And she's not really doing anything to shut me down."

"Doesn't sound like you want her to."

Shane could still taste her lips. Feel her body arch into him. Her hands holding his shoulders tight. "I kissed her earlier this week."

"So?"

"In the parking lot of a restaurant. Serious PDA. I mean a Fed and a cop engaged in a public display of affection of epic proportion."

"I don't see the problem," Dave said. "You've talked. You both understand each other. You still have feelings for her. You're both older and hopefully a lot wiser."

"We have to work together." Shane chugged his beer. "Having any kind of relationship with someone you're working with is a bad idea. Especially one that's a high-profile case. This kind of case could make a career or kill one."

"But just for the one case, right? Then you're not working together."

"Well, then she goes back to D.C., and I stay here." When Shane wasn't thinking about the case, he was thinking about all the reasons why he and Kara needed to stop whatever it was that was going on between them. It could only end badly.

"I don't know what to tell you," Dave said. "I know your brain is wired to overthink. And for your job, that's probably a good thing. But not for this. When she rolls back into town I think you should sit down and let her know what you're thinking. See what she has to say about things. What she's feeling, or not feeling. Otherwise you're just going to drive yourself crazy thinking about all the possibilities."

"You're right."

Dave pointed to the box. "Want company when you go through that?"

"Nope," Shane said. "If it's all the things I remember leaving behind, some might be a little embarrassing."

Dave laughed, pushing the second beer toward Shane. "I'd better head home then, so a second one is out of the question." Dave stood and gave Shane a good shoulder squeeze. "Talk to her. I mean really talk to her."

"I will." Shane felt his phone vibrate. He pulled it from his pocket and read the text. "Speak of the devil."

"The good ones always are," Dave said. "I'll see myself out."

The text from Kara asked if he was around and could talk. He grabbed his beer and the one he'd opened for his brother, and moved to the dining room where he opened the box and pulled out some of the contents. The first thing he picked up was their high school graduation picture. His black graduation robe was open, showing off his striped button-down shirt that was his mother's favorite. His hair was nearly to his shoulders, a bone of contention with his parents that he refused to cut his hair for graduation. Kara's yellow robe was zipped up, but he remembered the white strapless dress she had worn that day, along with the three-inch heels she sported that made her almost as tall as him. He tapped his phone, hitting call back on her name. She picked up on the first ring.

"Hey," she said. "Thanks for calling."

"What's up?"

"I just wanted to talk." Her voice sounded tired. Quiet. "Long day."

"Everything okay?" He set aside the picture, reached into the box, and pulled out a small photo album and smiled. It was from elementary school. Kara had made it for him for Christmas one year. At the time he thought it was kind of stupid, but flipping through the pages now, seeing him and Kara at six with their arms looped around each other... she'd always been his best friend. He had missed her dearly over the years, and was glad to have her back. That's what he had missed the most. She'd been the one person he could say anything to.

"It's been an exhausting few days," she said. "I just finished the M.E.'s report. Feel like I've been chasing my tail."

"I hear ya. Did you find out anything?"

"I sent you a draft of my report on the religious angle. But can we talk about that tomorrow? I'll get there in time to meet you at Emily's funeral."

"Sure," he said. "What's wrong?"

"Nothing, really. I'm tired and wanted to hear a friendly voice," she said. "So, what are you doing?"

"Truth?"

"Yes. Unless it has to do with porn and giving yourself a little treat."

He laughed, reaching in the box and taking out the snow globe she'd given him for his seventeenth birthday. "I'm looking at Lake Placid Winter Wonderland."

"Oh my God. You kept that? You thought that was the dumbest birthday present ever."

"Well, you did give me something else later that night."

"I don't know what you're talking about. I wasn't that kind of girl."

"Yeah, you were." He pulled out a group of cards. Birthday. Halloween. Love notes. He was a dork for keeping all this stuff. He plucked one out and unfolded the paper and laughed again.

"What's so funny?"

"I found a note you wrote to me, hinting at what we might do if we won states."

"You've got to be kidding me."

"We won states," he said, remembering sneaking her into his bedroom after the team had a big party in the village. "Twice in one night and once in the morning."

"Why is it that you remember every sexual thing we did?"

He set the notes aside and reached in the box, pulling out a picture frame. His breath hitched as he stared at a picture taken at Canandaigua Lake at a friend's cottage. It had been taken probably an hour after the first time they had made love. "I suppose because you were my first."

"My first everything," she said. "You know, this is highly inappropriate."

"Not really," he said. "Just being sentimental. Now if I started talking dirty to you, maybe tell you about how I'd like to take your breast—"

"I think we should stop," she said.

"I've barely begun." He saw lights pull into the drive. He quickly packed up the box. "I'd push, but Kevin just got home. I'll talk to you tomorrow."

"Good night," Kara said. "Sleep well."

"I will if you meet me in my dreams," he said. That had been the way they used to end every phone conversation since they were in high school. *Old habits die hard.*

11

KARA ROLLED THE SUV to a stop about ten car lengths behind the line of cars at the funeral for Emily Cleary, and right behind Shane's vehicle. She saw him and Jones standing in the background, flanked out about fifty paces from one another, along with a half dozen other plain-clothed officers who were there for security purposes.

Shane was on the north side, leaning against a tree. It was one of those days where the temperatures rose to about fifty degrees. Large piles of dirty snow littered the landscape, making winter look like a combination of mud and ice. You could always count on the weather to change drastically day to day in Rochester, and since it was January this warm weather wouldn't last.

Grey clouds floated above, and a light trickle of rain

drizzled from the sky. Fitting for the funeral of a murdered little girl.

Friday was always a bittersweet day. She held her two doughnuts in a bag in her hand.

"Being around him is still hard on you, isn't it?" Foster asked.

"Sometimes," she admitted. "I've known him since I was in grade school. He used to pull my ponytail and tease me on the playground. I would come home crying, and my mom would always tell me that boys who did that were being stupid because they actually liked you. That boys in general were illogical, even as grown men. In middle school, Shane and I began a secret romance. Everyone thought we were just friends. But we weren't."

"Ah, friends with benefits. I've had a few of those."

"We were in middle school." Kara glared at her partner. "And I was never easy."

"Never said you were." Foster laughed. "If he got to cop a feel, it was friends with benefits."

"What is it with men and 'copping a feel'?" She used her free hand to make the quotation marks.

"We're men. Breasts and swords. It's what we live for."

She shook her head. "Anyway, Shane and I have a good working relationship now."

"There's a lot of history between you and him."

She glanced at Foster, holding up the bag. "A lot of history in this town." Foster knew more about her than she liked anyone to know. He knew her routines now. Her rituals about only taking days off when forced, and working cases on vacation. She'd been avoiding life for fifteen years. Perhaps it was time for a change.

"You still care about him," he said matter-of-factly.

"Don't you still care about your first love?"

Foster stuffed his hands into his pockets. "No. She left me at the altar and married my cousin, who happened to be my best man."

"That sucks."

"It did," Foster said. "But then she left him for his accountant. She's forty-two and on her third husband. I'm really glad I never married her. Now, the first girl to let me in her pants? Yeah, I still got it bad for her. She still lets me in her pants now and then."

"You can be a real pig, you know that?"

He nodded. "Jones is a good detective. I like working with him."

"I've noticed," she said. "You two have a real bro crush going on. Odd, coming from a guy who gets into pissing contests with other men."

"As long as we don't cross streams."

Kara opened her mouth, then shut it tight before opening it again. "I got nothing."

Foster laughed "Let's go tell them what we've uncovered, which isn't much. Then, once the funeral is over, we can regroup back at the precinct."

"There's something I need to do first."

"What's that?"

"My parents are buried in this cemetery."

"What me to come with?" Foster asked.

She shook her head.

"Got it. I'll hitch a ride with Jones. You've got the SUV." Foster meandered toward Jones. Kara stood by the car for a moment, watching Shane. He wore his standard black coat and trousers. His shoulder against the tree. One ankle crossed over the other. He must have felt her presence, because he turned and waved her over.

It was time to face another demon. Only this time she realized she didn't have to be alone.

"Hey you," he said as he placed his hand on the small of her back and rubbed gently for a few seconds before letting his hand drop. "How was the flight?"

"Uneventful." She smiled. It did feel good here with him.

"I haven't had the chance to read your report. Been staked out here since seven."

"The religious angle is interesting. The one cult where the pastor was molesting small boys caught our attention because it was rumored he performed human sacrifices. I was able to interview five of his former followers. They said at one point they didn't have any electricity in the compound, so he used a lot of candles. They also said he used them in religious rituals like exorcisms and shit. One follower said she saw a human sacrifice. The details she gave were gruesome. Stuff like taking out human hearts...shit," she muttered. "I'm sorry."

"Don't be," Shane said. "Keep going."

"She's not a credible witness, but the details she gave us were a little too realistic and detailed to ignore. Can't make that stuff up."

"Do we know where the pastor is now?"

"Yes," Kara said as she studied Shane's profile. He'd always been confident in almost any situation. "Went dark a few years ago, but resurfaced this winter in Kentucky. My office is looking into his current church and working on getting an interview with him. Hoping to have something this afternoon."

"I was thinking about the black market," Shane said. "The killer wouldn't have known Gregory had a transplant, unless it was a friend or close family member. That information is kept under lock and key."

"I thought about that, too," she said. "Except for the scars. The killer would have had to see them on his back."

"So, then, why take the kidneys?"

"That I don't know," she said. "The guy who we think runs the black market is under surveillance, but it appears he's aware he's being watched. He barely moved from his house and we didn't see anyone coming or going. Nothing suspicious. I talked to a few people involved, and thus far everyone who has donated did so voluntarily. Did it for the money. Most of the organs don't stay in this country, but kidneys are a big bulk of the market, so my question is why murder someone when people are willing to sell them?"

"People will go to any length. Pay any amount of money," Shane said. "You'd be surprised what people might do if they can't get to the top of the organ recipient list." He glanced at her, his brow arched in an inquisitive stare. "You think we're on a wild goose chase, don't you?"

"With the black market? Yeah, I do," she said. "Both murders are too ritualistic. My gut says it's not the black market, but we've got four other different rings that we know are active, and we have to chase down every possible lead when we've got nothing solid."

"The funeral is over," Shane said, pointing at the sea of people moving away from the grave site. "I think we can leave now."

She noticed Shane picked up a bouquet of flowers and showed them to her. "Your parents," he said softly. "I thought you might want to pay them a visit."

"I was planning on it." She held out her bag that contained two fried cakes. "Treat O'Friday."

"You still do that?" Shane slipped his hand under her FBI rain jacket. His fingers gently rubbed against her lower back as they walked down the narrow path in silence, until she was standing in front of her parents' tombstones. Some brown grass and mud was mixed in with the snow. The tombstones had weathered over the last fifteen years, and the carvings of their names and dedication had darkened with age.

"The last time I was here was for their funeral," she whispered.

"I'll give you a few minutes." He began to pull away.

"No," she said, grabbing his arm. "I want you to stay. Please?"

He said nothing else. Just stood there next to her, arm looped around her waist, holding her steady like he'd done all those years ago.

"I have been so wrong about so many things," she said, leaning toward the graves. The stone above her mother's resting place felt cold and clammy. She ran her fingers across the lettering.

Patricia Murphy Martin. Loving Wife and Mother. A Friend to All.

She took the flowers Shane had brought and placed them in the holder next to each stone. A pang of guilt trickled down her spine as she looked at the engraving on her father's stone.

Edward Eric Martin. An Inspiration to All.

"I should have put more on his stone."

"Your dad was a man of few words to begin with. I'm sure he'd rather it be a simple statement with a positive sentiment." Shane squeezed her hip. "And that's exactly what that statement is."

She pulled out one of the doughnuts. "Here's to you, Dad." She raised it in the air. "Say hey to Mom." Kara stuffed her mouth and practically swallowed the doughnut whole. She coughed as she gently tossed the second one to the ground in front of her father's grave.

It was then she realized a few tears had rolled down her cheek.

Shane wrapped his powerful arms around her and drew her close. She leaned into him, sucking every ounce of energy he offered. She buried her face against Shane's chest, wrapping her arms around his strong midsection "I'm sorry," she whispered. "I didn't think I'd get emotional."

She felt his hands run up her arms, keeping her body from shivering. It was a gentle touch. Caring. His thumb lifted her chin. She blinked open her eyes as he pressed his lips against her forehead. "You're allowed to be emotional."

For a long moment, all she could feel was his thumb gently caressing her chin and cheek. His soft brown eyes locked in an intense gaze with hers. "Thank you," she managed, doing her best to pull herself together and step away from the embrace that had become way too familiar.

But he wouldn't let her go. He cupped her face with both hands as he lowered his head and gently, but firmly, pressed his lips against hers. The way he carefully parted her lips with his tongue sent a warm pulse straight through to her toes. He took away all the pain and filled it with something. She leaned into him, taking the strength his embrace had to offer. The kiss deepened. He drew her closer. It felt safe and warm, like she'd come home.

Her fingers dug into his back, demanding more.

Her tongue swirled around in his mouth in a wild, panicked frenzy. She couldn't get enough of him.

With his hands still firmly cupping her face he pulled back, dropping his forehead to hers. "I know I started this, but this isn't the time or place."

She let out a long sigh. "I think we need to talk about what's happening with us." Never did she think she'd be back in this town, in this cemetery, kissing Shane Rogers. Her heart ached for everything she'd walked away from.

"We do." He kissed her forehead, then stepped back. "Right now, we need to head back to the station. Jones and Foster are meeting us there."

They walked in silence, with space between them until they reached the gravel road where their cars were parked. Shane held the door of her SUV open after she'd climbed in and started the engine. He looked at her with a combination of understanding and something deeper. Something powerful and passionate.

12

SHANE LEANED BACK in his chair, feet up on his desk, tossing a crumpled piece of paper up in the air. He caught it and then repeated the motion, doing his best to rid his mind of that fantastic kiss. He wasn't in high school anymore, yet he couldn't seem to keep his hands or lips to himself.

Jones sat his desk, directly across from Shane. Kara was using the desk on the right side of Shane, and Foster sat on the edge of that desk. The bullpen was on the quiet side for a Friday afternoon.

"It doesn't look that similar," Shane said, comparing the markings on Emily's body to that of the church symbol of the pastor in Kentucky. "I mean, parts of it do, but not the whole thing. Honestly, it looks more like the tat from that case in Syracuse."

"That kid as a solid alibi," Foster said. "For both murders."

"Look at this." Kara shoved another piece of paper under Shane's nose. "That's from the pastor's previous church. It looks just like a butterfly with a very long midsection and short wings." Kara tapped the paper. "And these two oval things in the middle look like the incisions in Gregory's back."

"The killer used a black sharpie on Emily's body, and the M.E. found traces of a green one on Gregory. Could mean something," Jones said.

"Other than placement around the body, the candles used in each crime scene were different." Shane tossed Jones the crumpled paper. Jones immediately tossed it back.

Kara rolled her eyes.

"See, he doesn't need to be warned," Shane said.

"Let's get back to the case, shall we?" Kara said.

"The M.E. says the killer is left-handed on both murders," Jones said. "Also says that the incisions made on the body were done with precision, as if the killer knew what he was doing." Jones swiveled his chair in a complete rotation before tossing the paper back to Shane.

"Does the pastor have any medical training?" Shane asked.

"Not that we know of," Kara said. "But our reports show he's left-handed, so there's that."

"What about that case where some poor bastard had his intestines cut out?" Foster said. "Any leads on that one?"

"Not a one, but it's probably the closest we have to a similar case," Kara said. "If we have a serial killer, they have to start somewhere. Perfect their technique."

"Don't you think that's a bit premature?" Foster asked. "I know our time is limited, and our team leader might pull us at any moment since we're not officially here, but we shouldn't be tossing that word around."

Shane didn't like the idea that Kara could be pulled at any time. The thought threw him so much that he missed the paper Jones had tossed, and it landed on the top of his head with a soft thud. He expected a snide retort from Kara about the paper, but all he got was a frown.

"Were we able to put Emily, Doug, and Gregory at the museum at the same time?" Shane asked, focusing his energy on the case.

"Yes." Foster lifted his tablet and started tapping away on it. "But why are we even looking at Doug? He's got an airtight alibi."

Shane picked up the paper and tossed it to back to Jones. "Because he was sleeping with Emily," he said. "And I talked with Cleary about why he lied about knowing him, and he said he hadn't recognized the kid's name, and that once he told the boy and his parents Emily's age, Doug stopped coming around."

"You buy that?" Foster asked.

"I think he's been in a drunken haze since the day she was murdered," Shane said as he caught the crumpled paper. "I also think he doesn't want people to know his daughter was rebelling sexually, since we know she was sexting with other boys."

"Did you tell him what we found in her journals?" Kara asked.

Shane reached up in the air, grabbing the poorly-tossed paper. "Not yet. I want the analyst to finish with it, then we can give them back and let him read it for himself."

"Do you two do that all the time?" Foster asked. "It's annoying."

"Your fingers tapping loudly on the computer is annoying," Kara said. "You can turn the clicking noise off."

"I like to annoy you," Foster said. "Based on time cards, I've found five different occasions when Gregory was working in the museum at the same time Emily and Doug were taking classes."

"Anything on matching Emily's phone records with Gregory's?" Shane asked.

"Couldn't find a single call between the two of them," Jones said.

"I think we should go back and talk with Doug," Shane said. "Looking at Emily's photo history, she had quite a collection of naked pictures of herself. Not to mention images of male genitalia we don't know the origins of."

"What do you think Doug's going to give us?" Kara asked.

"I don't know, but I think he could provide some insight into her life."

"His parents aren't going to let us in," Jones said.

Shane snagged the wad of paper. "Catch." He tossed it at Kara, who barely glanced up and seized the ball with her right hand. "Impressive. Thought you might have lost those reflexes. Now toss it back."

Instead, she tossed it to Jones.

"All right. Let's go back and talk with Doug," she said. "It can't hurt."

Shane watched them toss it back and forth, and for some godforsaken reason he felt a pang of jealousy.

"What about Haughton?" Kara asked, as she continued to toss the paper to Jones.

"He's left-handed," Shane said as he glanced between Jones and Kara, frustration building in his gut. "He's got motive, but why would he wait so long to kill Emily?"

"Maybe he wanted to wait until she was closer to his daughter's age?" Jones asked, but it was more of a hypothesis.

Kara quickly tossed the ball to Jones and then flipped her laptop around, placing it on the center of the table. "Our analyst just sent this over. It seems that Gregory has a second cousin who went to the same school as Haughton's daughter and Rodney, the kid who raped her. Gregory's cousin's name is Barb Esters, and she was interviewed by a local news crew when Haughton's daughter killed herself."

"Interesting." Shane pulled the laptop closer. The browser was stuck on a link to a news channel YouTube video. Shane clicked the play button.

"It's terrible what happened," Barb Ester said into the newscaster's microphone. "I didn't know her well, but we all mourn her loss and pray for her family."

"I remember a slew of interviews from different girls who went to school with the Haughton girl." Jones quickly rolled his seat to his desk and started to pound on his keyboard. "Here we go."

"What do you have?" Kara asked.

"Looking up the old case files on Rodney. After he raped Lisa, other girls came forward with claims he'd harassed them. A couple even said he'd raped them as well. But none of them filed charges. Half of them recanted later. There was one girl who..." Jones tapped his computer screen. "...yeah, that's her."

"Who what?" Shane asked.

"Barb was Rodney's girlfriend." Jones continued to pound away on the keyboard. "She gave a statement when Lisa accused Rodney of the rape. Barb was his alibi. Swore he would never hurt anyone. That he was this great boyfriend. She had a bruise on her left eye during that interview. I'm sending the reports now."

"How the hell do you remember that? We had barely been made detective, and that wasn't our case."

"Gregory's mother's maiden name was Esters. I've been wracking my brain, trying to remember why it sounded familiar." Jones picked the paper up and started tossing it with Kara, leaving Shane out of the loop again.

Shane stood up and snagged the paper midair.

"Jealous much," Kara retorted.

"Sure am, when you cheat on me with a Fed." Shane put the paper in his top drawer, then glanced at his watch. "It's getting late."

"I think we should interview Esters today," Jones said.

"Good idea," Foster added. "But you and Shane are going to have to do it. Kara and I have a conference call with our team. We can regroup tomorrow."

Shane was about to suggest that he could wait for their call to be over, so he and Kara could do it, but then thought better of it.

Shane settled into the driver's seat and headed toward Alexander Street. The last known address for Barb Esters was a side street that ran between Alexander and South Union.

"So, what's going on with you and Kara?" Jones asked. "I thought you were getting along, and now you're acting like an immature teenager."

"We have a lot of history, and some of it is resurfacing."

"This has nothing to do with your past," Jones said. "What's going on right now? Something happened in the last twenty-four hours between the two of you."

"It's complicated," Shane said. "I need to talk to her, in private, and put a lid on this, I just haven't had the chance."

"It's always complicated with women. In my experience—"

Shane laughed. "Really funny coming from a guy who has serious commitment issues." He stopped at the light at the corner of Alexander and East Avenue. "I'm not taking advice from a guy who has never had a serious relationship."

"I'm single because I haven't met anyone I'm willing to risk feeling like a schmuck for."

"That's funny, because I heard a rumor a woman was spending a lot of time at your place."

"I'm single, not dead."

"I heard this woman has been living with you."

"Has the office turned into a bunch of gossips?" Jones shook his head. "I have sex. With a woman. Who is staying at my house. Temporarily, while her new apartment is being painted."

"At least you're having sex," Shane said. "I can't remember the last time I had sex."

"I bet you remember the last time you had sex with Ka—"

"Two days before she left me," Shane said. "Not that it's any of your business." He brought the car to a stop in front of a house that leaned a little too far to the left. The white paint on the siding had peeled so badly it showed the rotten wood. "Barb's apartment is upstairs."

Dogs barked from across the street. Jones looked around the side, while Shane checked out the porch area then rang the bell. They waited three minutes for a young woman with a small child to come down the stairs. "I'm not interested in whatever you're selling."

"Barb Esters?" Shane asked.

"Depends on who's asking."

Jones pulled out his badge. "Detective Jones. This is my partner, Detective Rogers. We want to ask you a few questions about John Rodney."

"Why?" She gave them a puzzled look, before telling her daughter to run upstairs and watch television. "He's still in prison, right?"

"Yes," Jones said.

"Good. I hope the bastard rots there. Now, what do you want with me?"

"Is Gregory Donegan your cousin?"

"Second cousin. Poor bastard. Heard he got killed or something. But what does that have to do with me or my loser ex?"

"You didn't think he was a loser when you gave a statement to the police when he was accused of rape." Shane flipped open his notebook. Not sure where this was going to lead them, so he jotted down a few more questions.

"Yeah, because the bastard hit me, and I was pregnant and scared. I'd say anything back then to protect him, because he was constantly threatening me, but then I wised up. Me and my kid are better off without that fucking bastard."

The woman certainly liked the word bastard. "You mentioned in an interview that you didn't know Lisa Haughton well. Is that true?"

"Well, sort of," Barb said. "Lisa was one of those privileged chicks who liked to slum it. She had a reputation of being easy and liked bad boys. Everyone knew it. Not a guy who didn't want a piece of that ass. I was jealous. But after I knew my loser boyfriend had really raped that poor girl, I turned on him. I even offered to testify against him, but he took another plea, so I was off the hook."

Shane noted he wanted to ask Cleary about Barb and her willingness to testify.

"Did your cousin, Gregory—"

Barb interrupted Jones. "My second cousin, and one that I don't know and probably haven't seen since I was two."

"Sorry," Jones continued. "Did your second cousin, Gregory, know John Rodney? Were they friends back in the day?"

Barb laughed. "I doubt they ever met. Hell, I didn't even know Gregory was living in Rochester until I saw on the news he'd been murdered." Her smile turned to a frown quickly. "Do I need to be worried? Is someone going to come after me?"

"I don't think so, but it doesn't hurt to be diligent in your safety," Shane said. "We're trying to get a feel for Gregory's life. Thought you might be able to help."

"Sorry. I can't help you with that." She glanced over her shoulder. "If there isn't anything else, I've got to get back to my kid."

"Have you ever met this girl?" Jones held out a picture of Emily Cleary.

"Never met her, but she's all over the news. Why? Do I need to be worried for my kid? What's really going on here?"

"Again, I don't think so, but I'd keep an eye out. If you notice anything suspicious, call 9-1-1," Shane said, handing her his card. "You can call me as well."

"I remember her father," Barb said. "He took my deposition; I think that's what it's called. I told him everything I could about that shithead, Rodney, but in the end, they didn't need me to testify, since Rodney took a deal. Jerk should have gone away for life."

"Did you cut a deal of some kind with Cleary?"

She shook her head. "I was happy to tell him about every rotten thing Rodney was into. I was clean. Other than covering up for him in the beginning. You're sure Rodney ain't out? Because if he is, I do have reason to worry."

"He's still in prison," Jones said.

"What about this kid?" Jones held out a picture of Doug. "Do you know him?"

She reached out and touched the picture, making a face as she studied it. "No. Not that I remember."

"Let us know if you think of anything that might help us."

"Okay."

"Keep your doors locked and don't hesitate to call." Shane checked his watch. "Let's go talk to Doug before we call it a night."

---

*S*hane shoved his phone into his pocket after texting Kara about their decision to interview Doug again, but also to ask her to stop by the house. He hadn't heard back from her yet.

He rang the bell, then put his hands on his hips, looking around the neighborhood. Both Doug and Emily lived walking distance to the Village of Pittsford. Lots of places to meet around the four corners. Sometimes he and Kara would meet down by the canal at the park. Or in the parking lot of Hilllard's Bar and Grill. Sometimes behind the teen center or even the train tracks. So many places.

Mrs. McCauley answered the door. She frowned the moment she laid eyes on Shane.

"Sorry to bother you," Shane started. "We'd like to talk to Doug again."

"Do I need a lawyer?" She kept the door close to her face.

"That's entirely up to you," Jones said. "We're just trying to find out what happened to Emily."

"My son didn't do anything wrong."

Shane wanted to remind the woman that, actually, her son had done something very wrong if he'd had sex with Emily, but refrained. "We need to gain insight into Emily's life, and since she was friends with your son at one point he might help guide us in the right direction. He might know something he doesn't realize could help us find her killer."

"Alright," she said. "Doug is in his room. I'll go get him."

"Can we talk to him there?"

"Why?"

"He might feel more comfortable there," Jones said. "His own space. Surrounded by his own things."

Shane and Jones followed Mrs. McCauley up a flight of stairs. The carpet was worn to the point it needed replacing. The wallpaper was dated back to the seventies. Vintage frames filled with family portraits lined the hallway.

She tapped on the door at the top of the stairs. "Doug? The detectives need to talk to you again." She pushed open the door. Doug sat at his desk, on his computer. He quickly slammed it shut and turned. "What?"

"Mind if we talk alone?" Jones asked.

"I'm staying," Mrs. McCauley said. "This is my house."

Doug's room was a typical teenage boy's room. Clothes on the floor. A couple of posters from the hit show *Breaking Bad* and one from the show *The Big Bang Theory*.

"What do you want to know now?" Doug asked.

"Did you know this gentleman from the museum when you and Emily took some classes there?" Jones held out picture of Gregory.

"I don't think so," Doug said.

"Are you sure? Take a good look." Jones continued to hold up the picture. "Take it."

Doug looked between Jones and his mother, who was now standing next to her son. "I don't know him. Why? Did he kill Emily?"

"We don't think so," Shane said. "And, unfortunately, he died recently."

"That's horrible," Mrs. McCauley said.

"What about you, Mrs. McCauley? Does this man look familiar to you? He worked part-time at the museum."

"I supposed I could have seen him there," she said. "But I don't recall."

"Doug, did Emily have any other boyfriends before you? Or anyone who was jealous of your friendship with her?" Shane asked.

Doug shook his head. "I have no idea. We didn't talk about stuff like that."

"What did you talk about?"

"Stuff," Doug said.

Jones had stuffed his hands into his pockets and was looking around the room.

"Sex stuff?" Shane asked.

"I don't like this line of questioning," Mrs. McCauley said.

"I didn't want to do this in front you," Shane admitted. "I could ask him to come down to the station for an interview. You can get a lawyer, but that isn't going to help us find Emily's killer and that's our top priority. It would be helpful if we had a moment alone with Doug."

She pursed her lips. "Five minutes." She grabbed her son's arm and whispered something in his ear. Shane craned his head, but all he got was a muffled sound. He figured Doug's parents knew there had been an inappropriate relationship and were doing their best to protect him.

"Why don't you have a seat?" Shane pointed to the chair across the room, in front of a messy desk.

"I'll stand," Doug said in a confident voice, but his shifting body and the constant movement of his hands, showed a nervous young man.

"We know there were pictures and a lot of sexting going on between you and Emily," Jones said.

"I didn't have sex with her."

"Did you know she was doing the same thing with other boys?" Shane asked.

Doug glanced to the floor, his eyes narrowing. "I don't know. I guess so." He looked up. "I didn't know she was fourteen. Really. She told me she was seventeen."

"You believed that?" Shane asked.

Doug shrugged.

"Do you know any of the other boys? Any of them have a reason to hurt her?"

"I don't know who else she was texting," Doug said. "All the kids do it."

"You sext with other girls?" Jones asked.

"I have," Doug said. "But it's not illegal or anything."

"There are laws about protecting minors and sending and receiving naked images," Shane said.

"I didn't do anything with the pictures. I can't control what she sent me."

"Can we see your phone?"

Doug shook his head. "Come on, man. I got private stuff on there that has nothing to do with Emily."

"But you might have a number we can trace back to Emily's phone that could help us find her killer."

"My father is going to kill me," Doug said as he turned to his desk, opening his top drawer and pulling out his phone. "I'm only doing this because Emily was my friend. When will I get it back?"

"Might want to get a new one." Shane carefully took the phone just as Mrs. McCauley stepped back into the room.

"Doug! What are you doing? Don't give them that."

"Jesus, Mom," Doug said. "She was my friend and

she's been murdered. If something on my phone can help, then, well...I should let them look at it."

"We're not out to get your son," Shane said. "We're only trying to find out who killed Emily."

"Since he's eighteen, I guess I can't force him to take it back," she said with a deflated tone.

"I'm afraid not," Shane said.

"You didn't have to meet me here," Kara said as Shane stepped from his vehicle in the driveway of Congressman Cleary's house. "I know you want to be home with your son."

"Turns out my niece is way cooler than the old man," Shane said. "Besides, I didn't want you to do this alone."

She smiled. "Chivalry at its best."

He chuckled.

"It has to be hard on your son when a case like this comes your way."

"I was working a double homicide when he was first diagnosed. I didn't pass it off, and it spurred many fights with Janet."

"There are other roles than active homicide." Kara knew it wasn't her place, but she really wanted to understand his relationship with his late wife. Might help her understand their rekindled feelings.

"I didn't want to face Kevin's illness, but a month

into his treatments I realized I wasn't doing anyone any favors."

"You're a good father," Kara said, noting Cleary had stepped out onto his front porch. By the scowl on his face he was none too happy to see them. "Ready to get our heads taken off?"

"I'm always ready."

They approached the front porch until they were face to face with Cleary.

"This is getting ridiculous!" Cleary barked.

"Your frustration is understandable." Kara stepped into the marble foyer.

"I doubt you understand anything," Cleary said.

"We want to talk to you about Barb Ester. She was John—"

Cleary cut Kara off. "I'm well aware of who she was. A key witness in our case against Rodney, the boy who raped Lisa Haughton."

"You resigned from the D.A.'s office a few weeks before Lisa killed herself."

"One day after Rodney took the second plea," Cleary said, not offering to move to the family room or living room. Instead, he kept one hand on the door, ready to kick them to the curb. "I know the timeline."

"How did you come to the plea offer?" Shane asked.

"We had him on multiple crimes. I offered the public defender two lighter sentences versus taking him to trial for rape, which we had rock solid. The key to the deal was he couldn't serve the sentences consecutively. So, he got fifteen years. Probably longer than if we'd gone to trial, which I didn't want to put Lisa Haughton through. She was a weak witness and the defense would have reduced her to rubble. Also, and no offense to the Rochester PD, but there were some issues with evidence collection. I didn't want to take a chance that Rodney would walk."

"Did Barb give you information that helped with making that offer?" Shane asked.

"She did." Cleary still had a death grip on the door. "Without her we couldn't have pushed him to take the deal."

"You cut her a deal as well?" Shane asked.

"She didn't do anything worth cutting a deal. Once he took the plea, she was no longer needed."

"Why wasn't any of this in the report?" Kara had read and reread the arrest report and the plea bargain for John Rodney, but there were no notes of this side deal and negotiations.

"It was my last case. I wanted it wrapped up before I left. The guy is in prison. I did my job. As far as the first offense," Cleary said, "you both know any other D.A. would have offered that kid a plea. Hell, most cops would have talked the parents into not filing charges or pursuing anything other than a restraining order. The kid had no priors. It was that simple."

"Do you know this man?" Kara showed him a picture of Gregory Donegan.

"Should I?" He held it in his hands, examining it

closely. "I don't recognize him. Does he know something about what happened?"

"No," Shane said. "He was murdered."

"You think this is related to my daughter's murder?" Cleary pulled the picture closer, then stretched his arm out, obviously needing cheaters to see better.

"We don't know yet," Kara said.

"How did he die?"

"Strangulation," Shane said. "He was related to Barb Esters. Thought maybe he was involved with Rodney somehow, trying to link it all back to Haughton."

"I've felt bad about Haughton's daughter for a very long time," Cleary said. "But hindsight is 20/20 and I still think that man killed my daughter. He hasn't been right since his daughter killed herself. I actually understand that."

"We have a sensitive topic we need to discuss." Kara held out the papers and notebooks they'd taken from the house.

"What are those?" Cleary took the bundle, but didn't open them. Just stared at them.

"Your daughter's journals," Shane said.

"The ones you took?"

Kara nodded. "There's a lot of graphic sexual details about her relationship with Doug McCauley."

"Excuse me?" Clear said behind gritted teeth. "My daughter was fourteen."

"I'm sorry, Congressman," Kara said. "But your

daughter was sexting and sending inappropriate images to more than one boy."

"You little bit—"

"That's uncalled for," Shane said. "We're on your side, but Emily was meeting and texting with this boy. And her journal talks about some very sexually explicit—"

"Don't you dare talk about my daughter that way! What the fuck do you know?"

"We know that your daughter was murdered," Shane said. "I know this is hard to hear—"

"You're lying."

Shane pointed to the journals. "I wish we were. Please look at these. Read them. Only one boy is named, but she talks about others. Any little thing you can think of may help us catch this bastard."

"You made copies of these?" Cleary looked at Kara with disgust and anguish. His bloodshot eyes glared at her with disdain.

Kara nodded.

"I don't want this getting out," Cleary muttered. "My little girl was murdered. I can't have…" he sniffled, "…her memory tainted like this. It would destroy her mother."

"We would never consider releasing the journals," Shane said. "But we *will* do what it takes to bring the killer to justice."

"Haven't you done enough damage?" Cleary asked

sarcastically. "You basically forced me to tell my wife about my affair with Heather."

"We did no such thing," Shane said.

"Right." Cleary's tone was dark and ominous. "Thanks to you I may have lost my wife as well."

Kara decided to ignore the statements. It wouldn't do any good to go at it with Cleary at this point. "We need to ask that you not contact the boy or his family. You need to let us handle this."

"I won't promise anything," Cleary said. "Anything else?"

"Not right now," Kara said.

"I need to get back to my family."

"We appreciate your time," Kara said. "We'll be in touch."

Cleary opened the door. No sooner did Kara cross the threshold than Cleary slammed the door.

"He is so not going to like what he reads in those," Shane said. "How old were we when we delved past just kissing?"

"Fourteen," she said. "And it's really not the time to discuss that."

"I'm just thinking." He leaned against the door of her SUV. "Did your parents know? Have any kind of clue what we were doing? My parents lectured me all the time about how to treat a lady, respect and all that. If I had a dollar for every time during our relationships that my parents brought up STDs, condoms, pregnancy, and every other thing related to sex, I'd be a billionaire. Hell, I was terrified to touch you."

"Not that terrified, because you did, but to answer the question, my parents talked to me about sex. They certainly weren't blind, or naïve, but they weren't as open as yours."

"You think the Cleary's ever talked to their daughter about that stuff?"

"I don't know," she said. "I got the impression he could have been aware, but in denial."

"Which is why I don't understand why he didn't tell us about Doug during that first interview. I would think if it were my kid, I'd be sucking up my pride and telling all."

"I hate to point out the double standard," Kara said, "but you're a boy. My parents didn't want to accept their little girl was growing up. They certainly didn't want to know if, and when I had sex, especially my father, who every time my mother decided it was time to rehash the sex talk and made him join us, turned fifty shades of red. He'd end the conversation with, 'I know you're a good girl,' even after we went to college and they showed up and found you half-dressed in my dorm room."

"I hadn't thought about those differences," he said. "My parents knew you spent the night. My father even gave me a box of condoms my senior year. Even talking with Kevin, I'm fairly open. He's not even close to hitting puberty, but he texts with some girl from school all the time. He's only been back a couple of days. I have to take his phone away sometimes and have a stern talk with him, but secretly I'm thinking 'that's my boy'."

She laughed. "You're a good father."

"I don't often feel like I am. But I'm doing my best." Shane bent over and kissed her cheek. "Drive safe."

"Sleep well."

"I will if you join me in my dreams."

13

SHANE SAT AT THE DINING ROOM table after eating a large breakfast that his niece had prepared. Theresa was in the kitchen, doing the dishes, while he enjoyed a few more moments with his son. For the last year he hadn't worked a single Saturday, and now it was two in a row. And probably tomorrow as well.

"I spoke to your teacher yesterday," Shane said. "You're lucky all she did was take the pocketknife away. Do I need to remind you it's considered a weapon?"

"No, Dad," Kevin said. His lower lip quivering. "I forgot it was in my pants pocket. Honest. I didn't mean to bring it to school."

"I believe you and so did your teacher, but you could be expelled from school." Shane lowered his chin and arched his brow, trying to channel his father's strong paternal look. "I know you don't want that to happen."

"Can I have a little dish like you have to empty my pockets out in every day? I think that will help me to remember."

"We can do that. And Theresa and I will remind you." Shane smiled. "So, tell me about this girl you've been talking to."

Kevin rolled his eyes. "She's in my tutoring group. She missed last semester, too."

"Why?"

"She had some kind of cancer. Doesn't like to talk about it."

"Going to tell me her name?" Shane knew her name, because he'd seen it in his son's phone. He only read a few of the texts. After knowing what was going on with the Cleary girl, he felt he needed to be more in tune with his son. So many changes.

"Gina," he said. "Besides having a hard time in math, she's having a hard time adjusting to being back. A lot more than I am, but it could be easier for me if I had a smartphone."

"Maybe next year." Shane shook his head. "How are you having a hard time?"

"I'm the only kid who doesn't have a smartphone."

"Nice try," Shane said. "So, you and Gina hang out a lot together?"

"In class," Kevin said. "And sometimes at lunch.

Some of the girls are mean to her because she wears one of those scarf things. It's taking a while for her hair to grow back in."

"You like her a lot."

"We're friends." Kevin's cheeks flushed.

At his age Shane had it bad for Kara, but he had no idea what that meant. Just that he liked being around her more than anyone else.

"Well, if you did, do you remember what I told you about how to treat girls?"

Kevin rolled his eyes again. "Really, Dad. We're just friends."

"Well, if you decide it's time to be more than just friends—"

"I'll treat her like a lady," he said. "Respect her. Go meet her parents. Blah, blah, blah. You and Grandpa are so old-fashioned."

"Trust me. It's not old-fashioned. It's how you get a good woman. It's how I ended up with your mom."

"I'm ten and not really in the market for a wife," Kevin said. "Can I be excused now? I've got a hot date with my Xbox."

Shane laughed. "Sure. I've got to get to work. I promise it won't always be like this."

"I'm not worried."

Shane figured he was in for one hell of a ride with this kid through his teenage years. "I'll see you all tonight!" he yelled as he snagged his keys.

The early afternoon sun was bright, as the sky was clear. But the temperatures had dropped again, and snow was on its way.

Shane headed to his favorite coffee shop to fetch four large cups, as requested by his partner, Kara, and her partner. The line was long, but the line was always long.

"Mr. Rogers?" a familiar voice rang out.

He turned to see the new nurse on the transplant wing standing behind him. "Hello, Tina," he said, hoping he'd gotten the name right.

"How's Kevin? Enjoying school?"

"He is," Shane said. "Thanks for asking."

"I've got an hour before I have to be at the hospital. Care to join me?"

He glanced at his watch. It was just past one. He was supposed to meet Kara, Foster, and Jones by one-thirty at the station. "Thanks for the offer." The two people in front of him were together and it was his turn to order. "Three large coffees and one mocha to go." He looked over his shoulder at Tina. "Sorry, I have to get to work."

"I understand," she said. "Tell Kevin, next time he comes in I want to see more magic tricks."

"Will do."

"Three large coffees and a mocha," the clerk said.

Shane took the tray in one hand and glanced at his phone in the other as it buzzed.

"Shane here."

"We've got another!" Captain Morrell barked. "Eight candles placed around a naked adult body. Three on each side. One at the head. One at the feet. Same weird butterfly-looking mark. Only, this time an incision was made in the belly."

Shane quickly put the address into his phone and raced to his car, putting the tray on the passenger seat.

Another dead body.

It took Shane fifteen minutes to drive across town, weaving in and out of traffic, which wasn't too bad this time of day on a Saturday.

Kara had beat Shane to the crime scene. He rolled his car to a stop behind her SUV. Jones's car was right in front of hers. He quickly pulled out his cell phone and texted his niece, indicating he had a situation and wasn't sure when he'd be home. He waited a moment, thankful when she texted back. It was nice to have her around to help.

Shane quickly scanned the scene, pushing his home life from his brain, and focused solely on the case. If this was the same killer, which Shane knew deep in his gut it was, he'd now be considered a serial killer. The press was already aware the FBI was involved, and they'd been speculating on the connection between Emily and Gregory. It was going to be nearly impossible to keep the press at bay.

This time, the killer had chosen a young single mother in a subsidized apartment building in the town of Greece. The victim's ex found the body when he went to drop off his son for an overnight visit.

Shane drew his sport coat tight around his body, then hefted the coffee tray from the passenger seat. The cold chilled him to the bone.

The apartment was on the second story. Shane stood at the bottom of the stairs after ducking under the police tape and signing the crime scene log. He glanced over his shoulder. The press was interviewing the neighbors and anyone who wanted to be put on camera. People stood around pointing, whispering among themselves. Faces lined with worry. Fear.

Slowly, he made his way to the top of the stairs, focusing on the white noise and trying to ignore the lingering smell of rotting flesh. Foster and Kara were talking with man who looked to be in his mid-thirties. His eyes were bloodshot. He kept shaking his head and running his hand across the top of his buzzed hair. He wore jeans and a nice button-down dress shirt. A black leather bomber jacket was folded over his arm. Shane also noted his expensive shoes. Kara stepped away briefly, took two of the tall paper mugs, and mouthed 'thank you' before turning her attention back to interviewing the man.

Jones stood in the kitchen, which was to the right of the front door, talking with a uniformed officer. The family room was straight ahead. Down the hall, he noticed three doors; he assumed two bedrooms and one bathroom. Through the door directly at the end of the hall he could see movement and lights flashing.

"What do we have?" he asked Jones, handing him his cup.

Jones thanked the uniformed officer, who then ducked into the hallway. "He was the first one to arrive with the EMT. First to interview the father."

"Is that who Kara and Foster are talking to?"

Jones nodded. "The victim is Iris Belton. The ex, Ray Lebinick, knew something was up when she didn't answer the door."

"The ex had a key?"

"Not really an ex," Jones said. "He and the victim never married. He has custody of their son. She sees her kid twice a week for dinner and one night over the weekend. The father pays for the apartment. It's in his name. The victim works at a local restaurant and bar as a waitress."

"Where was the boy?"

"The father said when she didn't answer the door, he took his son back down to the car with his wife. They're still in the parking lot. A uniform is with them, keeping the press away."

Shane pulled out his notepad and ran his fingers across the leather before flipping it open. "Approximate time of death for Gregory was two weeks ago. Approximate time of death for Emily was a little over a week ago. Both suspected to be killed on a Thursday."

"M.E. said, based on temperature of the body and

lividity, it could have been a day or two. Didn't say Thursday, but didn't say it wasn't Thursday. I'm thinking maybe Thursday means something," Jones said. "I also think the killer doesn't care when the bodies are found. Or where he kills. Emily was abducted. It appears Gregory and this one were killed where they lived."

"Morrell said there was an incision in the stomach."

Jones nodded again as he leaned against the counter. "M.E. says it's like the other ones. Done by someone who knows what they're doing, but wouldn't speculate on any internal body parts missing."

"Presentation of the body?"

"Naked. Face-up. Gagged and bound with duct tape and rope."

"Wonder if there's any significance to that."

"Could be," Jones said. "Clothes at this scene were folded and placed on the bed. Also, first time we have blood. The killer did try to clean it up, but there's a fair amount soaked into the carpet."

Shane jotted down a few notes in his pad, then nodded toward the bedroom. "All right," Shane said. "If the killer is taking organs for the black market, he's got to have help. Someone to transport the organ while he finishes his ritual."

"Agreed," Jones said.

Shane wandered through the family room toward the back bedroom. The apartment was sparsely furnished. One very old plaid sofa that had seen better days pushed against the back wall. One small coffee table on the side with a lamp. The other side of the room had a beat-up vinyl recliner in front of a sliding glass door. He snapped on a latex glove. "I take it this was locked when you arrived?" he asked Jones.

"Yep."

Shane continued to the short hallway. The room to the right was a small bedroom with a single bed. Just a box spring and a mattress on the floor. An old wooden desk under the window. The door on the left was the bathroom. Not much he could see, but it looked clean. The entire apartment looked and felt clean. Cared for. The furnishings might be old, but he got the sense that Iris took pride in what she had.

The smell of disinfectant and death hit his nostrils the moment he stepped into the master bedroom. The body was next to the double bed, also just a box spring and mattress on the floor.

"I think this one fought." Dr. Green, the M.E., held up one hand and pried it open a bit. "Small piece of cloth."

First piece of real evidence they had. "Care to wager a guess as to what organ might be missing?"

"Don't know that one *is* missing." Dr. Green motioned to one of his team members. "Let's get the body ready for transport."

"Hey, Doc," Shane said, "what about the markings? What do you make of those?"

The M.E. glanced up at Shane. "Looks like a

butterfly to me. But something to consider with the other two cases is that the organs that were taken can be harvested for transplant."

"How many organs can be donated?" Shane asked.

"Lungs, heart, liver, kidneys, pancreases, thymus, intestines, corneas. Those are the main ones. Other tissues, tendons, etc., can also be used."

Shane stepped from the bedroom, making room for the M.E.'s team and stretcher. "Jones," Shane barked, "let's push the crowd back to the other side of the parking lot."

"Already on it."

Shane took out his cell phone and called his captain.

"Tell me something good," Morrell answered.

"I think it's safe to say we've got a serial killer."

"That's not good news."

"We think this murder might have occurred on a Thursday, like the others. Won't know for sure until we get the report back. The M.E. believes he has found some fibers." Shane stood outside the door of the apartment, at the top of the stairs. Kara at his side. "I think we might want to dig deeper into the black market, while keeping an eye on Haughton."

"The Feds with you?"

"Yeah," Shane said.

"I think it's time we gave a statement to the press."

*S*hane wanted nothing to do with Kara's press conference. He always hated them, even if he was standing there, listening. His captain had given him permission to sit this one out, though he did want to catch it on the news. He pulled his sedan into the two-car garage, next to his niece's little car. He checked the time. Twenty minutes before the six o'clock news. Just enough time to 'kick it', as his niece would say, with his son, then watch the news.

When he pushed open the garage door that opened into the family room his nostrils were filled with his mother's special vodka sauce. He was going to get fat having Theresa around to cook.

"Hey, Dad," Kevin said. He sat on the sofa, Xbox controller in his hand, eyes focused on the television. "Thought you were going to be late."

"I thought I'd be home a few hours ago, but something came up." After Shane unclipped his weapon and stored it in the secure box in the closet, he sat down next to his son and ruffled his hair. "You need a haircut."

"So do you." Kevin glanced up from his game. "It's over your collar and you need a shave."

Shane rubbed his chin. "I forgot to do that this morning. How about we both get haircuts tomorrow?"

"Tomorrow is Sunday, and the barber isn't open on Sunday," Kevin said.

"What did you do today?"

"Went shopping for Grandma's birthday present. Don't forget. You know how she gets…"

"I already got my present," Shane said. "What did you get her?"

"I'm not telling," Kevin said. "It's a surprise."

"Hey, Uncle Shane." Theresa was in the kitchen. She looked just like her mother. On the taller side, but not quite as tall as his sister. Theresa wasn't shy, but she tended to be reserved. Quiet. Into her studies. She wanted to go to medical school and be a pediatrician. Anna had said her decision was based on all the problems Kevin had faced in his life. She wanted to make a difference in the world. "Dinner will be ready in forty-five minutes, give or take. Though I doubt this will be as good as Grandma's. I can never get it just right. I swear she doesn't give out all the ingredients just, so no one can make it as good as her."

"Probably right." Shane sat on the stool at the breakfast bar, watching Kevin fiddle with the Xbox remote. "Plan on six-thirty. I need to do something first. Do your chart?" Shane asked Kevin.

"I did. It's on the counter."

Shane glanced between Kevin and Theresa, realizing that neither one of them was going to show it to him. He waited two full minutes before standing, then checked the notebook, noting that everything appeared fine. "I need to go make a few calls and take care of something."

"That's code for, 'I'm going to watch the news and I

don't want you to watch it because it's about a case you're working on,'" Kevin said. "We're supposed to bring articles to school, so we can discuss current events both locally and globally. I've got one due on Monday." Kevin dropped the controller on the sofa and stood in front of his father. Hands on his hips. Feet shoulder-width apart. Much like Shane always stood. "I'm not a baby anymore. I'm double digits. And everyone in school is talking about the congressman's daughter who was killed. I assume that's your big case."

"He's right, Uncle Shane," Theresa said, still stirring the sauce. "Better to know what's going on in the world than to be ignorant."

Shane thought about it for a moment. So many changes, but it was difficult to ignore how happy his son was at school, and in life. "All right," Shane said. "But understand there are things I won't be able to talk to you about, and it's best you not tell the other kids at school that I could be working on anything they hear in the news. Got it?"

"Yep." Kevin quickly snagged the remote and turned on the television. "What news station do you like?"

"ABC," Shane said, still staring at his son. He looked so much like Janet. She'd been a good mother, the best, always attentive to Kevin's needs. She'd been Shane's rock for years and he'd just started to get used to the idea of living alone again when Kara walked back into his life, stirring things in him that were both thrilling and terrifying.

"Beer?" Theresa dangled one in front of him. "You look like you could use one."

"Thanks." He knew Janet would want him to get on with his life, but did that mean being with Kara again?

Kevin had sat back down on the sofa. He rifled through his backpack, pulling out a folder and a notebook.

Shane shook his head. "He's growing up too fast."

Theresa laughed. "My mother cried so hard when I left to come here, I thought she was going to change her mind and not let me bring my car."

"Your mother's always been emotional and dramatic. Being Mike's twin, and less than two years younger than Dave, and the only girl, she got picked on a lot."

"She says they were downright mean, but you not so bad."

"That's because I'm six years younger and she picked on me," Shane said. "Turn it up, little man."

"I really hate being called that," Kevin said.

"Is that your high school sweetheart standing behind the captain?" Theresa asked.

Shane's phone buzzed. He glanced at it quickly. It was Kara. "One and the same," he said as he lifted the phone to his ear. "I take it the press conference isn't live since I'm about to watch it?"

"Ended about fifteen minutes ago," she said. "Can we talk tonight?"

"Come on over. My niece made my mom's sauce."

"I'll be there soon."

Shane ended the call and sat on the sofa, looping his arm around his son. "Theresa, I hope you have enough food for one more. Kara is joining us."

"I'm just like Grandma. I only know how to cook for an army," she said.

"That FBI agent on TV was your girlfriend once?" Kevin pressed the volume button a few more times as Kara made her way to the podium to represent the FBI's interest in this investigation. "She looks familiar. Aren't there pictures of her at Grandma's?"

"I dated her before I met mom," Shane said. "I took her to my senior prom and she used to babysit a couple of your cousins."

"Are you---"

"*Shhh,*" Shane said. "After this is over."

"We're working with the Rochester Police Department in a joint task force," Kara said, her hands gripped the podium, eyes focused right at the cameras. The way she commanded the room was impressive. Shane was almost disappointed he'd missed it live.

"We have three victims we believe have all been killed by the same person."

Lights snapped, and a few reporters shouted out questions. A very poised Kara held up her hand. "All I can tell you right now is that we're talking with a few persons of interest. If anyone has any information they believe is pertinent to these murders, please call the number at the bottom of your screen. Thank you." She turned, and walked away gracefully, taking her place next to the Chief of Police as the reporter for the station recapped what they understood about the murders.

Then the news cut to commercial.

"Are you working with her?" Kevin asked.

Shane checked his phone. Kara had sent a text that she was ten minutes out. "I am," Shane said.

"And she's coming here?"

Shane nodded.

"That is so cool!" Kevin jumped off the sofa, but then stopped suddenly and turned to face Shane. "I don't get to tell the kids at school I met her, do I?"

Shane shook his head. "Maybe when this is all over I can talk her into coming to your school. Then you can tell them you met her way before they did."

"Okay," Kevin said. "I'll set another plate!"

"Aren't you supposed to watch *all* the news?" Shane asked.

"Oh. Yeah. We've got to write a paragraph about the stories. And then a paragraph about what we thought and felt. I could do it tomorrow, but we're going to Grandma's for the day."

"Better sit here then." Shane patted the sofa. "You need help, Theresa?"

"Nope. You're paying me the big bucks to cook, clean, and take care of my favorite little cousin."

"And I didn't even get the family discount." Shane glanced at his son's homework paper, forcing himself not to check his forehead, a habit he needed to break. The doctor had been right. School was good for him. Theresa was good for him.

And now he was going to meet Kara.

Would that be good for his son?

———————

*S*hane was a tad startled at how well dinner had gone. Kevin and Kara got along like they'd known each other their entire lives. There didn't seem to be any awkward silences, and Kara more than enjoyed the magic show Kevin had put on. All in all, it had been a good evening. But now that Kevin was in bed, and Theresa was studying, he had a moment to be alone with Kara.

He rubbed his sweaty palms like a boy on his first date. "Hey," he said as he turned the corner from the staircase to the living room. He wasn't much of a decorator, and when he bought this place he'd wanted a fresh start. It was too hard to have so many constant reminders of Janet. He'd kept all the things that really meant something to her and their son; otherwise, new digs, new furniture.

Kara sat on the brown leather sofa across from the fireplace, looking out the front window. His breath hitched. Her dark hair shone in the soft light from the lamp next to her. In a million years, he never thought he'd lay eyes on her again, much less see her sitting in his living room. "What did you want to talk about?" He settled in on the other side of the sofa, picking up the remote to the fireplace. It had felt weird to have a gas fireplace at first, but he'd gotten used to it. The flames crackled to life as they set off a soft fiery glow.

"A couple of things." Kara tucked her one foot under her butt and faced him. "Business first?"

Shane nodded.

"You okay with being the lead detective on an official joint task force?"

"I am," Shane said. "I like the team we've assembled so far. I also like the way we've been working. I don't want that to change."

"I'm not going to leave you hanging."

"Professionally," Shane said. "I believe that."

Kara leaned over, looking up the stairs. "You sure you want to talk about the case here? Maybe we should step outside."

"It's too cold," Shane said. "Besides, if he's not sound asleep from having a long day, he's under his blanket reading. And he knows that if I bring work home, unless he's on fire, he's to stay in his room."

"You don't think he's at the top of the stairs? Listening?"

"He's not the nosey type." Shane shook his head. "Besides, I'd hear him. The floorboards between his room and the stairs creak. Unless the television is on he's not getting passed that, and really, he gets it that sometimes work comes home. When Jones is here, he'll call from the top of the stairs before coming down."

Kara tucked her hair behind her ears. It was something she did when she was either excited or nervous. She didn't look like she was either. "We did a widespread search on the organ black market. We've got four large rings, as I told you, but the most interesting thing was that our analyst found a case from the early nineties where a man in Louisiana was collecting organs for some ritual to bring back the dead. He took them from people he referred to as witches. Nonbelievers to be sacrificed in the name of his god to cure the sick."

"I think that was a case I studied in school. It made national news." Shane's mind had splintered in all sorts of different directions once he realized the killer was collecting organs.

Shane leaned back on the sofa and closed his eyes, pinching the bridge of his nose. He mentally went over every detail stored in his memory about each of the cases. They weren't related. They didn't travel in the same circles. Didn't even live in the same area. Nothing added up. "Was Iris Catholic?" Shane knew the Cleary's were Catholic. So was Gregory, but according to his family and friends he didn't attend church at all. He didn't have much to go on with Iris. The second team of detectives was still interviewing family and friends. Those reports would be on his desk in the morning.

"No. Jewish actually." Kara pulled out her tablet and

fired it up before handing it to Shane. "I sent this to you, but take a look now."

Shane took the tablet. "What is it?"

"Victimology of Emily and Gregory. Waiting for your other detectives to file reports on Iris before we pull that one together."

Shane looked at the glowing tablet. "Give me the Cliffs Notes version."

"Gregory helped coach soccer at the YMCA and was a referee for travel youth soccer."

"Emily played travel soccer," Shane said.

Kara nodded. "Two years ago, Gregory volunteered as an assistant coach for the age level that Emily was in. His team played hers twice. Both times, they lost by a lot. Other than that, and the museum, we can't find anywhere else their lives might have crossed."

"We need to interview both coaches. See if they remember an incident involving either one of them. What about Iris's kid? Did he play soccer?"

"I called the father and, sure enough, Iris's boy is into soccer. She went to games as much as she could, according to the father. He says he and Iris didn't fight much. Did what was best for their son. The step-mother said she and Iris were friendly enough."

"It's Saturday, so we should get some forensics back by Monday." Shane held the tablet in his hand, looking at the words, but he preferred to listen to Kara's voice. "Curious to see what we get from the fibers the M.E. found in Iris's hand, or what organ is missing." Shane pulled out his phone and texted the second detective team to look into the soccer connection as best they could, considering the late hour. "Looks like we've got our work cut out for us tomorrow." Shane handed back the tablet, dropping his head to the cushion on the back of the sofa again. He rubbed his temples. "I suspect if we don't figure this out in the next couple of days, we'll have another dead body come Thursday."

"I want to taunt the killer," Kara said.

"You already did that."

"Not really," she said. "I want Cleary to give a statement when I do my next press conference."

"About what?"

"About how good a job we're doing tracking down the killer."

"He won't go for that."

"If we give him the details, he sure as shit will. Right now, all that he and the public know is that we have three murders that have brought the Feds to town. The press is asking questions, begging for details, and reporting on our presence. But they don't know about the candles or the organs, and I don't think we can keep that quiet much longer."

"Are you suggesting we leak information?"

"You know as well as I do that we're going to have to give them something before things are leaked from other sources and we lose control of how we want this to play out."

"Dangerous game." Shane rolled his head to gauge

Kara's expression. She sat on the other side of the couch, her back to the armrest. Her legs were folded over one another, her elbows on her knees as she leaned in a tad. Her facial expression was stoic. Unemotional. And impossible to read.

"The killer has left no clues that we understand. Normally in cases like these, the killer wants credit. He wants the press to give him a name. He wants notoriety."

"So, you just want to piss him off." Shane didn't like the sound of that any more than he liked the good congressman giving a press conference. "Just to try to get him to taunt back."

Kara nodded. "I've looked into two possible cases to use as a basis. The one that makes the most sense the press dubbed the Organ Slayer. He's currently in a psych ward. He killed nine people. Each time he'd take something from the body."

"Do we know why he did it? What do the shrinks all have to say?"

Kara contorted her face as if she'd just bitten into something sour. "He was frying the body parts and eating them. He's a psychopath and legally insane, with no concept of right and wrong."

"A regular Hannibal Lecter," Shane said. "So, what do you plan on doing to taunt *our* killer, exactly?"

"This other killer was dubbed the Organ Slayer by the media. We want to call this guy a copycat of him, and a bad one at that."

"Sounds like he could be, except we have no reason to believe our killer is eating body parts."

"We don't have any reason to believe he's not," Kara said. "Tomorrow, following the briefing and after we've all got our assignments, we'll make an announcement—"

"So, you've already decided taunting the killer is the best move?"

"With no leads, it's our only move."

Shane let out a long breath. She was right. They had nothing. Not even a direction. A long moment of silence followed. The only noise was the heater kicking on and off. It was odd how easy it was to converse with Kara about work. A natural ebb and flow between them. Like they'd been doing this for years, but it didn't help ease the growing tension between them.

"That it?" he asked.

"That's it for business," she said.

Shane rolled his head toward her again. She had pulled her knees up to her chest. Her arms folded around her legs and her cheek rested on her knees. Her eyes were focused out the window.

"Was there something else you wanted to talk about?" Shane asked.

"To say thank you for Friday. For bringing the flowers. For being there with me again after all these years. I really do appreciate it."

"You've already thanked me," he said, inching closer.

She turned her head, catching his gaze. Holding it

for a long moment. "I guess I just wanted to see you. Meet your son. Know your life."

"I'm glad you're here." His knee touched her toes as he rested his hand on the back of the sofa, running his fingers through her hair, ignoring the inner voice telling him to stop or at least slow down. "Kevin thinks you're cool."

"I like him." She raised her head, letting her one leg drop to the side; the other leaned against the back of the sofa. "We're playing with fire."

"I like things hot." He pressed his lips against hers, applying slight pressure before deepening the kiss. Her body relaxed as he felt her hands on his shoulders, her legs stretching out over his lap. He cupped the nape of her neck with one hand, the other hand rested just under the swell of her breast. Her lips and tongue danced with his like an old waltz. Slow. Tender, then occasionally picking up the pace, only to slow it down to a mere brushing of the lips.

Gently, he slid her body down the sofa alongside his. Their lips were still entwined in a wet and sloppy kiss. Carefully, as if he were doing it for the first time, he pulled her shirt out of her slacks and glided his hands across her stomach. His knee pressed between her legs. Her hands gripped his neck and shoulders, digging her fingers into his muscles. Her lips frantically rubbed against his. He wanted to ravish her, taking all that he could, filling himself with every inch of her body. He remembered every curve. Every sensitive spot.

Her chest heaved up and down with her raspy breath. He felt like a teenager all over again. It was both exciting and terrifying to have her in his arms. He pressed his hand over her lacy bra; he could feel her hard nipple through the thin layer of fabric. He fanned his thumb across the nub and was rewarded with a soft moan as she dropped her head back onto the arm of the sofa. He kissed her soft neck as he shifted his body, giving him a better view of her breasts. He found the small clasp of her front-clasping bra and worked it between his fingers until it popped open. He pushed the fabric aside and held the perky mound in his hand, sliding his tongue down her throat, second-guessing why he'd chosen to go under the shirt instead of unbuttoning the shirt. Now he had to release her perfect breast to open her blouse.

He shifted so both hands could work the buttons. He'd opened the top three, which gave him the perfect view of the most perfect taut nipple. "Still perky," he mused.

"Shane," she whispered. "Stop."

"I don't want to."

"I can tell." She quickly covered her breast by clutching at her shirt. "We forgot about Theresa, who just cleared her throat. I think she's at the top of the stairs."

"Shit." He reached inside Kara's shirt, groaning as he

pulled her bra back around her breasts. They had been just as he remembered. He'd never seen breasts like hers. Ever. Nothing could ever compare to Kara in any way. He sat up, helping Kara to a sitting position while she fumbled, trying to tuck in her shirt. "I didn't tell her about the rules when work comes home."

"That had nothing to do with work," Kara said.

"True. I'll have to add a new rule about women."

"Uncle Shane?" Theresa's voice rang out. "I need to get something."

"You can come down," he said. "I didn't hear the creak in the stairs," he whispered in Kara's ear.

"Oh hey, Kara," Theresa said. "Didn't know you were still here." But Theresa's smile said otherwise. "I left a couple of books I need. I'll be out of your way in a jiffy."

"I was just leaving," Kara said.

"You don't have to leave," he said.

"It's late and…" she paused. "It's late."

Taking the hint, he said, "I'll walk you to the car."

"Always the gentleman." Kara smiled sweetly.

"It was nice to meet you," Theresa said. "Hope to see you again soon."

"You too," Kara said.

Once outside, Shane pulled open the door of her SUV. His body shivered from the cold as it bit through his shirt. His trousers barely kept his legs warm. She tossed her stuff across to the passenger side, but then turned back.

"What are we doing?" she asked.

"I wish I knew," he said. "When this case is over, you'll go back to D.C. and I'll be here. With my son."

"I know." Her gaze dropped to the ground. "I still care about you."

He cupped her face and dropped his forehead to hers. "I care about you, too." He pressed her against the side of the SUV and took her mouth a little too harshly. Her tongue was as eager as his to engage in another dance, but he broke it off quickly. "We're different people than we were thirteen years ago."

"Sometimes we don't act like it," she whispered. "Not sure this can continue."

"Not sure we can stop it." To prove his point he kissed her again, this time cupping her breast, finding her nipple with his forefinger and thumb and twisting it gently.

"You don't play fair," she said.

"I just know what you like."

She smiled up at him, her hand on his chest, slowing lowering it until her fingers gripped his belt. He stared down at her hand for a moment. "I can play that game, too."

"I haven't had sex in two years, so I'm not past doing it in a car," he said. There was no control when it came Kara. He wanted her, and he was going to have her. If not right now, then tomorrow, or the next day. He'd deal with the consequences later.

"I have to go." She pushed him back, then climbed into her truck.

"Before you pull up to the hotel, you might want to fix your shirt. I managed to unbutton one or two again."

"Two Houdini's in the family. Great."

"Just horny," he said. "Drive safe. Text me when you get into your room, okay?"

She nodded. "Sleep well."

"Only if you join me in my dreams."

14

"*I*'D SAY THAT WAS A WASTE of a Sunday afternoon," Kara said. She snagged her coat out of Shane's car. "All we found out was that, in one soccer game, a father on Emily's team was tossed for being abusive toward Gregory."

"Not abusive," Shane said, picking up her small portable filing case. "He threatened Gregory bodily harm, and it's interesting that it was Cleary who escorted that father, Brad Johnson, off the field."

"And Cleary stated he doesn't remember the game. Said that lots of times parents were ejected from games for being assholes." Kara used her key card to get into the back entrance of the Holiday Inn Express, letting Shane go in first.

"Cleary was really drunk this afternoon," Shane said. "I don't think he knows what day it is."

Her room was only five in from the back door. Her

hand trembled slightly as she put the plastic key into the slot, pulling it out as soon as the lock clicked. She held the door open for Shane, grateful she'd let the maids clean this morning. Normally she'd go a couple of days without using the service. She didn't like her things messed with, but she'd been in the room too long. It needed cleaning. "We need him to sober up before going in front of the press."

"He will." Shane set her files on the desk.

"Put them on that bed," Kara said. "Did Mrs. Cleary read the journals?" Kara asked as she kicked her shoes off into the closet, then secured her weapon and hung up her coat. The room was your typical standard two-queen room. She always got two beds. One for her work, one to sleep in. She fluffed the pillow on the bed where Shane had dropped her case, then sat down, opening the files and placing them on the bed.

"She did." Shane sat in the chair at the desk, putting his feet on the bed while he leaned back and clasped his hands behind his head. "Had quite the talk with her while you were going over the press conference with Cleary."

"And?"

"She acted stunned," he said. "But she never looked me in the eye. I think they both knew but didn't want to know."

Kara nodded, tossing the files to the side. "Soccer right now is the only thing that connects all the victims."

"What did Cleary say about giving the press conference?"

"Not much," she admitted. "I didn't give him the details, just told him to show up tomorrow at 9am, sober. That we needed his help."

"I hope this works," Shane said.

"So do I," she said. "Anything from the M.E.?"

He shook his head. "I think we need a break. A good night's sleep and then come back at this fresh in the morning."

"I suppose you need to go." Her heart hammered in her chest. The last thing she wanted was for him to leave.

His feet hit the floor as he glanced at his watch. He was going to leave. She sucked in a deep breath. She had to be okay with his decision. Even though things had gotten out of hand last night on his sofa, and later in text messages, he had a son he needed to get home to. He stood, reaching into his coat pocket, and pulled out his keys. Tossing them on the desk, he took his sport coat off and carefully hung it on the back of the chair. He removed his weapon next, carefully checking the chamber, and then set it on the desk.

She swallowed the lump in her throat as he moved between the two beds, pulling what appeared to be his wallet out of his pants pocket, and then his phone out of the back pocket, and set them on the nightstand. "I don't need to be anywhere for a couple of hours," he said. His voice was husky and deep and filled with passion.

Her body tingled when he pushed her feet to the floor and lifted her off the bed. He tugged at her ponytail, pulling the hair band out. "I don't like it when you wear your hair up."

"I need to for work."

"We're done with work."

His fingers glided through her hair as it fell just past her shoulders. She shuddered as he traced his forefinger from the side of her earlobe, down her neck, to her cleavage. He smiled. "Your body always does that when I do this." He retraced the path. Her eyelids grew heavy and, once again, her body trembled slightly.

She pressed the back of her hand against his stomach, her fingertips sliding just inside his pants, her thumb wiggling at his belt buckle.

He batted her hand away.

She cocked her head and reached for him again, but this time he took her hand and placed it on his shoulder. "Not yet," he whispered.

With his eyes on hers, he unbuttoned her blouse. She dug her fingers into his strong shoulder blades while reaching for him with her other hand.

"Nope." He grabbed her wrist. "I've got cuffs if we need to go that route."

"So do I," she said.

"That's not going to happen." He draped her other hand on his shoulder while he pulled her blouse out of her pants, then rolled the shirt over her shoulders, but she wasn't about to move her arms now. "This is coming off," he said.

She batted her eyes. "But you put my hands here." She squeezed his shoulders. "And here they will stay."

He reached out and unsnapped her bra.

"Whoa." She jumped as her hands dropped to her sides, then they were yanked backwards as Shane pulled her blouse all the way to her wrists. Her bra straps fell off her shoulders. He held her arms behind her back with one hand and smiled triumphantly. She thought about squirming, but then opted to enjoy watching him look her up and down. His free hand cupped her breast. His thumb gently traced a tiny circle over her hard nipple. She leaned into him, wanting more and more, but he continued to keep his touch feather-light.

"Let my arms go." She wiggled. Her breasts burned for his touch, her panties wet with anticipation.

He leaned over and sucked her nipple into his mouth, rolling it with his tongue, increasing the pressure on the other one with his fingers. Even when they'd been new lovers, they knew how to instinctively please the other. He had always liked to tease her. Make her desperate to have him.

She was already desperate, and he'd barely begun.

He released her hands, but the buttons on her sleeves made it impossible to shed her shirt. "Get this thing off me."

He ran his tongue across her nipple, up her chest, kissing her neck. "Having difficulties?" he murmured, rubbing his thumb across her lips.

She'd freed one of her wrists by popping the button with a swift yank, and was close to freeing the other one. "There," she said as the button flew across the room. She dropped the shirt and her bra to the floor. "Two can play at this game." She shoved him, a little too hard, and he tumbled back onto the bed. She straddled him before he had a chance to move. She started unbuttoning his shirt. His hands kept coming up, toying with her nipples, making it impossible for her to concentrate on the buttons. She adjusted herself slightly, positioning herself in the perfect spot, grinding her hips ever so gently.

His eyes rolled back and he dropped his hands. "Fine. But hurry up."

She didn't waste any time removing his shirt. As he rose and lifted his undershirt over his head, she bent down and took one of his nipples in her mouth, toying with the other one.

He hissed, grabbing her hand. "My turn."

"Nope." She slid down to the floor, on her knees, and began undoing his belt.

He sat up. "You do that, and it just might end there."

"I doubt it." She pried the belt open, then the clasp on his trousers, before slowly and carefully tugging at the zipper, all the while looking up at him. His chest heaved up and down with labored breath.

"I wasn't kidding when I said it's been two years."

"I'm sure you've done something to release the pressure." She slid his slacks to his ankles then lifted the elastic on his boxers, releasing all of him.

"Not... the... same..." he let out a guttural groan.

Her body shivered at the sound. She took him in her hand, stroking softly, then licking the length of him.

He fisted her hair and pulled her away as he gasped. "You can't do that unless that's all you want." He looked at her with intent in his eyes. "It's my turn now."

She stood. "Only if you do that one thing that I—"

"That and more." He yanked her to the bed, rolling her to her back. His mouth moved from one breast to the other, his hands working on her belt. He paused, raising his head, and caught her gaze. He held it for a long moment before kissing her tenderly. His lips barely brushed hers. His tongue soft and slow against hers. "You're ready," he whispered.

All she could do was pant.

He smiled, then planted kisses on her neck, down her breasts and stomach. His hands pulling her slacks and thong off at the same time. Part of her wanted to just have him inside her. Forget the foreplay. The other part remembered just how good that foreplay was.

"That's different."

She lifted her head and looked down. Shane had one hand on her stomach. The other on her thigh. "What?"

JEN TALTY

"Last time I was down here you had a landing strip." He traced his fingers down her stomach to just above the point that throbbed with intense heat. "Now, nothing."

"I don't think you need the strip to find your way around." She raised her one leg, resting it on his back. His breath hot on her body. He was worried about lasting? She figured the moment he touched her, her body would be quivering with delight.

He took the other leg and dropped it over his shoulder, then fanned his thumb against her. Wetness poured out of her, ready to take all of him. She watched him gently part her as his tongue gently lapped at her. He inserted his fingers and pressed his tongue harder and faster. She arched her back, pulling his one hand to her breast. "Please," she begged.

But he continued to tease her. Stroking her insides slowly. His tongue intimately rolling over her throbbing nub. His fingers barely touching her nipple. Then he'd pick up the pace a little, bringing her so close, but not over the edge. "Yes," she whispered as he stroked faster again. Sucked harder. His thumb and forefinger twisting and plucking at her nipple.

Her body bucked and shivered. She clutched his head, squeezing her legs tight, trying to make him stop, but he continued. Her body convulsed in sheer ecstasy. "Shane." She let her legs fall to the side. "I'm begging."

He slid his fingers out slowly, then kissed her intimately, making her throb again. He stood, reaching for

214

his wallet. She watched him wrap himself with the condom. "Turn over," he demanded.

She smiled, rolling over to all fours, pressing herself against him. He leaned over, slamming himself into her, over and over. She arched her back, pushing against him as he reached around and rubbed his thumb against her again. "Oh, God," she moaned as her body quivered, convulsing in a million spams as he continued to pound her. It wasn't rough. But it was raw. Desperate.

He groaned as he clutched her hips, holding himself deep inside for a long moment before he moved in and out, but this time slowly, until he collapsed on the bed, drawing her back to his chest and holding her tight while kissing her neck. Part of her was home. The other part was stuck in a place where the past didn't exist and there was no future.

They lay there for a long time, catching their breath. His knees tucked in behind hers. His arms completely wrapped around her body. She held his forearms with both hands, not wanting to ever let go again.

"Are you cold?"

"A little."

He adjusted himself, holding her with one arm, pulling the comforter over their bodies. His lips pressed against her earlobe. "I wish I could stay here all night with you."

"But you can't," she said. It was going to be hard to

watch him walk out of this hotel room. To sleep in this bed alone after what they'd just shared.

"I could if I let Theresa know."

"No." She twisted her body, rolling to face him. "I wouldn't feel right about taking time away from Kevin."

Something buzzed on the nightstand.

"My phone," he said. "Mind handing it to me? Just want to make sure it's nothing important."

"You don't have to stay here now."

"I want to stay," he said. "Hoping I can regroup and act like a horny teenager who can do it more than once in an afternoon."

She laughed as she reached for his phone. "As I recall, you never had a problem with that." When she handed him the cell, the screen lit up with a picture of Janet and their son.

"Shit," he said. "I'm sorry. I'll change it." He took the phone from her hands, quickly tapping at the screen.

"You don't have to change it." She snuggled into the crook of his shoulder, wrapping her arms around his strong body. "She was your wife. Kevin's mother. You loved her...still love her." Closing her eyes, she kissed his chest. "I'd think there was something wrong with you if you didn't have pictures of her on your phone."

"It doesn't bother you?" He ran a finger up and down her arm.

"I'm not jealous of her or her memory," she said. "I respect it."

"You used to be jealous."

She laughed. "No. You wanted me to be jealous. But I never had any reason to be. And I still don't. I'm glad you were able to find someone like her to give you such a wonderful life and family. I know if she were still alive, we wouldn't be in this bed."

He reached down, tucking his thumb under her chin and tilting her head. "You know what's really weird?"

"What?"

"As odd as this conversation is," he said, smiling, "I'm really glad I stopped this morning to buy condoms," he said. "And not just one. I have more in my wallet."

She laughed. "Look in the nightstand drawer."

He reached over her and pulled the drawer open, looking inside. "Well, what do you know? A box of condoms."

"Last night on the way home."

"Great minds think alike," he said, caressing her thigh as he kissed her shoulder. "I was so hoping when you invited me in that this is how we'd end up."

"I needed help carrying my portable file cabinet."

"Right." He laughed. "So, that thing I stopped you from doing. I think I can handle it now."

Her heart fluttered. The ease she felt was like they'd never stopped loving each other.

But he had. And it didn't bother her.

15

SHANE SPREAD OUT IMAGES from the three crime scenes on the conference room table, then on the far side of the table, he put images from the crime scene from Boston that Kara had brought to his attention. The victim was a twenty-five-year-old male who had gone to Boston College, then worked at a local marketing firm. He'd been born and raised in Rochester, a fact that was too close to all the other cases to be a coincidence.

Across from the table were two large corkboards filled with suspects, possible connections, timelines, and other information. Kara had used the whiteboard to draw a diagram of victims to persons of interest, but it all led them to no one in particular. He leaned on the table, putting his weight on his knuckles. His gaze went from Emily, bound with rope, gagged with duct tape.

Face up. Her eyelids closed over empty sockets. Hair perfectly styled. Clothes folded neatly next to her. He compared that to the crime scene at Gregory's apartment. Still difficult to see such a badly-decayed body. Shane wasn't sure what was worse that, or a fourteen-year-old girl. Then he glanced at the case in Boston. His stomach churned looking at the young man with his gut sliced open and his intestines pulled out of his body.

Shane turned his attention back to Gregory's crime scene photos. The body was laid out on his belly. His wrists pulled overhead, held together with duct tape. Ankles crossed, also held together with duct tape. His clothes folded neatly next to his body.

Shane shifted his gaze to Iris. The only real difference in the crime scene was the stained carpet. He glanced back to the case in Boston. The body propped up on the bed. Blood everywhere. Hands and feet tied with rope. There were no candles. But his clothes were folded neatly on the chair next to the bed. Shane leaned in to get a closer look.

A light tap on the door jerked Shane from his thoughts.

Captain Morrell leaned against the doorjamb. "Are you sure you're up for this?"

"I told you I was when I agreed to be lead."

"You didn't agree," Morrell said. "You were assigned, and I didn't really give you a choice." Morrell was a good cop, but he was better at being a leader than in the field.

"Then why ask me now?"

"With everything that has happened—"

"Are you worried I'm going to be distracted? Unable to do my job?"

"I wouldn't have given it to you if I thought that," Morrell said. "But after everything we've been through over the years, I owed you a private conversation."

"I appreciate that. But I'm good to go. I've got full-time help and Kevin is in school." Shane looked back down at his images. "You good with the team I put together?"

"I approved it," Morrell said. "I've got to head back to my office. Kara is prepping Cleary for the press conference."

"Is Cleary sober?"

"Probably for the first time since his daughter was murdered. His hands are shaking. Not sure we really want to put him in front of a camera."

"Kara told me they're going to give the press conference together."

"Almost rather the Feds do it alone. Kara is quite impressive." Morrell pushed off from the doorjamb. "But, then again, it shows Cleary is backing all of us. On board. We need that in the eyes of the public." With that, Morrell disappeared into the hallway and Shane scanned the images once more, slowly blinking once between photographs, hoping something would jump out at him.

Shane heard more footsteps approaching. So much for spending some alone time with the victims.

Pollack and Benster stood at the door. "Iris's apartment was clean. No prints other than hers, her kid, and the kid's father, whose alibis checks out."

"I figured," Shane said. "What about the candles?"

"They come from all over the place. We've got requests in to get batch numbers to see what stores," Pollack said.

"We've got the BrightLite candles narrowed down to two consultants in this area," Benster added. "One in the city and the other consultant is in Fairport. We're going to talk with them today."

"After that," Pollack continued, "we're going to head out and interview some of the soccer coaches and refs again. See what else we can dig up."

"Appreciate it," Shane said. "I'm going to ask you the same thing Morrell just asked me." Shane turned his head. Pollack stood in the doorway, while Benster leaned against the wall, both hands behind his back.

"No need," Benster said. "We know what being part of this task force means."

"Pollack? You good? You've got a wife and a couple of kids."

"My wife has only known me as cop. She's got my back. I'll make it up to the kids when I can."

"Alright," Shane said. "But after you're done with the two interviews, go home. Take a few hours with your family."

Pollack nodded.

"I'm not married. Hell, I don't even have a girl-friend," Benster said. "I can come back."

"No," Shane said. "We work in the same teams we've been working. Take a nap. Watch a movie. Get laid. We're all going to need to take time to rest and release."

"Just call me if you need anything," Benster said.

"Will do." Shane turned his focus back to the images as the two detectives headed down the hallway. Shane had arranged the images so the bodies were all exactly as they were at the scene. If the head pointed north, he placed the image that way. He studied every detail of each one, trying to match something to each scene. He even measured out the placement of the candles around the body. They weren't exact, but they were close.

For the Boston case, he used the notes filed from the detectives to arrange the photos, but there were more differences than similarities.

The ticking of the clock on the wall taunted him. He didn't look up. There was something in these images he was missing.

The alarm on his phone was set for two different times. First was the press conference. Second was when his son would be getting out of school. Until then, he wanted only to focus on these four cases.

He pressed his knuckles into the wooden conference table. He glanced between the first image of Emily and the corkboard across the room, checking the timeline, the connections to the other victims, and persons of interest.

Still didn't give him any insight.

He decided to rearrange the images, putting the four victims at the top of the table. Below them the different images from the crime scenes, trying to match them this way. He did this for another forty-five minutes.

He smelled Kara's perfume before she walked into the room. He allowed himself a reprieve and glanced in her direction. Her hair flowed just over her shoulders. He was glad she hadn't worn it up. It was a nice distraction for a moment. "You're a sight for sore eyes." He was rewarded with a smile, but it faded quickly.

"How long have you been in here looking at those?"

He glanced at his watch. "Going on two hours." He let out a long sigh and then sat down, tapping on one of the images from the Boston case. "Can you make that out?"

Kara lifted the image. "Looks like a tattoo."

"The report doesn't mention a tattoo. I want to find out what that is."

"I can see if our tech can blow up the image, and I'll call our Boston office.

"Thanks." He leaned back in his chair, taking in the

beautiful woman leaning against the corner of the conference table. "What's on your mind?" he asked.

"Just talked to the M.E."

"And?"

"Did you know that the medical school reported five cadavers missing?"

"Yeah," Shane said. "Months ago. I think they were found. Some stupid prank a bunch of pre-med students thought would be funny."

"Not all were recovered. We just found one."

"Where?"

"Genesee River," Kara said.

"What does that have to do with our cases?"

"The cadaver had new incisions; the medical school checked their records and this particular one was scheduled for a class at the university, so all of the organs should have been inside the cadaver."

"I take it this cadaver was missing organs."

Kara nodded. "All the ones that can be harvested."

Shane pinched the bridge of his nose. His pounding headache returned at full force. "So, you're thinking our killer also has a thing for cadaver organs?"

"I'm saying anything to do with organs could be connected," she said. "Most serial killers perfect their kills over time. I've seen many where their first kills are so different from what they ended up with that we had no idea it was them."

"But why a cadaver?"

"Profiler doesn't think it has much to do with the

person, but the organ, which brings me to weird item number two from the M.E.: Iris was strangled. But what's really disturbing is that her liver was taken."

Shane had believed Iris had an organ removed, so this wasn't shocking news. "We've got eyes, kidneys, and maybe a cadaver's organs. What makes a liver more disturbing?"

She handed Shane a folder. "Because she'd had a partial liver transplant eight months ago."

"You've got to be kidding me." Shane snagged the report and starting reading. "That's two vics who had the same organ they received as a transplant removed."

"Make it three."

"Excuse me?" Shane looked up over the report. His eye twitched, along with his right thumb, itching to text his son, but he'd still be in school. In class. With his phone off.

"I was just in with Cleary, going over the points of the press conference. He informed us that Emily had a cornea transplant in her right eye because of an accident. The transplant was less than a year ago."

"Way to bury the lead, Kara." Shane slammed his fist on the table. "You should have started with that."

"I started with a chain of events," she said calmly. "All important for different reasons."

"Whatever." Shane's mood didn't improve with her calm voice. "I can't believe Cleary is just telling us this now." Shane stood quickly, dropping his chair to the floor with a loud thud. "His daughter is murdered, her eyes cut out of her head, and he doesn't think to tell us about an eye transplant?"

Kara lowered her chin, tilting her head, and raised one eyebrow. "He was certain, after that note, that Haughton killed his daughter in a drunken rage, and frankly so were we."

"Why didn't the M.E. know this? Her medical records. Why wasn't that cross-referenced?"

"He couldn't tell looking at Emily's eye sockets, and her medical reports were delayed in getting to him. Gregory's body was too decayed, but with Iris he could tell as soon as he opened her up."

"Fuck." Shane paced the width of the table. He could feel Kara's eyes on him, but he didn't look at her. The fact that they missed this very important piece of information from day one was on him. No one else. Just him. He didn't ask the right questions. He didn't look in the right places. "We're dealing with a method-ical killer, and it's not about the victims now as much as it is the organs."

He heard Kara's feet scuff on the floor.

He glanced in her direction. She stood in front of the whiteboard. Eraser in one hand, pen in the other, scribbling the new information.

"This isn't going to be easy on you," she said.

"I'll be fine." But he wasn't entirely sure about that as his hand covered his cell phone in his pocket. "We need dates of the transplants and, just to be thorough, I want to know if the Boston victim had a transplant."

"Already on it." Kara pointed to the papers she'd brought in. "Those are the dates of the three transplants. They were all in the last year. No more than nine months out but no sooner than six months. But what stood out was they were all on a—"

"A Thursday," Shane said. He picked up the report on the Boston case. "This guy was murdered on a Thursday as well."

"Could be a coincidence."

"You know better," he said, knowing her statement was meant to calm his nerves. "We need to know when the cadaver went missing." Shane pulled out his phone and tapped the calendar, scrolling back… "Shit."

"What?" Kara asked.

"Kevin's heart transplant was on a Thursday."

Kara dropped her pen. The sound of it bouncing on the tile file echoed. Shane's heart hammered. His breath caught, causing him to cough. In his experience, there was never such a thing as a coincidence.

"We need to get the donor list for the last year," Kara said. She quickly moved across the room. Her fingers wrapped tightly around his bicep.

"Not that easy," he said. "There are strict protocols in place protecting where organs come from. Besides, what would be the basis for the warrant? They're so far apart there's no way that all the organs came from the same person. What's the motive? We don't know why this person is taking organs. Could be several different reasons. Until we find that motive no way are we going

JEN TALTY

to get the United Network for Organ Sharing to give up their records, except for maybe our victims. Beyond that, neither they nor the government are going to release any names outside of that."

"But if all of our vics were murdered on Thursdays and they all received organs on a Thursday—"

"I'm sure we can get the donors for our vics, but I doubt we can go any more widespread than that."

"We need to know," she said. "We need to try."

"We can try," Shane said, knowing exactly where she was going. He placed his hand over hers, which was still curled around his arm. "I'm worried my son may be in danger. But we need to write the warrant for our vics. For the case, specifically. Work out from there."

"But if we—"

"No." He laced his fingers through hers, guiding her into a chair as he sat across from her. Even if his son's transplant hadn't been on a Thursday, he'd be troubled by the current findings. "If we go for too much, we might get nothing. We start with our victims and then we gather more information to get more."

"It's Monday. If our killer hasn't already killed by Thursday we're going to have another dead body."

"You don't think I'm aware of that?"

"We're at ground zero, and I don't like the unknown and how that unknown might be connected to your son."

"We don't know that it is." Shane felt his vocal cords shake. It obviously hadn't gone unnoticed by Kara, as she raised her brow. "Look," he said, "besides knowing where my son's heart came from could fuck with both my psyche and Kevin's; we're only in one aspect of the equation. And—"

He pressed his finger over her lips when she opened her mouth.

"If my son hadn't had a transplant, you know what I'm saying is the best, most logical, course of action."

"But Kevin did have a trans—"

He shut her up this time by pressing his lips against hers in a tender, but quick, kiss. "I know," he whispered, "but we have to follow protocol to the letter on this one."

She leaned back in her chair, breaking off all contact except her one hand grasping his. "I really don't want to give this press conference."

"You have to," he said.

"I know."

"What are we going to give up?"

"Butterflies and organs," she said.

"So, everything but the candles. Why not leave out the organs?"

"Because we're going ahead with calling him a bad copycat of the Organ Slayer."

"No matter what we tell the public, we're going to have panic." He leaned back, still holding her hand, rubbing his thumb across her soft skin.

She leaned forward. "Yesterday..."

"Was perfect," he said. "I told you I care about you. That hasn't changed."

She jumped when Foster's voice echoed across the room, "Excuse me."

"What?" Shane asked, not caring that he was still holding Kara's hand and his gaze with her eyes was unbreakable.

"Cleary's ready."

"$\mathcal{T}$HE BUTTERFLY MURDERS," Kara said. "Not what I had in mind when I mentioned the removal of organs." She tossed her napkin over her half-eaten buffalo chicken sub that she had ordered at a local sandwich shop not far from the precinct. Foster had gone to Boston to find out more about that case. "I mean, we said this looked just like the Organ Slayer."

"But you mentioned butterflies more times than organs," Shane said. "And it sounds better than The Organ Murders."

"You're not making me feel better," she said.

"We could go into the back seat of my car and I could find a half dozen ways to make you *feel better*." He winked as he took a huge bite of his turkey club.

"Tempting," she said. After the press conference yesterday, he'd practically begged her to come over to

JEN TALTY

his house, but by the time she managed to pry herself away from the precinct it was well into the midnight hour. As much as she wanted to spend even an hour in his arms, she needed a good night's sleep. Of course, she spent the first hour in bed texting and talking to him.

"We could drive down to the tracks. You remember. The ones across from the golf course. You gave me my first—"

"You have sex on the brain."

He shrugged. "I'm a guy. And really, that sexting stuff doesn't do it for me."

She laughed. "You certainly were into it last night."

"Till you fell asleep on me, and what's with this no picture rule?"

She picked up a napkin, wadded it up, and tossed it at his face. "I don't think I have to explain myself there."

"I would have sent one of me."

"Oh, just stop," she said. "It's never going to happen."

"What about when the case is over? When you go back to D.C.?" he asked. "You're going to need to give me something."

She swallowed. "I'll think about it."

"We could video chat." He cocked his head and waggled his brow.

"You know that's never going to happen."

"Why not?"

"Please tell me you've never done video sex chats before."

He shook his head. "I haven't. I've also never sexted before. I mean, not really. A few normal comments with Janet about getting lucky if I behaved." He smiled. "But after our little chat last night, I'm not opposed."

"I am."

"Can't blame a guy for trying," he said. "But seriously, what are we going to do when this case is over? Your life is in D.C. and mine is here. I can't uproot my son, and I wouldn't ask you to give up your career."

Her breath came in short pants, making her dizzy. "I'm not sure I know what to say."

He reached across the table, taking her hand in his. His thumb rubbed her palm. She wanted to jump across the table like a silly school girl and kiss him all over. But this wasn't a school girl crush, and she and Shane weren't the only ones in the equation. He had a son. A son who would always come before her, as he should.

"I think we're moving a little bit too fast," she said.

"We passed fast a long time ago. So, what are we going to do about it?"

She shook her head, trying to clear a path for logical reasoning. "I don't know, but it doesn't involve webcam sex."

He laughed. "I bet I could talk you into that." He laced his fingers through hers. "I'm being serious about a long-distance relationship. About giving it a shot."

"I know you are," she said. Her heart hammered in her chest. She held up her hand as he opened his mouth. "How do you feel about us? About being with me more than the time I'm here?"

His thumb continued to rub tiny circles on her palm. "Comfortable," he said. "This." He held up her hand. "Us. It feels comfortable. I don't know what it will feel like when you leave. Only, the thought of you leaving makes me uncomfortable."

"You have such a way with words." He could be romantic, but it was never when you expected it. When you did expect it, he came up with words like comfortable.

"When we have video sex, I'll have better words."

"Seriously, that's not happening." She squeezed his hand as the table vibrated. "One day at a time."

"All right." He leaned back in his seat "One day at a time. Now, I think we need to set that aside and talk about the case."

She was glad to be off the relationship discussion. "We've officially ruled out many of our suspects."

"Not all of them," Shane said. "We've got two religious nut jobs."

"Who we have no record of stepping foot in New York State." Kara couldn't get past the idea that someone was targeting people who had organ transplants on Thursdays, which put Kevin right in the line of fire. "The only other real suspect is Haughton, and that's only for Emily's murder."

The table vibrated again as Shane's screen lock lit

up. She swallowed, noticing he had changed his screen-saver picture to one of just of Kevin.

"Anything important?"

He glanced at it again. "Not the office. Not Kevin. Not anyone in my family. And not you. Therefore, not important."

A smile tugged at her lips. It was nice to be put on a list of important people. "We can also rule out the finger-chopper in Syracuse when it comes to Iris. He was in county lock-up for drunk and disorderly."

The table vibrated again. Shane picked up his phone. "Office. And it's interesting."

"What is it?"

He handed her his phone after tapping on it. "Got the CSI report on the fiber found in Iris's hand."

She took the phone and scanned the report. "The fiber is used in scrubs," she said. "Someone who works in the hospital."

"Sort of narrows it down," Shane said. "Also gives us a starting place. I know just about everyone in the organ donor wing."

"That really doesn't make me feel better, considering the profile we've put together." She handed Shane his phone back. "I don't mean to harp on this," she said, "but you told me that the M.E. said there are eight main organs that can be donated."

"Along with other tissues."

"Hang on," Kara pulled out her phone, which had started vibrating in her pocket. "More interesting news." She held up the image that Foster had sent over of a marking of a butterfly on the back of the victim found in Boston.

"Did he have a transplant?"

Kara nodded. "Intestines. And candles were found in the bathroom—specifically around the tub. No one thought that odd, but one officer did document it since it was a single guy living alone. If this is our killer, he must have been interrupted before finishing his ritual."

"And the victim is from Rochester." Shane chomped down on his lower lip, something Kara noticed he'd do when something troubled him.

"Let me put a car on Kevin and Theresa." She'd wanted to do that yesterday, but he'd said it was a waste of resources.

"That won't get approved, but some of my buddies are checking on things on and off duty." He continued to chew on his lip. "Corneas, kidneys, liver, intestines," he said. "That leaves lungs, pancreas, thymus, and heart."

"What are you thinking?" she asked, glad he seemed to be rethinking the idea of protection for his son.

"Well, my first thought was that maybe someone was collecting organs that they believed came from one person."

"A modern-day Frankenstein."

"Something like that, but the dates of the transplants don't jibe."

"But Thursdays do," she said, following his train of

thought. "So, it's possible that someone is trying to rebuild someone or something symbo—"

"Symbolically," Shane said, finished her thought. "What was the date the cadaver went missing?"

Kara quickly pulled out her notepad. "August eleventh. A Thursday."

"When was the Boston murder?"

"December first. A Thursday," Kara said. "That's a lot of time between the two incidents."

"Let's go."

"Where are we going?" she asked.

"Medical school. I want to find out more about the other cadavers that went missing."

"Why?"

"Because I think our killer has been practicing on them. Like a doctor would. Perfecting his technique until he thought he was ready to harvest organs himself."

———

*A*fter spending forty-five minutes on the phone while waiting in a hallway, Shane was finally given the name of the professor who initially reported the missing cadavers.

"Thanks for meeting with us," Shane said as Dr. Miles met them in the lobby of the Medical School Building.

"Not a problem. What is it that you want to know?"

Dr. Miles waved to a few chairs around a small table. Shane sat down, Kara next to him, and Dr. Miles across the table. Shane pulled out his leather notebook and ran his fingers across the top.

"The cadavers that went missing—" Kara started, but Dr. Miles cut her off.

"We've stepped up security protocols since then. We used to give key passes to various medical students, doctors, and nurses. But now it's just the teaching staff. Anyone else has to be buzzed in. A pain in the ass, but I don't want that to happen again."

"Buzzed into classrooms?"

"No," Dr. Miles said, "the storage facility where the cadavers are warehoused."

"What exactly happened to the cadavers?" Shane asked.

"The students assigned to helping transport the cadavers said they were approached by a staff member, asking to help them in an annual prank. Five cadavers were taken. Only three were recovered that day. The other two were gone."

"Gone where?" Shane asked.

"Well, one was just found as you know," Dr. Miles said. "The other one we still have no idea where it is."

"Don't you think that's odd?" Kara asked. "Someone just walks off with cadavers?"

"Of course," Dr. Miles said. "But the bigger problem is that we haven't identified the cadavers."

"What do you mean?" Kara asked.

"We just updated our system. UCLA lost track of identities of over fifty donated cadavers, which is what prompted us to do it. But while we made the transfer, we realized some were already mismanaged. There are better protocols in place now, but the cadavers that went missing? We're not sure who they are...were."

"So, you're saying this happens often?" Kara asked.

"Oh, no. Not like this. What I'm saying is that bodies are often donated to science, but we lose track of the identities, which has made this particular case difficult because we can't be certain we're even missing a cadaver."

"So, you don't know how many were in that room?" Shane asked, completely dumbfounded.

"No, there were five. Four have been recovered, but without proper tracking information we don't have a tag that goes with the missing cadaver. I'm ashamed to admit that, but with our new system and protocols it won't happen again.

"Do you remember the students who pulled this prank?" Shane asked.

"Sure do." Dr. Miles pulled a piece of paper from his pocket. "Here are their names. There was a hearing, but not much came from that. They had to pay fines, but were not expelled or removed from the medical school."

"Anything else you think we should know?" Kara asked.

"Not that I can think of, but I'll give you a ring if anything comes to mind."

"Thanks." Shane tucked the piece of paper into his notebook and shoved it in his pocket. Once the doctor had disappeared into another classroom, Shane said to Kara, "I think we need to set up one single meeting with these students."

17

*K*ARA SAT IN THE PASSENGER seat of Shane's car as he rounded the corner outside of the Village of Pittsford, not far from where he used to live. "What are you doing?"

He didn't answer as he pulled into his childhood neighborhood.

"Oh no," Kara said. "I'm not going to go spend time with your family."

"Look," he said, "we've got two hours before the students we want to talk to get out of class. Kevin and Theresa are having dinner here." He rolled to a stop in front of his parents' single-story house, which exactly as she remembered, with its white siding and black shutters. It was situated on a short cul-de-sac, encompassing only five houses on the street all together.

"From the look of all the cars in the driveway, half your family is here."

"Just Dave and Mike's families. Anna lives in Albany now, so she's not here."

"That's more than half your family."

"Well, we have to eat."

"We ate lunch three hours ago. I'm not hungry."

"I want to see my son," Shane said as he shifted into park then shut off the engine, taking the key out of the ignition and dangling it in her face. "If you really don't want to come in, here, take the key. Meet me back here in an hour and a half."

She looked out the window. She could see his mother standing in the kitchen window. Kevin right next to her, leaning over the sink. "That would make me look like a bitch."

"I wouldn't let that happen." He rested his hand on her thigh. "I'd tell them you had to chase down a lead and I was taking some time to see Kevin because we're going to be working late, which is true."

"Yeah, everything except the fact that there is no lead I'm chasing down currently, and even if I did have one I'd still look like a bitch for not at least coming in to say hello."

"I want you to come with me, but I respect your decision not to if that's what you really want."

"You don't get it." She turned to face him. His soft brown eyes were filled with kindness and caring. He'd always been a difficult man to say no to. "I'm completely and utterly aware of what I did… and not just to you, but to your family. Your mother, especially. If I were any of them, I wouldn't like me much."

He took her hand, raised it to his mouth, and gently pressed his lips against her skin. A slight shock trickled between them. "I'm the only one who really gets to be upset by what you did, and I'm over it."

"Not sure they'll see it that way."

"You won't know unless you come in. Either way, I choose to be with you. That has nothing to do with them. The only one who gets a say, besides you and me, is my son. I hope you understand that he will always come first."

That was actually something she could grasp. "I'd be worried if he didn't," she said. "Okay. Let's do this." She sucked in a deep breath and let it out slowly. During her first twenty years, she didn't remember a time when the Rogers family wasn't part of her daily existence. She'd gone on their family vacations. They came to her field hockey games and cheered her on. Looking at the house, she realized just how much she'd missed all of them.

He nodded and in true Shane fashion, leapt from the car and raced around the front end, practically sliding across the hood just to open the door for her.

"Do you know how many times I've wanted to open the door before you got to it?" She took his hand and let him guide her out of the car.

"Why do you think I race to open the door, Miss Independent?"

"Chivalry. Old-fashioned values."

"Ha!" He placed his hand on her back, rubbing that one spot that made her want to ravish him in any place at any time. "Truth is," he said. "You always wore V-neck shirts, and I could get a nice view of your cleavage by leaning over and—"

"Tits and ass." She shook her head.

His hand slid down over her round bottom and he gave it a little pat.

"Don't do that in front of your family."

"Okay," he said.

"I'm not really ready for this. And while I like where things are going, I don't know what's going to happen—"

"One day at a time," he said. "One thing at a time."

The front door opened and there stood George Rogers, Shane's father. George had aged some in the last thirteen years. His hair had thinned, and it had turned completely gray. His face was filled with deeper lines, but he was still handsome and distinguished-looking.

"If it isn't Kara Martin," George said. "You're as pretty as ever." He pulled her in for a tight hug before even saying hello to his son. "Come in." He pushed open the door. "It's so good to see you after all these years."

Shane winked and gave her a big smile, like all was good in the world. That didn't help her nerves.

"Dad!" Kevin bolted into the foyer, giving him a bear hug. "Hey, Kara."

"Hey, squirt. How goes tricks?"

"Other than I screwed one up and spilled milk on Grandma's new carpet, just fine."

"I think magic shows will remain in the kitchen from now on," Edna Rogers said as she entered the foyer. She looked exactly the same. Same dark hair cut in a bob. Perfect-looking skin with very few wrinkles. "Hello, Kara. Glad my son finally brought you around." She, too, pulled Kara in for a hug, giving her a little extra squeeze. "Shane, you know what to do with that." She pointed to the weapon on his hip.

"Yeah. We'll take care of them." Shane held out his hand.

Kara carefully handed him her weapon, watching as he secured them in a box on the top shelf in the hall closet.

"Thanks," Edna said. "Everyone is in the family room."

Kara followed Kevin and his grandparents through the kitchen, noting they'd recently updated the appliances and replaced the Formica countertop with granite. His mother had always had impeccable taste.

"Are you both going to be able to stay for dinner?" Edna asked.

"Depends on when it's served," Shane said. "We can only stay about an hour or so."

"Then I'll have to make you something to go. Even if I put it in the oven now, it won't be ready in time." Edna paused at the entranceway to the family room. It was an older house, so the kitchen was closed off from all the other rooms. "Look who's here."

Kara glanced around the room. They had put an addition on, doubling the size of the family room. Off the back they'd added a sunroom next to the deck that overlooked the pool.

Kara recognized Dave and his wife Shari, along with Shane's other brother, Mike. But the woman sitting next to Mike, Kara didn't know. Nor did she recognize any of the four other children sitting in the sunroom playing video games.

"Heard you were back in town." Mike got up and extended his hand to Kara. "I don't think you were around when I met my wife. This is Mary Jo."

Mary Jo looked younger than Shane, so she was maybe ten years younger than Mike. She rubbed her very round, large belly, waving. "I'd get up, but it takes two people to pull me off this sofa. I'm a week overdue."

"Nice to meet you. Congratulations," Kara said.

"Number three," Mike said. "Alison. Tyler. Get in here and say hello to your Uncle Shane and meet his friend."

The two younger children jumped up from their

THE BUTTERFLY MURDERS

beanbag chairs and raced through the open double doors into the family room. "I'm Alison." She waved. She looked to be about six or so.

"I'm Tyler." He was maybe a year or two younger.

They looked at each other and giggled. "Can we go back to watching the twins play video games?"

"It's 'may we,'" Mary Jo said. "And, yes, you may."

"She's an English teacher," Shane said. "Corrects everybody."

"Sometimes we use bad grammar just to get a rise out of her," Dave said.

"With you," Mary Jo said, pointing to Dave, "I doubt it's on purpose."

Shane's family had always been a bit on the sarcastic side, and it felt good to be back in that environment, but it didn't settle her upset stomach, or make her feel any less uncomfortable. They were also a very close-knit family and she was sure there had been a few choice words tossed around about her and the way she'd left Shane.

Shane guided her to the sofa, where she got a warm embrace from Dave and Shari. The couch was large, but not really meant for four adults, but Shane pretty much didn't give her a say as he squished her between him and Shari.

Without thinking, Kara grabbed Shane's hand, lacing her fingers between his.

Edna and George sat on the loveseat against the

other wall, and Theresa settled in a recliner next to that.

She waved to Kara. "Wish my mom was here. She's been dying to see you."

"Tell her I said hello," Kara said. It was all so familiar, but awkward at the same time.

"Last time we saw each other I only had two kids," Shari said. "You did a fair amount of babysitting for those two."

"I did," Kara said. "Jeff and Haley. I remember Jeff was quite the handful and Haley, as a baby, liked to scream a lot."

"She's still very dramatic. Just like my sister," Dave said. "Everything is such a big deal."

Kara smiled. These were good memories, but it still didn't stop the ticking time bomb of her pulse. "Jeff has to be eighteen by now."

"He is," Dave said. "And he goes to THE Ohio State and he's playing D1 football."

"That's awesome." Kara's voice sounded unsteady to her own ears, her fingers still clutching at Shane's hand, though she'd wedged them between their thighs hoping no one would notice. Everyone acted as though this was just any other day, but she could tell there was some stiffness in the air.

"Haley's at her boyfriend's," Shari said. "She'll be by later. The twins over there, being RUDE while they play a video game, are Jake and Cameron. They're thirteen."

"Put down the controllers and come in here and say hello to Uncle Shane and Kara."

"As soon as we finish—"

Dave cut his son off. "Now, Jake."

"Fine."

Both boys dropped their controllers and scuffed into the family room. They weren't identical; both favored their father with their dark hair, and were well on their way to puberty. They were both at least five foot eight or so, and muscular.

"Hey, Uncle Shane and his friend Kara," Jake said.

"Nice to meet you," Cameron said, then turned to his brother. "Theresa was right, she's hot."

"I never said that," Theresa protested.

Cameron smiled. "You also said you caught them on the sofa maki—"

"That's enough!" Dave barked. "Not the way to behave in front of Uncle Shane's friend."

"You mean girlfriend," one twin muttered.

"Seriously," Dave said in a much louder voice. "Stop it or we'll go a week without electronics."

"Sorry," the boys said in unison and then went back to their game, Kevin joining them on the floor.

Kara felt the heat rise in her face. The back of her neck was clammy. Her hairline damp.

"Sorry about that," Dave said. "As you can see, not much has changed around here, except it's no longer us razzing Shane, but his own nieces and nephews."

"I'm sorry," Theresa said. "They totally took what I said out of context and twisted it."

"Perhaps," Edna said, "you shouldn't be saying anything at all, young lady."

"Yes, Grandma."

"So, tell us, Kara," George said. "How long have you been an FBI agent?"

"Seven years," Kara said. "When I graduated from college I worked for the D.C. Police Department in their violent crimes division, then applied to Quantico and landed back in Violent Crimes Division with the FBI."

"Just sounds so gruesome and depressing," Mary Jo said. "I don't know how you and Shane do it. And all these murders lately, totally freaks me out."

"We've got a couple of tough cases," Shane said. His thumb gently rubbed her trembling forefinger, as if to tell her to relax. "But I can't remember a time when I ever wanted to be anything else."

"You wanted to be Evil Knievel," Kara blurted out, forgetting about everyone in the room as she turned and smiled at Shane. "You set up that ramp and totaled your brother's dirt bike—"

"You little liar," Mike said.

"That was you?" George said. "We thought the bike had been stolen…"

"Oh," Kara said. "Sorry… I forgot I was supposed to take that to my grave."

Shane stared at her with a playful smile. She held his gaze for a long moment, getting lost in his eyes.

"That's two bikes you totaled," Dave said.

"So, what *did* happen to my dirt bike?" Mike asked.

"Since Kara opened this can of worms, I think she should tell the story." He winked.

She let out a nervous chuckle. "We were ten, I think. That would have made Mike sixteen, right?"

Mike nodded. "That bike cost me an entire summer's salary and that little brat," he pointed to Shane, "was told to keep his hands off."

"Maybe if you'd let me ride it just once, I wouldn't have felt the need to take it," Shane said. "I watched you, day in and day out, ride it up down those fields behind the house. I figured if Mike, the least coordinated person in the family, could do it, I could do it. So, I took it out to the field, set up a small ramp. I floored it, lost control, and bailed. The bike hit a tree."

"I know," Mike said. "It was found mangled next to that tree."

"Shane and I then went back to the house," Kara said, "and collected a few other items from the garage and ditched them in a dumpster in the village. Left the garage door open and went to get ice cream."

"We collected insurance money on that," Edna said. "I think that would be considered a crime."

"Statute of limitations," Kara started, "has run out on that, so nobody will be getting arrested today."

"Except maybe you," Mike said. "You're the one who flooded the bathroom."

Kara turned bright red. "That's not funny," she whispered to Shane.

"Actually," Shane said, "it's hysterical, but she wasn't alone. Probably more my fault than hers."

"We did know that Kara and Shane flooded the guest bathroom," Edna said, waving her hand dismissively. "But no point in embarrassing the girl, letting her know we knew she had stayed the night."

"The girl is embarrassed now," Kara said softly.

"Don't be," Edna said. "We had way too much fun torturing Shane."

"You grounded me for a week, made me do all the repairs," Shane said. "And now it makes sense why I was grounded from seeing Kara."

"Like that worked," Mike interjected. "You snuck out more than we did."

"No, I didn't," Shane said.

"He's right," Dave added. "He just snuck Kara in. Hence the flooding of the bathroom."

Her cheeks flushed again. She looked to Shane for some moral support, but all he did was wink at her and then said, "I learned how to sneak her in from Dave. He was the master at getting away with stuff in this house. Of course, I made a small fortune threatening to blab if big bro didn't pay me to keep my trap shut."

"Money well spent," Dave said. "Though I'm still a bit shocked that Mom and Dad had no idea."

Edna scowled. "We tried to catch all of you, but we just weren't very successful, except for the bathroom incident, but then, Shane's ski team had just won states. We let it slide, sort of. But just you wait." She wagged her finger. "Your kids are going to do things someday that will shock you, and you will have no idea they were doing it."

"I'm not sure I want to know," Dave said. "I'm all too aware of what I was doing at their ages, and it wasn't pretty. I'm sure Haley has snuck out. I set the alarm to catch her, but half the time I sleep right through it...and those twins are going to be the death of me."

"At least with boys," Mike said. "you only have one penis to worry about. Girls? Lots of penises to worry about."

"I can't believe you just said that." Edna scowled at her son. "And in front of your niece."

"She's a grown up," Mike said. "And it's true. We boys got away with a lot, but Anna, she got caught once sneaking out and you grounded her for a month; not just from going out, but from practically everything and everyone."

"He's got a point, Ma," Dave said. "And I know we treat our daughter differently than we treat the boys."

"It's not the point I take offense to. It's the verbiage."

The room burst out in laughter, Kara included.

"Oh honey," George said. "If I had a dollar for every time you corrected the boys when they used any other word to describe a penis, then demand they only called it a penis, I'd be rich."

"I can't listen to this," Theresa said getting up. "This family is crazy."

"Welcome to the nut house," Shane said.

Theresa just shook her head, but with a smile, as she left the room. "I have studying to do."

"I have some food to prepare," Edna said. "Kara, will you help me, so I can pack something for you and Shane to take with you? I know you have to leave soon."

"Sure," Kara said. It's not like she could say no, even though she wanted to. She wasn't sure what was worse: staying in this room with Shane, his brothers, and their wives or being alone with his mother. Both presented the possibility of more equally embarrassing moments. She tried to unlace her fingers from Shane's, but he wouldn't let go. He just sat there and smiled at her like a stupid kid. She leaned forward, trying to pry her hand from his, but he held it tighter.

"Don't make my mother wait," he said.

She cocked her head, scooting to the very edge of the couch, but he still wouldn't let go.

She stood quickly, hoping that the sheer force of her movement would pry his hand from hers before anyone saw, but all it did was pull her back down on the sofa. He leaned in and kissed her cheek. "You'd better go."

"Let go," she whispered as she stood again, but this

time slowly, knowing he wasn't going to release her until she started to walk away. Of course, she had to step over him, and as she did he released her hand, then he gave her one small pat on the ass. She shouldn't have been surprised. Thirteen years ago, she'd been used to his unique display of affection. Today? Well, she was still used to it. The only thing that bothered her was how she believed his family had to perceive her based on how she'd left him. "What can I help you with?" Kara asked Shane's mother as she stepped into the kitchen.

"I wish you could stay for dinner, or that it was ready to be put in a container. I made my famous eggplant lasagna, only they still have no idea there's eggplant in it." Edna opened the fridge and started pulling out what looked like fixings for sandwiches.

Kara laughed. "Shane knows. I accidentally told him one night."

"That means everyone knows," Edna said.

"I'm sorry." Kara's chest tightened. The last thing she wanted to do was upset Shane's mother.

"Don't be." Edna reached out and touched Kara's arm. "It's impossible to keep a secret in this family anyway. I don't think most of the grandkids know yet, so let's not tell them, okay?"

"You bet."

"You still like turkey, provolone, lettuce, tomato, bacon, and mayo sandwiches?"

Kara swallowed the lump in her throat. "Toasted?"

The sandwich itself wasn't anything special. Didn't have any unique ingredients. But after all this time it warmed Kara's heart that Shane's mother remembered it was her go-to sandwich.

"I think we can handle that." Edna handed Kara the bread. "Toaster is over there."

For the next few minutes, Kara quietly worked on toasting and putting together two sandwiches while Edna rummaged through the pantry. It was weird, but then again it wasn't., to be back in this house, making sandwiches like she used to do when she and Shane would go skiing, or down to the lake, or just hanging out at the house. As nervous as she was to be around Shane's family, she felt a sense of belonging she hadn't felt since she'd left.

"Here." Edna set a couple of plastic bags on the counter next to the sandwiches. "I packed some chips, homemade cookies, and a couple of waters."

"Thanks." Kara stuffed the sandwiches into the bags and then placed them into a small tote bag Edna handed her. "This is great."

"Kara?" Edna questioned softly, holding her shoulders in a death-grip. "I know things are different. A lot has changed. But one thing that hasn't changed is that we have always thought of you as family. You're welcome here anytime. I just wanted you to know that."

Kara swallowed her breath. She'd never expected any of his family to be mean. Cold maybe. A little standoffish, perhaps. But certainly not nice and welcoming, which is exactly how they all had been. Shane had told her a long time ago, and she'd seen it first-hand, that his family didn't hold grudges. Life was too short to stay mad. She fought the tears welling in her eyes. "That means a lot, considering everything."

Edna pulled her in for a long hug. "Shane and Kevin have been through a lot. All I want for everyone in my family is to be happy. I want that for you, too, and I can tell coming back here hasn't been easy."

"Easier than I thought it would be." But it was going to be even more difficult to leave again.

---

*S*hane watched Kara's hips sway as she stepped from the family room to the kitchen, knowing his father was going to say something the moment she disappeared.

"Sometimes you act like a child," his father said. "Some of that teasing was uncalled for and not very gentlemanly."

"If that were Mike," Mary Jo said, "I would have turned around and smacked him for embarrassing me like that in front of his family."

"Mike's the one who brought up the bathroom," Shane protested.

"You didn't shut him down," Shane's father said.

"My husband shouldn't have said anything to begin with," Mary Jo countered back.

"You weren't around thirteen years ago," Mike said. "Those two couldn't keep their hands off each other."

"I think it was a little different back then," Shari said. "We all constantly walked in on them making out. Just now he was—"

"He," Shane pointed to himself, "is sitting right here, so let's not talk about me as if I'm not in the room. And, yeah, I know. I was being childish. But I still care about her and she still cares about me. I was trying to show her that you all were fine with her being around."

"I think we could have managed to do that on our own," his father said. "Now imagine if you witnessed that behavior coming from Kevin."

"He's ten," Shane said.

"The point that Dad is trying to make is that—"

Shane interrupted Dave, "I get his point. But that doesn't change three very important things."

"And what's that?" his father asked.

"First, I'm still in love with her. Second, she lives in D.C. And third, I'm trying to figure out how the hell I'm going to make a long-distance relationship work with her until she figures out that we do still belong together, because I'm not letting her go this time." Shane looked around the room, gauging each person's expression. Mike had a smirk on his face. His wife, however, looked thoroughly shocked. His father's expression was solemn and concerned, but he nodded. Kara had hurt his father, leaving more than anyone else in the family. He'd taken a real shine to her ever since she was little. Dave and Shari, however, were doing their best to suppress a couple of large smiles and perhaps laughter.

"Shane?" Kara's voice rang out.

"Yeah?" He hoped she hadn't heard any of his rant.

She held up her phone. "We've got a situation…" She mouthed the word 'Cleary.' "We need to go."

"Kevin!" Shane called for his son. "I've got to go back to work."

Kevin appeared in the family room through the door to the sunroom. "Okay," he said. "Will you be home before bedtime?"

"I'm hoping I will be." He gave his son a hug with a kiss on the top of his head. "I'll text you in a little while when I know more about what's going on."

"Where's Kara?" Kevin looked up at him.

"Kitchen. Or maybe already heading to the car."

"Kara!" Kevin bolted from the family room.

Shane followed him, watching as Kara turned right before she stepped into the foyer.

"Kara," Kevin said again as he wrapped his arms around her. "Be safe."

"I will." She hugged him, glancing over the top of his head. Her eyes narrowed, showing concern.

"Are you going to come back to the house tonight?" Kevin asked. "I want you to."

"I don't know," she said. "Depends on how late we have to work."

Shane had stopped in the middle of the kitchen, gripping the counter, his heart pounding painfully in his chest. He felt a strong hand squeeze his shoulder. His father stood behind him. "It will work out," he whispered. "Trust that."

"If I don't see you tonight, then will you come by tomorrow?" Kevin asked Kara.

Shane let out a long breath. He really hoped his father was right and that things would work out. Not only was he attached to Kara again, but now his son had developed his own special bond with her.

"I'll make it happen," Kara said.

Shane made his way into the foyer, took his weapon from Kara, and clipped it to his belt. "Love you, little man."

"Please stop calling me that," Kevin said. "Love you, too."

Shane stepped out onto the walkway after Kara. He followed her in silence, his hand gently on her back, knowing his entire family was watching.

"What was that all about?" she asked as he opened the door. "Kevin was really upset."

"He's worried," Shane said. "Worried something will happen to you."

18

KARA STARED OUT the window while Shane drove through the Village of Pittsford, turning onto Rand Place. Two police cars were blocking the McCauley driveway. Cleary stood next to one of the police cars with a uniformed officer.

"This is going to be a real shit storm," Shane said.

Kara quickly compartmentalized and focused on her job. "I don't see Foster or Jones."

"They're coming from Greece. Probably another ten minutes out, depending on traffic. It's rush hour."

Kara stepped from the vehicle before Shane could open her door, pulling her wool coat around her body. The temperature had dropped again, and a light snow fell from the sky. "Let's stick together on this one," Kara said. "Interview Cleary first, then go inside and talk to the McCauley's."

"Alright."

She scanned the area as they made their way from the pavement to the sidewalk and then onto the driveway. Cleary was waving his finger at the uniformed officer.

"If it isn't Frick and Frack," Cleary said. His words slurred. He swayed when he talked.

Kara looked around again and that's when she saw Cleary's car halfway on the sidewalk two doors down.

Both Kara and Shane showed the officer their badge. He nodded and stepped back.

"What happened?" Shane asked.

Cleary laughed. "That little piece of shit in there raped my daughter." He fidgeted, and sniffed a few times, rubbing his nose. White powder still lined his nostrils.

Kara stepped closer. "Congressman Cleary," she started. "You're drunk. And high. I'd say on coke."

"Fuck you," he said.

"What did you do here?" Shane rephrased his original question.

"I knocked on the door and told them I was going to haul their son into court for rape. I've got all the proof in my daughter's journals. He's eighteen. She was fourteen. He took advantage of her. Probably why she left our house that day and is now dead. All because of that little shit."

Shane tapped Kara on the shoulder, then pointed down the street. "Nothing we can do about the news, but keep them at bay." Shane waved the officer back over. "Put him in the back of your car, then rope off the area."

"You have no jurisdic—"

Kara cut the officer off. "I do, so do what he says."

The officer nodded.

"No fucking way. I'm not getting in the back of a police car. I didn't do anything wrong. Hell, I left his property when he told me to."

"You're wasted." Shane pointed to Cleary's car. "Not to mention you ran over a mailbox, you're illegally parked, and you've got a flat. Get in the fucking car or we'll cuff you and *put* you in the car."

Cleary got in the car.

"Not going to get anywhere with him when he's higher than a kite," Shane said. "Let's go inside and see what else we're going to be hauling the good congressman down to the county lock-up for."

Kara felt Shane's hand on the small of her back as they walked toward the McCauley house. "As much as I like your hands all over me, you really need to stop doing it at crime scenes or anytime we're at work."

He dropped his hand. "Can't seem to help myself," he said. "Besides, it's calming. I really wanted to haul off and hit Cleary. What the fuck was he thinking? Especially after giving that press conference with you."

"He's not thinking," Kara said. "He's in pain. He's grieving not only the loss of his daughter, but her innocence as well. The parallels to what's happening to him and what happened to Haughton are a little too similar in a weird way."

"I know," he said. "But this isn't going to make either of our bosses happy, and considering I'm lead, Morrell is going to chew my ass out." He waved his hand in front, indicating ladies before gentlemen when they approached the door, but he kept his hand from the small of her back.

Once again, they both showed their badges to the officer who stood in the foyer near the porch where Shane and Kara had questioned Doug a few days ago. There was no log to sign, because it wasn't a crime scene, but they were still going to have to file a report.

"I see you finally arrested that asshole," Mr. McCauley said. "He had no right coming in here and making all sorts of accusations and threatening my family."

"What exactly did he say?" Shane asked.

"Accused my son of… of… raping his daughter. Said he was the reason she's dead."

Kara glanced past Mr. McCauley into the living room, where Doug and Mrs. McCauley sat on the sofa. Doug leaned back, arms crossed, anger and fear etched on his face. Mrs. McCauley sat upright with a stiff back, while she gnawed on a fingernail.

"Did he enter the home?" Shane asked.

"I wouldn't let him. He shoved me, trying to get in, so I hit him and locked the door. He tossed a rock through my window." Mr. McCauley pointed to the porch. "He was screaming and shouting all sorts of obscenities. He left me no choice but to call the cops."

"You did the right thing," Shane said. "Do you want to press charges?"

"Of course I do!" Mr. McCauley shouted.

"We haul him in and charge him with a few misdemeanors," Kara said. "He'll pay a fine, maybe do some community service, possibly have to step down as congressman, but that puts your son and his relationship with Emily front and center."

"What the hell is that supposed to mean?" Mr. McCauley asked.

"We need a few words with Doug," Shane said calmly.

"Why?"

"To clarify some things so we can put all this in perspective," Shane said. "Please."

Mr. McCauley nodded.

Kara followed Shane into the living room, where Mrs. McCauley greeted them with a weak smile.

"Sorry to have to do this," Shane said, "but we need to ask Doug some very candid questions." Shane sat down in the chair on the other side of the room, closest to Doug.

Kara opted to stand and let Shane handle this one. Might be better man-to-man.

"I need you to be honest with me," Shane said. "No matter the question."

The boy nodded, but never uncrossed his arms.

"Did you have sex with Emily Cleary?" Shane had leaned forward, clasping his hands while resting his arms against his thighs.

"Of course he didn't!" Mrs. McCauley yelled.

"Please," Kara said. "Let Doug answer."

"Not without a lawyer," Mr. McCauley said.

"You can call one," Shane said. "I actually suggest you call one, but that isn't going to change the outcome of tonight."

"Then he'll answer that question with his lawyer," Mr. McCauley said. "And I'm sure his answer will be no."

"We had sex, but I didn't rape her," Doug said softly. "She came onto me. She pushed me. She sent me—"

"Goddamn it," Mr. McCauley said under his breath. "Stop talking, now."

"Thanks, Doug," Shane said. "Being honest will help you in the long run, trust me on that."

Kara turned to Mr. McCauley, who stood against the far wall, rubbing his chin. "Is he in real trouble?"

"He could be," Kara admitted.

"So, what do we do?" Mr. McCauley asked.

"Right now, nothing except get a good attorney." Kara watched Shane walk through the foyer and out the front door. She could see Jones and Foster standing at the bottom of the steps. "We'll also need you to file a statement about what happened tonight."

"Alright," Mr. McCauley said.

Kara handed Mr. McCauley her card. "If Cleary does show up here again, call me directly."

Mr. McCauley nodded.

"Let's give this family some privacy," she said to the officer.

Kara closed the front door, thankful that Shane had the other officer turn off the lights on the patrol car. The news crew was still a problem, standing across the street, their cameras rolling, lights glaring, newscasters trying to talk to anyone who would give them a hint as to what went down. She checked her watch. It was after six.

"Things wrap up well in there?" Shane asked as she approached him, Foster, and Jones, who stood next to the sheriff's car that currently contained the congressman.

"I think so," she said. "But we still have to deal with the charges the McCauley's are going to bring, which include vandalism, trespassing, assault, not to mention the DUI that we can charge him for."

"He blew a .25," Jones said. "One neighbor said he nearly hit her as he barreled down the street."

"Fucking wonderful," Shane said. "I'm shocked he agreed to even take the blood alcohol test."

"I'm sure he'll manage to find a way to say the test was faulty, wrong, and that he took it because he knew he was sober," Kara said.

"I know you still need to talk with the medical students," Jones said. "Then I'm sure you want to get home to Kevin. Cleary might take a while, so unless Foster has something else going on I think we'll handle Cleary."

"I'm good with that," Foster said.

"Let's get Cleary out of here then," Kara said. "Regroup early tomorrow. We've got a lot of ground to cover."

"Shoot for seven?" Jones said.

"I can make that work," Shane said. "Let's roll."

19

SHANE LEANED BACK on the sofa in his family room, plopping his legs onto the coffee table as he watched Kara beat his son in a game of NHL hockey on Xbox. He wondered if Kara knew he was letting her win, though Kara had some skills, which was shocking, but she did play the game well.

"No... No... crap," Kevin said as the buzzer went off, ending the game. The final score was Kara with 3 goals, Kevin with 2. "Two out of three?" Kevin asked.

"It's already almost ten and you've got school tomorrow."

"Oh," Kevin said. "I didn't realize it was that late." He pushed himself off the floor, reaching his hand out to Kara. "But I demand a rematch."

"Sure thing." She took his hand and let him help her up. "See you tomorrow."

"Goodnight," Kevin said.

"Not so fast. Come over here and give your old man a hug."

Kevin rolled his eyes, but relented. "And before you say it, meds and brush my teeth, and blah blah blah." Kevin then gave Kara a big hug before heading through kitchen and disappearing up the stairs.

"I know he let me win," Kara said. "But it felt damn good."

Shane laughed as he wagged his finger and patted the cushion next to him.

"I'm not in the mood to get caught necking by your niece again."

"Just sit down," he said. Theresa had actually made a point of saying she was up for the night. At least that's how he took it when she said, 'I won't be back down, too much homework, and then I need some sleep', but he also didn't want to neck on the sofa. He wanted to wait half an hour, then take her to his bedroom, lock the door, and ravish her body seven different ways.

She snuggled in next to him, putting her feet on the coffee table and her hand on his thigh.

It was a good start. "Thanks for coming back here. It meant a lot to him."

"He's a really great kid. Kind of impossible not to love him," she said. "Shall we catch the last few minutes of the news?"

He wanted to respond to the word *love*, but also

wanted to watch some of the news. He'd approach the love subject later. He clicked on the television, then scooted all the way to the far end of the sofa, pulling her between his legs as he leaned against the armrest, the television angled in front of him. One thing he didn't like about the family room was that the sofa and television were perpendicular.

He wrapped his arms around her, resting his chin on the top of her head. For the next twenty minutes they watched the news, saying nothing, even after the incident at the McCauley's' had been reported, which lead right into how Cleary had been picked up for a DUI. Once the newscaster closed the program, Shane clicked off the television. He pressed his lips against her temple, rubbing his hands up and down her arms. "Sorry I was an ass at my parents' house."

"Had I not grabbed your hand, it wouldn't have happened."

"What did you and my mother talk about?"

"Not much, but she made me feel welcome."

"I told you they all would," Shane said.

"Mike's wife seems so different from everyone else," Kara said.

"She is, but it was going to take someone very different to get Mike to settle down. We were all shocked when he said they were serious. He met her and six months later they were married."

"They look happy."

"They are," Shane said. "Come on." He pushed her from his chest, then took her by the hand as he turned off the family room light, then the kitchen light. She followed him until they got to the stairs, then she stopped, tugging her hand free.

"I don't think this is a good idea."

"I'm not taking you to the hotel. If you want to leave, I'll give the keys to my car. You can come back and get me in the morning." He reached out, hoping she'd take his hand. "I don't want you to go."

"It's not that I want to go," she said. "I just don't think—"

"Just stay with me. I don't care if all we do is sleep."

She cocked her head. "Right."

He laughed. "Okay, so I do care, but I won't push."

"I don't believe that." She reached out and took his hand. "You're irresistible."

He smiled, lacing his fingers through hers, and led her to the top of the stairs. Kevin's door was open slightly. He tiptoed over, and peeked his head in. His son lay on his back, a book resting against his chest. Shane quickly and quietly entered his son's room, shutting off the reading lamp, then gently closed his door. Theresa's door was shut tight and Shane could hear the faint rumble of music.

Kara was already in his bedroom, leaning against his dresser. He shut the door, locked it, and turned on the television, which was hung on the wall across from his king-size bed. "I always fall asleep with the TV on," he said.

She laughed. "When you used to sneak me in at night, we'd turn the TV on so no one would hear us."

"That, too." There was something very real about having her in his bedroom. In his home. "There's a T-shirt in the top drawer you can sleep in. If you want, I have some pajama bottoms."

She nodded. "Extra toothbrush?"

"I've got some new ones in the linen closet in the bathroom. I think I have everything you might need."

"What about tomorrow morning?"

That reality hadn't hit him. He thought for a moment. "Wake up early, take my car back to the hotel, then come back and pick me up."

"I can do that." She turned and opened the dresser drawer, pulling out one of his shirts. "Mind if I use the bathroom first?"

"Go ahead." He pulled the black comforter and gray sheets back on both sides of the bed. It had been a long time since he'd slept with a woman. It felt like a lifetime ago that he'd held Kara in his arms all night long. He turned off the lights. The glow of the television was enough. He tapped on the bathroom door.

"Come in," she said. She stood there in his T-shirt, which barely came down over her ass. He tilted his head. Her ass cheeks peeked out from under the fabric. He reached out and lifted it, noting a tiny thong before she batted his hand away.

"Well, my shirt doesn't cover your butt and I was just checking to see what you had on under there."

"Right." She rinsed out the toothbrush. "You still like the left side of the bed?"

"I'm going to be on whatever side of the bed you're on, so I don't care."

She pulled the shirt down over her ass as she padded out of the bathroom, shutting the door behind her.

He groaned and quickly got ready for bed.

He clicked off the light, and stepped into the bedroom. She was tucked under the covers on the right side of the bed. She smiled at him as he slid himself under the sheets. He lay on his side, staring at her for a moment. "I've never had anyone here before."

"I've heard that line before," she said. "I think the first time you tried to get into my pants was in your bedroom."

"As I recall, I wasn't very successful that night."

"You got in there."

"Not that night. I thought you were going to make me wait forever."

His breath hitched at the sight of her wide, teasing smile.

"Was I worth the wait?"

"Hell, yeah." He palmed her cheek. "Perhaps this isn't the most appropriate thing to say while you're half-naked in my bed, but while I moved on, fell in love again, and had a son, I never stopped thinking about you. I've always only wanted you to be happy."

"I think that's the sweetest thing anyone has ever said to me."

"Janet and I sometimes talked about you. She knew how important you'd been to my childhood, and she never tried to erase your memory or take away how much I loved you."

"Are you trying to make me cry?" She leaned closer, brushing her plump lips against his, then abruptly pulled back. "Did you hear that?"

"It's the heater kicking in," he said with a slight chuckle.

"I should go," she whispered. "What if Kevin wakes up? Or needs you in the middle of the night?"

"He'll knock on the door." Shane could understand her reservations. He had his own set, but since his time with her was limited he wanted to spend every moment he could with her...outside the confines of a murder investigation. "He suspects something is going on with us anyway."

"He said that?"

"No," Shane admitted, "but I know my son; the way he is around you is like no other woman he's met since his mother died, and I think part of that is that you're the only woman I've had any interest in." He slipped his hand under the sheets, tugging at the hem of his shirt that draped over the middle of her thigh. "I want you."

"It's not that I don't want you, but—"

"No buts." Swiftly, he lifted her shirt over her head. He pulled back the covers and groaned at the sight of her mostly-naked body. She propped her head up with one hand, while she'd pulled her other hand away from his body and let it drop along the side of her leg. All her curves exposed. Her nipples tight and ready. He reached out and traced his finger from just under her earlobe, across her neck, and down the center of her cleavage. Her body quivered.

"God, I love that," he said as he continued to trace a path with his forefinger across her flat stomach, circling her belly button, then down a little further, stopping at the top of her tiny thong. "This has to go." He rolled it down her hips and yanked it off her legs. "You're more beautiful than you were when you were eighteen."

"You're really working the lines."

"It's the truth." He smiled. "I was thinking about the night I suckered Dave into letting me use his car even though I didn't have a license yet, and I took you to the train tracks near his house. You surprised me that night."

"I surprised myself." Her sweet smile made every inch of his body ache for her gentle touch.

"I liked that very much."

"I remember," she said. "Why don't you take your boxers off and see if you still like it?"

He didn't hesitate, tossing them onto the floor.

She reached out and ran her finger across his chest, grazing one of his nipples.

He hissed.

Then she did the same thing to the other one before running her hand down his side, moving closer as she squeezed his ass. Her hand then slid down his thigh, then up again, this time cupping him in the most intimate way.

A guttural groan escaped his lips. It took every ounce of control not to stop her. She could do things to him that would bring him to an immediate climax, but she knew that, and enjoyed teasing him as much as he did her. So he let her gently stroke him, wrapping her fingers around him, then sliding one finger over the head, and down the shaft as she cupped him again. He stared into her eyes as she toyed with him. She smiled, licking her full, rosy lips.

She scooted halfway down the bed before rising to her knees. Brushing her hair to the side, she bent over, her tongue darting out of her mouth, licking the length of him. She looked up at him as she took him into her hot, moist mouth. He propped himself up on his elbows, fisting the sheets, watching as she held him with her hand, moving him in and out of her mouth. Her tongue danced across the tip before taking all of him in again.

He took a fistful of her hair and tugged, pulling her mouth off. "Come here," he said. His mouth found hers, thrusting his tongue deep, swirling around inside, desperate to love her again.

He cupped her breast, rubbing his thumb over her nipple, twirling it, pinching it, tugging at it. He pushed her down onto her back, sucking hard on her nipple. He dug his fingers into her ass, pulling her all the way to him, pressing his knee between her legs. He could feel her wetness dripping onto his thigh. He reached between her legs, shoving two fingers inside her, while his thumb fanned across the swollen, hard nub. She moaned, panting. Her hands cupped his head, eagerly pushing him from one breast to the other. Her legs spread wide open for him, her body rocking with his strokes. His name spilled from her lips, perhaps a little too loudly.

He lifted his head and looked in her passion-filled eyes before gently covering her mouth with the palm of his hand. He continued to rub and finger her, while stifling her loud moans. She was close to the edge, so he eased up and reached for the condom. He fumbled with the package, finally tearing it with his teeth, but not having much success removing it from the package.

She took it from his hands and pulled the condom out, then gently rolled it over him before straddling him, taking him inside her, grinding her hips back and forth. He propped himself up on one hand, the other holding the small of her back, his tongue toying with her nipple.

She rocked her body faster and her moans became louder.

"You always were a bit noisy," he whispered, before shoving his tongue deep in her mouth, capturing her moans. Their bodies rocked back and forth, her hips grinding wildly. He could see her riding him in the small mirror on his dresser and his release exploded at the erotic sight. He wrapped his arms around her and fell backward while she continued to grind her hips in a panicked frenzy. He rolled her over. "Be quiet," he said as he lowered his head, running his tongue down her belly, lapping at her while stroking her with three of his fingers. When he knew she was right there he sucked on her nub, pulling it into his mouth, holding his fingers all the way inside. Her body convulsed violently, and he heard a few muted groans. When he lifted his head, he let out a soft chuckle when he saw she'd covered her face with a pillow. He kept one hand on her stomach, enjoying the small trembles that continued to ripple across her body.

When her breathing slowed, he lifted the pillow from her face. "Everything okay?"

"It's amazing we never got caught having sex in your parents' house."

"I do remember covering your mouth a lot." He lay down next to her, drawing the covers over them and pulling her close. "Don't get me wrong. I like the noises. The other day at the hotel, I wanted to make you scream."

"I think I did." She rested her head on his chest, looping her arm over his middle. "We need to set an alarm for me," she said.

"I already did." Shane clicked the television off. "Set for five. Should give you enough time to go to the hotel, get dressed, and come back and pick me up."

"Thanks."

"We're going to have to figure out how to make this work," he said. "I still love you."

"I've never stopped loving you," she whispered.

$\mathcal{K}$ARA SAT ON THE windowsill across from a classroom in the medical building of the University of Rochester, which was right across the street from the hospital. It looked like any other college campus, with lounges tucked in hallways, students and staff sitting on sofas having study sessions.

Shane leaned against the wall directly across from her, next to the door. She'd successfully snuck out of his house at five-fifteen and made it back just in time to have breakfast with everyone. However, it seemed that both Theresa and Kevin were under the impression she'd spent the night.

Well, she had, but wasn't sure how they knew it. And she wasn't sure how she felt about them knowing. Not so much Theresa, but Kevin. All through breakfast Kevin stared at her, spilling his juice because he wasn't paying attention to what he was doing while giving her sideways glances. It wasn't an accusatory glare, but more of a questioning one. She cared for Kevin deeply. If she ever hurt him, she'd never forgive herself. It was bad enough she'd hurt Shane, but hurting his son would be a hundred times worse.

She checked her watch. The door should be opening at any moment. Two of the three students they wanted to talk to were in that classroom.

The wood door flung wide and students filed out like a swarm of bees. Kara held up the photo of the student she was looking for, while Shane went looking for his. Five students walked past before a blonde haired, blue eyed, six-foot-two white male stepped from the classroom. Kara called his name and he looked her way.

"Yes?" he asked.

She flashed her badge. "Special Agent Kara Martin. I need to ask you some questions about the cadavers you put into the hallway."

"I thought that was all settled." His pupils dilated as he frowned.

"It was," she said, noting Shane had found his man. "Not sure if you heard, but one of the missing cadavers was found."

The man nodded. "I feel really bad about that. I just did what I was asked."

"By whom?"

"Someone from the hospital. She said it was a tradition. That each year she and some of the other staff played a prank on each other."

"What kind of prank?"

"I didn't really ask. She said she'd be keeping an eye on everything, so not to worry."

"What was her name?"

"I don't recall," the boy said. "But I do remember she had a proper ID. I did look at the badge hanging around her neck. And she wore full scrubs."

"What do you mean full scrubs?" Kara asked.

"Like she was going into surgery. Head cover, booties. She gave us each fifty bucks. If I could go back in time, I would have told her to do it herself. It was pretty stupid."

"Remember anything else about this woman? What was her build like? Could you estimate her age?"

"I wouldn't dare estimate her age. But she was thin. Maybe a little shorter than you, but not by much."

"Did she wear makeup?" Kara asked.

"Not that I recollect."

Kara pulled out her card. "If you can think of anything else that can help us, please give me a call."

"I will," he said. "I truly am sorry."

She nodded and then watched the medical student walk down the hallway, scuffing his heels.

"Anything?" Shane asked as he approached her. His student was walking in the other direction. "Says a woman paid him and his friends."

"Same story I got. Didn't know who she was. Said

her hair was covered, she wore scrubs, mask, the whole thing."

"That's what mine said, too." Kara let out a long breath. "The doctor blames the students, the students sort of blame themselves, but say they were paid to do it as a prank."

"We need to find this female doctor or nurse," Shane said. "And we could narrow it down by left-handed doctors."

"Good point," Kara said. "But I think we need to widen it to other hospital staff."

"Agreed," he said. "The woman could have posed as a member of the medical staff. My guy said he didn't get a good look at her ID tag, only said she had one."

"Same thing here."

"Why don't we head over to the Transplant wing. There isn't a nurse or doctor over there who doesn't know me; we might be able to find something useful."

"Sounds like a plan."

"There is this one nurse," Shane said. "She's new to the transplant unit. I think I remember her saying she worked in the ER, which means she'd know about patients being put on life support waiting to donate. Maybe she's on duty. She seemed like the talkative type."

"Sounds like you want to flirt with a nurse for information."

"Why, Kara Martin, are you jealous?"

"Maybe a little," she said, holding up her forefinger

and thumb. "You actually sound excited to go talk to her."

"Not excited to talk to her," he said. "But I feel like we're finally making progress." He pointed to the exit sign of the medical building. "Across the street and then red elevators to the seventh floor."

As soon as they stepped through the doors, the wind blew her coat open. She felt Shane's warm hand on the small of her back. She glanced over at him and arched her brow.

"Seriously? No one's around."

"It's not professional."

"Neither is making out in a parking lot with each of us having a gun on our hip. And by the way," he winked, "my mother's Bunco friends saw us."

"Wonderful," she said. "Speaking of being caught, I think—"

"Kevin got up to use the bathroom and saw you heading out the door. I'll have a talk with him tonight. See how he feels. But you owe him another NHL battle. He's not going to let you off the hook."

"I hate it when you do that." She pushed the button on the metal post, waiting for the light to change so they could cross the street. The sun was bright, which was rare, but it was still biting cold.

"I'm not redirecting the conversation," he said. "I'm not going to lie to my son about my feelings for you. He has a stake in our relationship, and just because he saw you leave doesn't mean he won't want to see you. It just means I need to talk to him and see how knowing you spent the night made him feel."

"And if that feeling is negative? What then?" The light changed, and they headed across the street with quick steps.

"Then you don't spend the night again," Shane said. "But I doubt that's the case. The way he casually mentioned to me that he saw you leaving so early—"

"What did he say?" Her pulse went wild with concern.

"He was more concerned about whether you would be getting breakfast and if you were coming back."

"I see." It was hard to keep from smiling.

"I do need to talk to him and find out how he really feels about me having a girlfriend, having my girlfriend around, a lot, and make sure his needs are being met... as well as mine." He looked over at her as he opened the door to the hospital. "He and I are a package deal."

"I know that," she said. "I'm concerned about what having me spend the night could do to him." She followed Shane through the lobby and down a long corridor.

"I don't think it's done anything negative to him. I heard him say something to Theresa about it and he was giggling. I couldn't hear everything, but I did hear him say how much he liked you. Then you showed back up and we didn't have time to discuss it further. I will tonight. Right before the epic hockey battle."

"Your son is as irresistible as you are."

Shane pushed the elevator button. "That's twice you've told me I'm irresistible in twenty-four hours. I'm going to remember you said that later tonight."

As soon as the elevator doors closed, and he and Kara were alone, he grabbed her, shoving her up against the back wall, and meshed his mouth with hers. It wasn't a pretty kiss. But it was effective.

"What the hell was that about?" she asked, wiping her swollen lips. Her breath was raspy. "Not that I'm complaining."

He shrugged. "Making sure I'm really irresistible."

The elevator dinged and jolted to a stop. The doors opened and no sooner did Shane step foot in the hallway than he saw Tina, the new nurse, standing at the other end. She smiled. "What brings you by?"

"I was hoping you could answer a few questions for me," he said. "This is Special Agent Kara Martin."

"I've seen you on the news."

"Is there someplace we can sit down?" Kara asked.

"Sure." Tina pointed to an empty lounge, which looked like it had a coffee machine and some snacks along with a table. "Do you want some coffee?"

"That would be great," Kara said.

Tina poured three cups, placing them one by one on the table off to the right side of the room.

"How difficult would it be," Shane started, "for someone to find out which deaths led to organ donation?"

"Well, medical records are private, but most people

tell their family, friends, co-workers. We protect the rights of all our patients, but as you know it's the donor who remains completely anonymous, except in some rare cases."

"What would those cases be?" Kara asked.

"Mainly kidney transplants from parent to child, sibling to sibling, friend to friend," Tina said. "But some people want to know, or their families want to know, and then extensive counseling is done. It's rare that the information is given out."

"Do you keep donor records at the hospital?" Shane asked.

Tina leaned across the table. "You're not seeking information on Kevin's—"

"No," Shane said. "We're working on a couple of homicides and trying to find out how someone might obtain information about transplant recipients and donors."

"Ah, the Butterfly Murders." Tina leaned back in her chair. "United Network for Organ Sharing keeps all the records, and they're sealed."

"Nothing remains in the hospital?" Shane asked.

"We keep records, but donor records are duplicated and then assigned numbers. That's how we reference them."

"Do you ever teach or do anything at the medical school?" Kara asked, noting Tina seemed to be left-hand dominant when she stirred her coffee.

Shane gave her a sideways glance.

"No," Tina said. "Why?"

"Did you hear about some cadavers going missing?" Kara asked. "A few months back."

"I saw on the news that one was recovered," Tina said. "What does that have to do with your murder case?"

"We don't know," Shane said. "Just checking all angles." He stood. "Thanks for your time."

"Glad to help," she said. "Let me know if you have any other questions."

The last thing Shane wanted to do was have Kara spend the night at the hotel, but he needed to talk to his son, alone. Kevin was happy she'd come over for dinner and played video games, and he did seem disappointed she'd left relatively early. Shane took that as a good sign.

He sat in his small makeshift office between the dining room and living room, while Kevin was upstairs finishing his homework. Shane filled out the paperwork for more warrants, specifically the names in the last year of organ recipients and donors in the Rochester area. He also wanted to know who had died on a Thursday in the last year. Not all of them would be donors, but it would help the search. Deaths were public records, so obtaining them would just be time-consuming.

His phone buzzed. A text from Kara.

u r being unreasonable

He laughed and texted back.

told u, not talking to u until I get a pic

He set the phone down and opened Kara's email about the FBI profile, which listed the perp as being male, between 35 and 50. A professional. Held a good-paying job. A bit of a loner, but mastered social situations. Possibly married. A recent trigger set him off, but the tendencies were always right under the surface. Of course, the profile now needed to be tweaked since they were possibly looking for a woman; female serial killers were an entirely different kind of murderer.

The floorboard at the top of the stairs creaked. Shane closed his laptop and moved to the family room.

"You wanted to talk to me?" Kevin asked, already in his pajamas. He had his mother's eyes, her smile, and her gentle soul. It was hard not to look at him and see his late wife, and all the things Shane had loved about Janet.

"All your homework done?"

Kevin nodded. "Also took my meds."

"Have a seat." Shane sat in the recliner while Kevin plopped himself on the sofa. There were moments that Kevin seemed like a little boy, and other times he carried himself with an air of maturity that even a thirty-three-year-old detective didn't possess.

"This sounds serious." Kevin sat crossed-legged, his

elbows on his knees, fists holding up his face, scrunching his cheeks. "Am I in trouble?"

"No." Shane didn't know where to start. He and his son had many serious conversations over the last two years, and Shane had always tried to be as honest as he could without giving the boy more than he could handle. "What do you think about Kara?"

Kevin bolted upright, dropping his hands to his lap, and smiled. "She's cool. I like her."

"So do I."

"Duh," Kevin said. "That is soooo obvious it's almost gross."

Shane smiled. "I want to have her around a lot more."

"You mean like stay over again?"

"How did you feel when you saw her this morning? Did it upset you in any way?"

"No," Kevin said. "You're a lot less uptight when she's here, which makes things easier."

Shane laughed. "I like having her with us, but when this case is over I'm afraid she has to go back to D.C. How does that make you feel?"

Kevin's smile faded. "I'd miss her."

"I'll want her to come visit. Maybe come up for a holiday or two. I'd like us to go visit her on long weekends. Some vacations. Maybe take a vacation together. Would you like that?"

"So, you'd have a girlfriend who lives seven hours away?"

JEN TALTY

"I like her so much that I'd be willing to try that, but only if you're willing to try it, too. We've never talked about me dating someone. I didn't expect I would be any time soon, but then Kara showed up."

Kevin continued to sit up tall, his face somber and serious. He held Shane's gaze like a man. "I like Kara, too."

"I promised you I'd be honest," Shane said as he moved swiftly to the sofa, putting his arm around Kevin. "You and I are a team, and no one will come between us."

Kevin rested his head on Shane's shoulder. "I miss Mom."

"I've been thinking a lot about Mom lately," Shane said. "She'd be so proud of you. You're a lot like her, you know?"

Kevin nodded. "I like Kara so much I feel bad that when she's around it makes not having Mom here a little easier."

Shane could hear the tremble in his son's voice. "I feel bad sometimes, too. No one can replace your mom. There is nothing we can do to bring her back. But we can honor her by living our lives. Being happy. Because, at the end of the day, all she wanted was for you to be healthy and for us to be happy."

Kevin looked up, water welling in his eyes. "Kara makes you happy?"

Shane swallowed his breath and it felt like someone had just sucker-punched him. "There isn't anyone in the world who could ever be more important in my life than you. Not even Kara, but I do feel a bit happier when she's around."

"She makes me happy, too."

"I care very much for Kara. She understands that you come first in my life. Before her. She also cares a great deal about you, and if she didn't I wouldn't bring her around. She's got to be able to put you first, and I believe she can."

Kevin wiped his eyes. "I like being with Kara. She's easy to talk to. Fun. And you're a lot less neurotic when she's with you."

"That's a big word." Shane chuckled as he ruffled his son's hair. "I suppose I am."

"So, she coming back tonight?"

Shane shook his head. "I'll see if I can get her to stop by for breakfast before work."

"That would be nice." Kevin wrapped his arms around Shane's shoulders. "I love you, Dad."

"I love you, too. Now let's both shut off all the lights and go to bed."

Shane made sure all the doors were locked while Kevin turned out all the lights but the one going up the stairs. Kevin was beyond being tucked in, so Shane said his goodnight and then closed Kevin's door. He pulled his phone out of his back pocket. Only one text from Kara.

I'll meet u in ur dreams...

"You'll see me now." He closed his bedroom door,

and clicked on the TV as he propped himself up on his pillows. He opened Facetime, calling Kara.

He could barely see her face when she answered.

"I hate this." She was lying on her side, her head resting on a pillow.

"What are you wearing? I can barely see you."

"Because all the lights are out, and no, I'm not turning any on. I'm tired."

"Still haven't told me what you're wearing." A light flashed across behind her and he heard noise in the background. Her beautiful face filled his screen.

"If you must know, a T-shirt and your boxers."

"That's hot."

She smiled. "How'd things go with Kevin?"

"He's a very insightful young man."

"You're just figuring this out now?"

"He wants you to come over—"

"For breakfast. I know. He texted me right before you called. I told him only if he turned his phone off and went to bed. He hasn't texted back."

There were so many thoughts floating through Shane's brain. But the one that struck him the hardest was that if Janet were still alive she and Kara would really like each other.

"We'll make this work," Shane said.

"One thing at a time," she said. "Sleep well."

"Only if you join me in my dreams."

---

21

*S*HANE HATED BRIEFINGS almost as much as he hated press conferences. He glanced around the small conference room. Captain Morrell leaned against the doorjamb, hands stuffed in his pockets, looking none too happy. Kara and Foster leaned against the windowsills on the other side of the room. Pollack, Benster, and three other detectives sat at the table, looking disheveled and tired, as they'd been out half the night following a few leads while working their own cases. Jones took his place next to Shane, in front of the whiteboard, corkboard, and wall of images. Shane disliked these kinds of briefings because it was a rehashing of things they already knew, a slew of questions they didn't have answers for, leaving them no better off than when they started.

"I've put Doug on the far wall." Shane pointed to the

other side. "He's involved with Emily, but not any of the other murders."

"We also put Haughton there, since we can only link him to Emily so far," Kara said.

"What about the religious whack jobs?" Benster asked.

Kara rose and tapped the back wall. "The one from Kentucky is still a suspect. One of my team members has eyes on him. No movement and no record of him coming into New York, but that doesn't mean he doesn't have someone doing his dirty work. However, we need to consider that our perp is someone in the medical field, or at least had some training. And is left-handed," Kara said.

"I got word this morning," Shane interjected, "that the judge granted us partial access to donor records of our victims," Shane said. "I glanced at them. All died on a Thursday, but not all of them in Rochester."

"But," Jones started, "all of our recipients had their transplants in Rochester."

"We've been pulling deaths on Thursdays in this area so we can interview family members about organ donation, but if the donors are from all over the place, it makes things more difficult."

"Excuse me," a uniformed officer said, standing at the door, holding an official confidential envelope. "This just came for Agent Martin."

Kara strode across the room, exuding power. She

thanked the officer and opened the envelope. Shane waited patiently as she scanned the documents.

Jones, on the other hand, couldn't wait. "What is it?"

"I had our analyst check for missing cadavers around the country. I'm shocked by the numbers," she said. "I also had her look at all open missing person cases in the Rochester area in the last year."

"How many cases?" Pollock asked. "

"Too many," Kara said. "But we need to go talk to the family members and see if any of them had a transplant in the last year."

"Anything else?" Shane asked.

Kara shook her head, nose still in the papers.

"Where are we on the soccer connection?" Shane asked.

"Nowhere," Pollock said. "Doesn't connect all the victims when we add in the case from Boston. Even Iris is a stretch for that connection."

"I'd say that's a dead end," Foster said.

"Agreed." Shane nodded. "Then we focus on the organ connection."

"So, let's address the elephant in the room," Foster said. "It's Thursday. Thursday means something to our killer. If he hasn't already killed today, or a Thursday weeks ago, then we're looking at another homicide by morning."

"If our theory is correct," Shane said, doing his best to remain impartial. As if his son wasn't a heart recipient. "We have only four organs left, and I requested a list nationwide of all donors and recipients of those four organs."

"We already know one of those recipients," Morrell said.

The room fell silent for a long moment. The tension was palpable. The implications deafening.

"Foster," Kara started, "why don't you and Jones pound the pavement with these missing person cases? Shane and I will dig through public records for deaths on Thursdays."

"Pollock and Benster," Shane said, doing his best to cover his annoyance. This was still his case, not the FBI's. While he wanted her help, he didn't like how she hijacked that call-in front of his boss. Not because he would have done anything different; just, it was his call. "Take a break, then connect with Jones, splitting the rest of the list."

Shane stood in front of the wall as everyone but Morrell and Kara filed out of the conference room.

"Agent Martin," Morrell said. "Can you give us a moment?"

"Sure." She stepped out into the hallway. When Shane turned to face his captain, Kara stood just outside the door, waiting.

"How are you holding up?" Morrell asked.

"I'm fine."

"We need to discuss the obvious conflict. Everyone in the office is painfully aware that Kevin could be a target if your theory is correct."

"And you're worried I won't stay focused," Shane said.

Morrell nodded.

"You can't pull me off this case."

"I'm not going to," Morrell said. "For now. But I will if you give me a reason, or if anyone on that task force does."

Shane nodded. No use in arguing with the captain.

"We're putting a car on Kevin. Won't be 'round the clock, we don't have the resources, but I'll check with Kara as well."

"I appreciate that."

"One more thing." Morrell pointed to Kara. "She really was your girlfriend all through high school?"

"Yeah, why?"

"Shocked that a dumb jock like you could get a girl like that," Morrell said.

"Stranger things have happened."

"I suppose," Morrell said as he moved toward the door. "Good for you back then. Not a good idea now." He stepped into the hallway and disappeared down the corridor.

"What did he want?" Kara asked, tucking her hair behind her ear.

"Not much," Shane said, letting his frustration out with his tone. "Next time, don't go assigning people shit on my task force. You had no right."

"Would you have done it differently?"

"Not the point." He pushed one of the chairs into

the table. "Not only did you take over, you did it in front of my boss."

"What are you really mad about? Because it certainly isn't that."

"Really?" He glared at her. "Because of that he thinks I'm not focused. Considering taking me off."

She clicked the door closed and took a few steps toward him, resting her hands on the table. "Maybe you should take yourself off. No one would blame you."

"Screw you," he said, turning his back. "I'm not stepping down. Kevin wouldn't understand."

"Yes, he would," Kara said.

He laughed. "You've been around a couple of days, and you think you know my son? Please."

"That hurt." Her fingers wrapped around his bicep with a gentle squeeze. "I know you, so tell me what this is all about."

"It's Thursday. I hate briefings. The woman I'm sleeping with just hijacked my briefing. My boss thinks I'm screwing the FBI agent who is here helping."

"We all know you're not Foster's type."

He chuckled, but his mood turned serious again. "Morell is putting a car on Kevin, but it won't be all the time. I can't leave Theresa and Kevin alone at night."

"I agree," she said. "So, let's come up with a plan that works so you don't have to drop lead and your son is safe."

"I texted Theresa and told her to go to my parents'

after she picks up Kevin, then come home when I get there."

"We can take our paperwork back to your place," she said. "That's why I wanted to make sure we got that task."

"I know." He looked down at the hand still firmly around his bicep. "Not professional."

THE BUTTERFLY MURDERS

area, she picks up Kevin that comes home when I get

he said. That's when I...

make sure ...

22

a CLICKING NOISE PULLED Shane from a light sleep. He stretched as he opened his eyes. Kara had propped herself against the headboard, sitting cross-legged, her laptop balancing on her knees. "What time is it?"

"Five-thirty."

He pushed her laptop.

"Hey," she said. "What are you doing?"

"Trying to look up your skirt to see if you're wearing that tiny little thong I took off you last night."

She smiled. "Nothing but skin under this skirt."

"That doesn't help the morning hard-on."

"You really are insatiable." She set her laptop on the nightstand.

"I noticed a little landing strip growing back."

"Why do you like that so much?"

He kissed her knee, sliding his finger up her thigh.

"The very first time I saw you naked, that's what you had. Kind of stuck with me."

Her laugh was cut short by Shane's phone going off. "That can't be good." He rolled over, snagging his phone. "It's Pollock. Hello?"

"Double homicide," Pollock said. "Two kids…"

Shane jumped from the bed, his feet hitting the floor with a loud thud. He yanked up a pair of underwear and tossed Kara her duffle bag.

"…both bound and naked. Candles," Pollok continued.

"Text me the address. We'll be there as fast as we can. Did you call Jones?"

"Next," Pollock said. "What about the Feds?"

"I'll get a hold of Kara and Foster." Shane ended the call and tossed the phone to the bed. "Call Foster. Double homicide." Shane paused for a moment, taking a huge breath. "Two kids."

"Fuck," Kara said.

"I have to wake Theresa. Let her know I'm heading out."

"Maybe you should leave a note."

"No," Shane said. "I promised Theresa I'd let her know if I ever had to leave before she woke up. Me telling her to go to my parents' yesterday freaked her out."

"Probably a good thing," Kara said. "She'll be more aware of Kevin's and her surroundings."

Shane grabbed a new shirt from the closet before

opening the bedroom door, to find Kevin walking across the hallway. "What are you doing up?" He pulled the door shut.

"Bathroom." Kevin rubbed his eyes. "Why are you getting dressed when you obviously haven't showered?"

Shane ran a hand through his hair. "I have to go into work, so waking—"

"I'm up." Theresa stood in her doorway. "Been studying."

"You really need to sleep more," Shane said. "And do something other than studying."

Theresa shrugged. "I'll go make a breakfast sandwich for you to take."

"Make it two," Shane said as Kara stepped from the master bedroom.

"Will do." Theresa headed down the stairs.

"Morning, Kara." Kevin scuffled his feet until he was close enough to give her a hug. "Dad said you have to go into work."

"We do."

Shane watched as Kara wrapped her arms around his son, then kissed the top of his head.

"Is it really bad?" Kevin stepped back, looking up at Kara.

"We don't know yet."

Shane stared at the two most important people in his life in awe. Their bond had developed quickly, which did concern him on some levels. Part of the reason he hadn't dated. Kevin missed his mother, and he craved that kind of connection.

"Come on," Kara said, looping her arm over Kevin's shoulder. "Let's go make a couple of coffees to go and wrap up those sandwiches."

Shane stood at the top of the stairs, watching Kara and Kevin as they carried on a conversation. After they disappeared into the living room, Shane snagged his tie and sport coat. No way was he letting Kara walk out of his life this time.

*K*ara stepped from Shane's car in the parking lot of one of the town parks in front of a lodge, which was out of Shane's jurisdiction; but at this point, it didn't matter. The Sheriff's office, the Rochester PD, and the Feds were all in bed together on this one. The sky brightened with the morning sun. A fresh layer of snow covered the ground. Kara pulled her coat tight and walked toward the police line, Foster giving her the evil eye. She showed her badge, signed the log, then stepped under the yellow tape. Shane did the same, but he went straight inside the cabin.

"Save the lecture," Kara said to Foster as she watched Shane disappear into the lodge. "Tell me what we have."

"Two kids were reported missing last night," Foster said.

"From where?"

"A support group for transplant patients."

"Christ," she said. "How old?"

"Both seventeen."

That explained why no Amber Alert went out. "Organs?"

"Parents stated one had a pancreas transplant, the other had a lung transplant."

"What's it like in there?"

"Fresh," Foster said. "Lots of blood."

Kara scanned the area, noting the CSI team working on a possible tire tread. "We haven't had two victims at once before."

"We haven't had an eye witness before either," Foster said.

She closed her eyes for a moment, savoring the word 'witness.' "To what, exactly?"

"A park worker who noticed a small SUV, maybe a CRV or Tucson, something that size, parked next to the cabin." Foster pointed toward the CSI truck. "Worker noticed flashes of light, so he went to the door and opened it. Said he saw a figure over one of the bodies. Next thing he knows our killer whacks him upside the head, knocking him out."

"Can he give us anything on the suspect? Height? Build? Eye color? Female? Anything."

"Didn't think our perp was too tall. Maybe five-seven or eight, but he couldn't be sure."

"Did you talk to the witness?" Kara blew into her hands and then rubbed them together.

"I did," Foster said. "He's not in a very good head space after seeing those two bodies. It's brutal."

"Guess I'd better go take a look."

Foster grabbed her arm before she took a step. "I'm not going to lecture you, but I am going to say my peace."

"Not the time or place."

"Just listen," he said. "I don't care you're screwing him. I got no problem working with Jones, but I'm concerned you're putting your career on the line and going to get your heart broke—"

"Don't go there." She turned, looking Foster in the eye. "I might be riding a little too close, but I'm doing that so this case doesn't derail if Shane...if something goes wrong, and if Kevin is a target, then consider me extra protection for both Kevin's safety and Shane's ability to do his job." She poked Foster in the chest. "We've got a lead detective who is too close, but it's not our call to pull him—"

"I don't want Shane to be pulled off. He's a good detective and has valuable insight. I just want you to see what everyone will see, or already does see, and the impact it could have on your career."

"I can't worry about that right now," she said. "Until this killer is caught, I'm glued to Shane and Kevin. So back the fuck off."

Foster held up his hands. "I said my peace. Now let's go inside."

The temperature was in the high teens, but Kara's blood boiled. She took long strides across the parking lot, not caring if Foster was one step behind or not. Squaring her shoulders, she checked her emotions at the door as she stepped into the small cabin, her nostrils immediately assaulted with the smell of pumpkin, vanilla, and copper. She covered her mouth as some acid hit the back of her throat.

A couple of quick flashes of light illuminated the dark room. She snapped on a pair of latex gloves. The CSI team had labeled evidence and was now cataloging them with the camera. The M.E. and his team were hovering over the two bodies. Jones was talking with a tech and Shane stood behind the M.E., his notebook in hand, his face pale.

She took a couple of tentative steps forward, then looked left and right. Clothes were folded neatly and placed on the counter.

"Hey Kara," Jones said.

"When Foster said fresh, he wasn't kidding."

"M.E. said both victims haven't been dead very long."

She focused her attention on the victim closest to the door. A blonde girl. Her blue eyes still open, but dull and lifeless. Her head turned toward the door. The victim's hands were above her head, wrists bound with duct tape. Ankles crossed, and bound with duct tape as well. Kara stepped closer, pulling out her notepad. The victim had a large incision on her stomach, and some of her internal organs were piled on the floor in a pool of sticky blood.

"M.E. said it's probable that the victims were alive when our killer sliced into their bodies."

"Jesus," she whispered. The second victim was presented in the same way. She was a redhead, and her eyes were thankfully closed. She had two long incisions on both sides of her body, starting from under the armpit and ending about twelve inches later. Kara pointed. "Lungs?"

"M.E. hasn't confirmed, but yeah, says that would be how to get to them. We've confirmed she had a lung transplant in the last six months. On a Thursday," Jones said.

"Pancreas for the other victim," she said. "That leaves the thymus and the heart." She lifted her gaze, studying Shane. He'd put his notebook away and was currently talking with one of the CSI team members. He stood tall, one hand stuffed in his pants pocket. His other hand twitched at his side, something he always did right before he strapped on his helmet before a ski race. To anyone who didn't know him well, he looked calm.

But his stiff, closed-off exterior told her otherwise.

"There are two doors," she said, pointing to the kitchen. "Which door did the witness come in?"

"Front door," Jones said, motioning behind him.

"Witness says the killer was kneeling over, lighting a candle at the foot of one of the victims. He was so stunned and shocked, he said he couldn't move. Next thing he knew, he'd woken up on the floor next to the victim. He ran out and then called the cops."

"How close was he to the victims?"

"In their blood close," Jones said as he pointed to the bloody hand- and footprints where the witness obviously scrambled to his feet and made a beeline for the door. "But according to the witness, the killer's car was parked on the other side of the lodge, in a grouping of trees."

"Do we know how long the witness was unconscious?"

"Based on the time he thought he pulled in and the time he called 9-1-1, it was twenty minutes," Jones said. "Why wouldn't our killer murder the witness?"

"I'm guessing it's some moral code or something. Only killing those who had a transplant." Kara stepped carefully around an evidence marker and to the foot of one of the victims, Jones following. "All the other crime scenes, the killer cleaned up the blood, or at least tried before lighting the candles. Or even putting them down. Why are these different?"

"And why two at the same time?" Jones added. "Feels rushed, doesn't it?"

"Something happened to our killer. Something that forced him to change his ritual."

"That's not good," Jones said.

Shane nodded to Kara, and pointed to the kitchen.

"Foster give you shit this morning?" Jones asked.

She whipped her head around, glaring at Jones. "What do you know about that?"

He held his hands up. "For what it's worth, I think Shane needs someone with him all the time," Jones said. "He was barely pulling it together after Janet died. Then Kevin's health went downhill. The pressure of it all nearly broke him."

"How was his job performance during that time?" She swallowed the lump of guilt that formed her throat.

"Had he not put himself on administrative duty when Janet died he would have been fired, but not because he wasn't doing his job. His record is one of the best in the station. The problem was his anger, which made him a loose cannon to work with. Never knew what he was going to do next."

Kara figured outside of Shane's family, Jones was the closest thing he had to a best friend. "Professionally, you know him better than I do."

"If you're asking me if I think he needs to step down from lead, I honestly don't know. He's been hyper-focused since he came back to work. Crossing every 't', dotting every 'i'. Even more so working with you, but this is a lot to take in."

"But he's not angry, like he was back then?"

"No," Jones said. "But he is scared, and that can be just as bad."

Kara pulled out her phone and hit*3.

"What are you doing?"

"Making sure we've got a car on Kevin and Theresa around the clock."

"He'll never forgive you for going behind his back, or using resources on him when there are dozens of other kids in this town just like Kevin with a target on their back. Besides, we have a rotation."

"I'm willing to risk Shane hating me. I've lived through that. I'm not willing to let anything happen to his son."

S hane stepped from the cabin, using the back door, careful not to disrupt a few evidence tags. The crisp morning air burned his lungs as he struggled to catch his breath. He'd worked some nasty homicides in his day. He'd seen some gruesome crime scenes over the years. But nothing in his life could have prepared him for this one. He rounded the corner of the cabin and faced the woods, needing a short break from it all. The inch of snow they'd gotten overnight lined the tree branches, forcing them to sag.

"Hey," Kara's voice echoed through the air. "Holding up okay?"

"Not really," he admitted. "What those two girls went through to get a transplant is hell. Surviving one, equally hard. And it's a constant battle. Organ rejection can happen at any time. You learn to live with that fact. I know it's very possible my son won't outlive me. His life is never going to be normal." He waved toward the cabin. "But to have all the possibilities of a future that you fought so hard to get, wiped out by a...it's just senseless." He stuffed his hands in his pockets and kept his gaze on the snow-covered path leading to the hiking trails that surrounded the park. "How are you holding up?"

"Not too well either," she said. "This is one of the toughest cases I've ever worked, and I've been assigned some pretty crazy ones. But this one is exceptionally tough because there are now only two organs left to be collected, and your son—"

"Could be more," Shane said, not wanting her to state the obvious. "There are other tissues that can be harvested. Not to mention the killer could start all over again."

"I thought of that, too," she said.

"I called Pollock and asked him to get in touch with your analyst to see if we can't match the description of the car with someone who works in the hospital."

"Narrow that down to someone who's left-handed."

"I know your profiler says a male," Shane said. "But we've got missing cadavers that appear to be orches-trated by a woman, based on what those students told us, and our witness here stated the perp was not very tall."

"At this point, we can't rule out either sex," Kara

said. "If we get the organ donation and recipient list, we'll have to just start interviewing everyone."

"That's going to be a grueling process." Shane heard the blip of the ambulance siren. He glanced over his shoulder as it pulled out, taking the witness to the hospital. "We've got less than one week to stop this fucker before he or she strikes again."

"The press is going to have a field day with this one," Kara said. "Not to mention the public fear it will create," Kara said. "My boss is considering sending the rest of the team."

"Jones won't like that too much, but I'll take all the help I can get."

She tapped his shoulder. "What's going on? Something is really bothering you."

He shouldn't have been surprised she would be so in tune with his emotions. When they were kids, she knew him better than anyone in his family.

"When I was a beat cop, shortly before making detective, I was dispatched to a DUI which ended up being vehicular manslaughter. The driver was a young mother. Two toddlers in car seats in the back. She blew a .18. Both kids were unharmed, but they screamed like they were dying as Social Services took them away. Once they were gone, I read her her rights and handcuffed her, hoping...praying, those two babies wouldn't be emotionally traumatized for life."

"That had to have been rough," Kara said

"The victim was a sixteen-year-old girl. The accident happened at Twelve Corners near Brighton High School. She'd been walking home after staying with some academic group. It was near five, so it was getting dark."

"There have been a few accidents over the years at that light."

"She'd been pinned between the car and the stop light. Her body leaning over the hood. When I got to the scene, the driver was trying to run, though a few good Samaritans made sure she didn't. The worst part, however, was that the two children were in front-facing car seats, staring at the dead girl's body for at least fifteen minutes."

"Jesus," Kara said softly.

Shane turned his head, catching her intense, but caring gaze. "Janet joined a bunch of support groups at the hospital when Kevin first got sick. I dived into work. That's how I dealt with Kevin's illness. Then Janet died and, other than my family and Jones, I had no one. I cut myself off from the world. I felt alone. Janet had always found comfort in these groups, and Kevin's doctor kept nagging me to go, so I went. The group moderator was the father of the girl who had been killed that day. She'd had a heart transplant when she was six, only to be killed ten years later."

Kara held his gaze, saying nothing. Just stood there with him for a long moment.

"The parents of the girl who died back then still run those support—"

"Oh, no," Kara whispered. "They were the ones leading the group the victims attended?"

Shane nodded. "They're taking it pretty hard. Blame themselves."

"You talked with them."

"They called me right after seeing the morning news. I've got interviews set up with them and Dr. Nads, who did Kevin's heart transplant, along with the head of the transplant department." He looked around toward the cabin. Jones stood in the back door, signaling.

"Let's go catch this fucker."

23

*S*HANE STEPPED THROUGH the elevator doors on the maternity wing at Strong Hospital, flowers in hand. He'd spent the last three hours interviewing left-handed hospital staff and he needed a short break to clear his thoughts before he went back at it.

He checked the board for his sister-in-law's name.

The birthing center was nothing like the rest of the hospital. It smelled like fresh shampoo and lilacs. The rooms were large, with a comfortable lounge chair and even a table. The concept was to make it feel more like home, and it worked. He tapped on the door before entering.

"Hey, little brother." Mike greeted him at the door. "Glad you could make it."

Shane set the flowers down on the counter, before taking a good look at the latest addition to the Rogers family. "Oh my God," Shane said. "He looks just like Dad."

"I know," Mary Jo said. "It's uncanny."

Shane bent over to give his sister-in-law a kiss on the cheek. "How are you feeling?"

"Better," she said. "But tired."

"He's a big one." Shane held his arms out as Mary Jo gently placed her son in the crook of his elbow, then he settled down in the chair, staring at the baby. Infants used to scare Shane. His older nieces and nephews he wouldn't consider holding, and if he did he was always afraid he was going to drop them. When his older brother Dave had the first grandchild, Kara used to push Shane to hold him. Had it not been for her, he might have always been awkward with babies.

"Biggest Rogers yet," Mike said.

Shane laughed. "Where is everyone?"

"Mom and Dad took Alison and Tyler home," Mike said. "They're both exhausted. You missed Dave and Shari by a half hour."

"How long are they keeping you?" Shane asked as he leaned over and pressed his nose against Timothy's head, taking a good whiff of fresh baby smell. The baby twitched, his eyes popping open for a moment, then settling back down into a deep sleep.

"At least two more days, maybe more," Mary Jo said. "But at least that little guy gets to stay with his mama."

"That's good. Any complications since surgery?"

"Recovering better than expected," Mary Jo said. "But I have no energy at all."

"I'm not surprised. You've been through quite an ordeal." Shane pressed his lips against the bald head of his nephew.

"Where's Kara?" Mike asked.

"Federal Building, buried under a pile of paperwork, trying to find us a lead. This case has us both pretty frazzled."

"Some scary stuff," Mike said. "Mom is totally freaking over Kevin."

"I know," Shane said. "Honestly, I'm troubled as well."

"We read that the killer only kills on Thursdays. Is that true?" Mike asked.

Shane nodded. "If my theory is correct, we've got two more organs this psycho is collecting, and one is the heart."

"Where is Kevin now?" Mary Jo asked, her weak voice laced with concern.

"School. There's only one point of entry, as all the other doors are locked, and he has to be signed out by someone on my approved list. Theresa will pick him up today. She always gets there about ten minutes before dismissal, checks in with me. I'm not sure what to do tonight. We have a ton of interviews to finish up. I've got ten more here at the hospital today."

"Are Theresa and Kevin going home right after school?" Mike asked.

Shane nodded.

Mike reached down and scooped up his new son, giving him a quick kiss on the check before setting him in the bassinet "Mary Jo needs a nap, and she should do that while this little guy is sleeping."

A sliver of jealousy tickled Shane's heart. He never begrudged his brothers or sister their families. He adored all his nieces and nephews, but he'd wanted to have more kids. Janet had two miscarriages after Kevin was born, and they had been equally devastating.

"Let's sit in here." Mike pointed to a small room, much like the one outside the transplant wing.

Shane poured himself a cup of coffee and sat on the sofa facing the windows to the hallway. Mike sat across from him, sipping his coffee, looking like he hadn't slept in days.

"Mom told me how bad things were in the delivery room," Shane said. "Sorry."

"I'm just glad Mary Jo is okay." Mike ran a hand across his unshaven face. "It was bad enough they moved us from the birthing room to a delivery room when they realized she was going to need a C-section, but then they kicked me out when she lost consciousness right after they lifted Timothy up for her to see. I could hear them yelling that they couldn't find a pulse. I thought I was going to lose it. She had lost so much blood and was white as a ghost. I sat with Tim in the nursery for two hours before they came and got me. I thought I lost her."

"But you didn't," Shane said. "How is she doing with not being able to have more children?"

"We're both fine with it. Three is more than enough," Mike said. "I would have had more, but she's done. This last pregnancy sucked for her, and then seeing her like that..." Mike wiped a tear that had escaped his eye. "I don't know how you handle being a single father. Kevin's illness. Your work. You're a stronger man than me."

"Some days it isn't easy, but Kevin is my world and he makes it easy. Just like Mary Jo and the kids are yours."

Mike took a slow slip of coffee. "What about Kara? Where does she fit in all this?"

"I don't know," Shane said. "It's complicated."

"Mom says she's been staying at your house every night."

"That's true," Shane said. "I want her, too. Kevin seems fine with it. But she's also there because she's worried about Kevin. She thinks I don't know she's got friends of hers watching the school, the house, me."

"Why wouldn't she tell you?"

"Because she knows that I don't agree with using taxpayer dollars to protect one person, when there are other children and adults with heart transplants who could be this killer's target and don't have a detective as a father or his FBI agent girlfriend. But, frankly, I don't have it in me to fight her and I'm glad she did it."

"Or maybe you don't want to fight her because you

might push her away," Mike said. "You made it very clear you weren't going to let her go this time."

"I don't want to, but this isn't an easy situation. We've moved past what happened years ago. We're both in a good place, but that doesn't make it any less complicated."

"Mom thinks you and Kara are going to ride off into the sunset."

"Mom has always been optimistic and positive about everything." Shane pulled his cell phone out of his pocket, checking his texts and messages. Nothing from anyone about the case or anything important. No news is good news was no longer the case in this situation. "Her life is in D.C., and I can't ask her to up and leave a career she's worked hard to achieve. She's really good at what she does, and I'd be an asshole to expect her to drop it just because we still love each other."

"What if she wants to?" Mike asked.

"She hasn't said so one way or another, and we're both under a lot of pressure with the case."

"Would you leave Rochester?"

"No," Shane said sternly.

"So where does that leave you and Kara?"

"A long-distance relationship, because I can't uproot Kevin's life. Our family is here, and that has been key in his recovery. So are his doctors, support system, and friends. As much as I love Kara, Kevin comes first."

"Kevin's a smart kid. He's also more in tune with the

world because of his life circumstances; I'm sure he has an opinion about all this. What has he said?"

"He and Kara have developed a strong bond. He texts her a lot and she him. They have a relationship outside of her being my girlfriend. And she's so good with him that the idea she's going to leave us both...I also can't afford to have Kevin's emotions crushed. He lost his mother. He nearly died. And now he's attached to Kara."

"I thought it would be weird seeing Kara after all these years," Mike said. "I thought I'd still be mad, and wanted to hate her."

Shane laughed. "Impossible to hate that woman."

"Speaking of women, I need to get back to mine. She insists on only breastfeeding, so I need to be there to do the diaper changing thing and taking Tim for walks so she can sleep."

"Understood," Shane said. "I'm going to sit here, finish my coffee, then head over to the transplant wing and finish my interviews. Jones is probably feeling like I totally ditched him."

No sooner did his brother disappear in the hallway than Shane's phone rang.

Kara.

"Hello?"

"I've got something," Kara said. "Remember Brad Johnson? The soccer dad escorted off the field for harassing Gregory?"

"Hold that thought," Shane said, tapping the call

waiting. "Jones is calling. I'll make it a three-way." Once all three calls were connected he said, "Jones, you're on with me and Kara."

"I went back to the car to get a file," Jones said, "and heard over the radio that Theresa was in a car accident."

"What the fuck?" Shane bolted from his seat. "Where? Is she okay? What about Kevin?"

"Three miles from school," Jones said in a calm voice. "Minor scrapes and cuts, but taking her to Strong now. She complained of neck pain. Kevin wasn't with her. She hadn't made it to the school."

Shane checked his watch. "He gets out in five minutes."

"I'm less than ten from his school," Kara said. "In the car, so I'll go get him."

"Bring him to my parents' house." Shane sprinted from the waiting area and hit the elevator button over and over. "I'll let them know you're on your way. And Kara?"

"What?"

"Don't tell him too much."

"Understood," she said. "But something you need to know."

"What's that?" Shane asked.

"Brad Johnson killed himself three months ago. Six months ago, his daughter died in a car accident. On a Thursday. Her mother is Tina Vallen."

"Who?" Jones said.

"The new nurse?" Shane paused mid-step as he entered the elevator. "Kara, get my son."

K ara gripped the steering wheel as she turned way too fast onto the street where Kevin's school was located, knowing she was five minutes after dismissal. Two buses were still in the bus loop as she pulled into the side parking lot. The two double doors opened as a couple of children stepped out with an adult.

Slamming the car into park, she jumped out and raced up the steps and into the lobby of the elementary school. Ten children stood or sat in front of the office.

No Kevin.

Panic gripping her chest, she flashed her badge at the secretary in the main office. "I'm Kara Martin. I'm here to pick up Kevin Rogers. I'm on the list."

The woman blinked at her a few times. "But you called and said someone else—"

"I didn't call," Kara said. "Where's Kevin?"

She shook her head. "I spoke to you. You told me you had to meet Mr. Rogers and said a nurse from the hospital was coming."

"Tina Vallen?"

The woman nodded. "We wouldn't normally let a student go without parental permission, but you were on the list and we asked Kevin if he knew the nurse and he did. She told us what happened to Kevin's cousin and she was from the hospital...!" the woman screeched. "I...I..."

"How long ago?" Kara pushed her panic aside, focusing only on her training.

The woman grabbed a piece of paper from her desk. "Sign out sheet says less than ten minutes ago."

Kara had probably passed them on the way out. "I'm going to have to ask that you don't let anyone leave," Kara said. "I'll have officers over here quickly, but we need statements from everyone in the building right now as well as those who were here when Kevin was picked up."

The woman nodded.

Kara turned her back to the office as she called the Captain Morrell's direct line. Her pulse was raging out of control. There was no way she was standing in this school waiting for the locals.

"Agent Martin," Morrell said.

"Need a couple of officers at Kevin's elementary school to take statements." She bolted through the main door, nearly falling down the steps as she made her way to her car. "I'm heading to where I think he's been taken."

"Jesus Christ," Morrell said. "Does Shane know?"

"No." She slipped into the driver's seat of her car. "I'm fifteen minutes from Tina Vallen's house. I need back-up there."

"On it," he said. "Kara?"

"What?"

"Let me call Shane. I need you to focus on getting to the scene; don't do anything stupid like going it alone."

Kara tapped the phone, ending the call. Her heart raced so fast she could barely breathe. Clicking her police lights off, she pulled onto the street where Vallen lived. Kara parked two houses down on the opposite side of the street, noting the SUV in Vallen's driveway.

Kara got out of her vehicle, eyeing the two-story house and the two sets of footprints in the snow leading up the path to Vallen's house. She was contemplating her next move; it was decided for her when the front door opened and Kevin appeared, Vallen standing next to him with a knife to his neck.

"Come join the party," Tina called. "If you don't, I'll kill him now."

Kara held her hands up and started walking, eyes locked with Kevin's.

"Give me your weapon," Vallen said, once Kara was standing three paces from them.

She did as instructed.

"Go into the house."

She took one step in before a crushing pain slammed her head and the world went black...

24

SHANE SLAMMED HIS CAR into park in front Tina Vallen's house. Jones had said he was five minutes behind. Shane wasn't going to wait, considering Kara's car was just across the street and she was nowhere to be found. He reached for his weapon just as his phone rang. He glanced at the screen and recognized the number.

Kara.

"Where are you?" He stepped from the vehicle, phone to his ear, weapon in hand.

"Kara? She's right here," Tina said. "Come to the front of the house."

He took a controlled breath as he eased his way toward the front door. "Where's my son?"

The curtain in the large picture window to the right of the door slid open a few inches.

"He's safe," she said. "But I'd put that gun down or I'll shoot Agent Martin."

Tina drew back the curtain, showing the back of Kara tied to a chair, her head slumped to the side, a gun pressed against her temple. Kevin was only inches away.

"You don't want to do this." Shane holstered his weapon, raising his hand to the side. "Let them go and then we can negotiate—"

"No," Tina said. Her hand held the weapon with a steady grip. "I see your partner just rolled in. Better tell him to stay back."

Looking over his shoulder, he held his hand up. Jones stopped in the middle of the street.

"Smart man," Tina said. "Now back away and keep your people out of my house. Anyone comes in, I'll kill Kara." Tina pushed the gun, forcing Kara's head to the side.

The hairs on the back of his neck prickled. If he made a move and Tina pulled the trigger, Kara had no chance. Based on the angle of the shot and the chairs, the bullet would most likely hit Kevin.

"What do you want?"

"Right now, I want you to back up. I'll call you back in twenty minutes."

The curtain closed. He stood there for a long moment, his hand hovering over the butt of his gun. His pulse beat out of control. The urge to storm the house, grabbing

Vallen's neck with his bare hands, was so strong it took every ounce of energy he had to turn and walk toward Jones. Sirens echoed in the distance, growing stronger.

"She's got both Kevin and Kara," Shane said, now standing behind Kara's SUV, his forefinger itching to feel the trigger of his Glock. "Both tied up in the front room. I'm sure she's watching us, and if we try to get in the house she'll shoot Kara and kill Kevin with the same shot."

"Fuck," Jones muttered. "Let's clear these houses and barricade both ends of the street."

"She's calling me back in twenty. We've got to figure out how to get in there before that."

"We will," Jones said.

Shane rested his hand on the hood of Kara's SUV and sucked in a deep breath. "I've got a plan."

"No, you don't," Jones said.

"We go one street over, both of us entering through the back door. Catch her by surprise."

"We don't know the layout of the house," Jones said.

"We don't need to. We just need to draw her from the front room. You know it could work."

"Could," Jones repeated. "But it's too risky and you know it."

"I'm not going to stand around here and do nothing." Foster and the SWAT team had arrived. They were currently exiting their van, one of them pointing at various things while others leapt to action. Shane took a step in their direction, but Foster stepped in his way.

"You need to stay out of this."

"No fucking way." Shane took a few steps sideways.

Foster put a firm hand in the center of Shane's chest.

He glanced down. "Get out of my way." Shaking himself free he pushed forward, but was given a good shove back. "Jones and I have a plan."

"You're not going anywhere near that house," Foster said. "You need to sit this one out."

"That's my fucking son in there." He glared at Foster as heat rose from his toes to his face.

"And my partner's in there, too," Foster said. "SWAT is going to cover the house; they have a green light to take the shot, if they have one. Until then, we need you to talk with the hostage negotiator."

"Right. Because that's going to stop that psycho from killing Kevin and Kara," Shane muttered as he followed Foster to the SWAT van. The sound of the helicopter overhead only added to the gripping pain pulsing at his temples. He stared at the house as he leaned against the van.

"You talked to the woman holding your son and Agent Martin?" Tillman, the hostage negotiator, asked.

"I did." Shane scanned the area as various SWAT members situated themselves in key locations, trying to get a visual inside the house.

"No demands?"

Shane shook his head, forcing himself to concentrate on the case. "We believe she's the Butterfly Murderer. We have six dead. All had a different organ transplanted. All within the last eight months. All on a Thursday."

"I've been told your son had a transplant."

"On a Thursday, a little over six months ago," Shane said. "Just moments before my son was abducted, it came to our attention that Tina's daughter died the day of my son's transplant." His voice trembled. He kept his hand firmly planted on his weapon, his forefinger tracing the side of the cold metal. Fear and anger were a dangerous mixture. Fear and rage were worse.

His anger bubbled toward rage, and if something didn't happen, and quick, no one was going to be able to stop him from going in.

"We've also found out," Foster began, "that Vallen's ex-husband donated all her organs."

"So, it's possible Vallen's daughter could have been the donor for your son's heart?

"That's the working theory," Shane said. "We don't know if she's trying to rebuild her daughter, or taking the lives of people she believes should be dead. The profile on this is split right down the middle."

"Could be a bit of both," Tillman said. "When did she say she'd call back?"

"Should be any minute now."

*K*ara's vision continued to be blurry and her mind remained a tad on the foggy side, but she didn't need to be fully alert to understand the gravity of the situation. She scanned the room, but didn't see Vallen.

"Where'd she go?" she whispered to Kevin.

"I don't know," he said softly. "Are you okay?" His voice quivered.

"I will be once I get us out of here."

"This might help." He shoved his hand toward her, holding out a pocketknife that he placed in her bound hand.

"How did you get it out of your...where did you get this?"

"Don't tell Dad I had it. I'm not supposed to take it to school."

Kara tried not to smile, but it was impossible. "Sit back down and keep that rope around your wrists so she doesn't know, okay?"

He nodded.

"Try to let me do all the talking; if I tell you to do something, no matter how scared you are, do it."

He nodded.

She continued to fiddle with the small knife, scanning the room, assessing what she'd do once her hands were free. Footsteps echoed from the right side of the house, so Kara had to slow her process down as Vallen entered the room.

"I never wanted it to come to this," Vallen said, waving the gun in the air.

"How did you see this ending?" Kara blinked a few times, glancing toward Kevin, who kept his eyes wide and locked on her. His chest heaved up and down with his labored breath.

"Had you not shown up," Tina said, "I'd be reconnecting my daughter with her heart."

"But why kill all the others?" Kara knew she had to keep Tina talking. Explaining. Buy some time as she continued to work her hands from the rope tied around her wrists. "We got the donor lists, and the others didn't have your daughter's organs."

"Perhaps," Tina said. "But it wasn't just about *her* organs. It was about removing what didn't belong to those people. Fate dictated their time was up."

"Wouldn't fate say the same about your daughter?"

Tina nodded. "But I didn't get a say in what happened to her body. She was kept alive for hours as they harvested her organs. They had no right to do that."

"You were her mother. You had a say."

"Not that it's any of your business," Vallen narrowed her stare, "but her father had both physical and legal custody, stripping me of all my rights as a parent to make any decisions about my daughter. I barely got to see her."

"That seems a bit drastic in today's world." Kara hadn't had a chance to go over Vallen's file once they had made the connection, so she was totally flying blind. The clock was ticking and she needed to slow it down. "How did he manage that?"

"According to him," Vallen said, her voice laced with venom, "I willfully violated his legal custody rights so many times that it wasn't considered an isolated incident. He said I continually denied him his rights as a father after our divorce, which was a crock of shit. By the time my daughter was three, he'd stolen her from me."

"Did you fight him?" Kara kept her voice as sympathetic as she could. "It's rare courts strip parents of all custodial rights."

Vallen laughed. "The courts didn't understand what a horrible and abusive father he was, and actually handed down court orders that he'd have her half the time during the first custody hearing. That wasn't going to happen."

"You ignored the court order." Kara felt the rope loosen around her wrists. "What about the abuse? You weren't able to prove it?"

"Worse," Vallen said. "He was able to make the courts believe I made it up and that I was the one who posed a threat to my daughter."

"I'm so sorry," Kara said. "That had to have been very difficult for you."

Vallen nodded, but she kept her gun pointed at

Kara's head. "Acting like you care isn't going to help you. I'm still going to kill you."

Vallen pulled up a chair and sat across from Kara, gun pointed at her head, cell phone in her lap. Out of the corner of her eye Kara could see Kevin, sitting stoic and brave, but his little body trembled slightly.

"I was working when they brought my daughter to the emergency room," Vallen said. "She'd been hit by a car. Her stupid father let her walk everywhere. Never protected her from anything. I tried to fight the organ harvesting once I realized there was no saving her, but he had all the paperwork at his fingertips, and hours later Kevin got his new heart."

"You don't know for a fact that Kevin has your daughter's heart."

"Do you know how many heart transplants are done in this country per year?"

Kara shook her head.

"Somewhere between ten and thirty. I'd say the odds are pretty damn good he's got my baby girl's heart. I intend to take it back."

"It doesn't have to be this way," Kara said, swallowing the bile rising in her throat. "You let us go and I can make sure you don't—"

"I can't let you go."

"You know this place is surrounded now. You're not getting out of here alive if you kill us."

"Maybe I don't care."

"What about your daughter's heart? How can you get it back if they kill you first?"

"The point is to make sure her heart stops beating." Tina laughed. "I need to call Shane."

Kara continued to work the small dull knife through the rope while Tina made her call.

"You want to see your son?" Tina asked into the phone. "You've got five minutes to drop your weapon and come to the front door. You try anything, and either Kara or your son dies."

Shane took his holster off his belt and handed it to Jones. "I'm going in."

"Before you do that," Tillman said, "we need to have a plan."

"The plan is, I'm going in," Shane said. "We know there's a back door. I'll keep her to the front of the house; send someone in and we'll take her down before anything happens."

"At least wear a bulletproof vest," Jones said.

"Too antagonistic." Shane ignored his partner's plea. "Just get in through the back of the house."

Jones nodded.

"I don't think this is a good idea," Tillman said, standing in front of Shane.

"I don't fucking care." Shane pointed to the house then

stepped closer to Tillman, who had to crane his neck to look up at Shane. "My son is in there, not to mention a Federal agent. If I don't go in, that bitch will kill one of them. I'm not willing to risk that. Now get out of my way."

Tillman stepped to the side.

Shane shed his suit coat so that Vallen could see he was unarmed. He kept his arms out to the side, palms raised to the sky. He forced himself not to look around and concentrated only on the front door, though out of the corner of his eye he could see members of the SWAT team scurry to the other side of the house.

This had to work.

He swallowed. His pulse beat so fast his hands shook. As soon as he crossed the porch, the front door opened.

He clutched his chest at the sight of his son. Kevin's face was stoic. His body rigid. Vallen stood behind him, gun pointed at the back of his head. Shane couldn't fill his lungs with air. "You okay?" he said softly.

Kevin nodded.

It didn't ease the crushing pain in Shane's chest.

"Come on in," Tina said, pulling Kevin by the arm. "Glad you could finally make it."

"What do you want?" Shane scanned the empty foyer that led to the main room. His knees went weak when he saw Kara on the far end, her face bruised, eyes swollen, and a thick wad of dried blood clinging to her hair just above her ear.

"Go sit down." Vallen shoved Kevin, then pressed her gun firmly against Kara's temple.

Shane noticed that Tina had positioned herself in front of the window and had a good view of the back door. That wasn't good. He stood across the room, back to the wall, facing both Kara and Kevin.

"You haven't told me what you want," Shane said. "I can make it happen, whatever it is, but I need you to let Kevin go as a show of good faith."

Vallen laughed. "I'm not going to let anyone go. This isn't a negotiation."

"This isn't going to end well for you." Out of the corner of Shane's eye, he saw Kevin's hand on the side of chair for a brief second before he wrapped the rope around it again.

Regular Houdini.

"This isn't going to end well for anyone," Vallen said.

"If those cops out there hear a gunshot, the bullet storm that will come down on this house—"

"You know that's not going to happen. Not when they have no idea who got shot. Might bring them in sooner, but then..." She raised the weapon, turning it toward Kevin. "I see the back door open, I shoot Kevin."

"Then what?" Shane asked.

"I kill myself, leaving you to suffer for the rest of your miserable life."

"But that's not what you really want, is it?" He inched forward.

"Don't move!" Vallen yelled. "Sit down on the floor."

"All right." He did as instructed, noticing slight movement in Kara's arms. Then she lifted her finger, showing a frayed rope and Kevin's pocket knife.

He forced his breath to continue, keeping his elation from bubbling to the surface.

"Put your hands together." Vallen stood over him. She moved the gun from Kara's head, pointing it at Kevin while she sidestepped and removed some rope from the mantel. She dropped the rope onto his lap. "Hold one end in your mouth, the other with one hand, and twist it around your wrists." She held the gun steady. A little too steady. "Hold your hands up to me."

"Tell me something," he said, holding up his hands. "Why draw butterflies on the body?"

"A few reasons," she said. "Butterflies can represent new life or hope. People who get new organs think they're given a new life; in reality, the new life comes in death. I freed those souls."

"Other reasons?"

"Last time I was with my daughter was four years ago at a butterfly exhibit."

Shane swallowed, truly sorry for the woman's loss, but it didn't change the current situation. "What do the candles mean?"

She laughed. "The eight organs stolen from my daughter."

"But you've only collected six." Shane needed to keep her talking so Kara could finish sawing through the rope, but he also had a few questions he wanted answered.

"No," she said, "I got my thymus last night and I'm about to get my heart."

He closed his eyes briefly.

She tightened the rope with her free hand, looping the end to form a couple half-hitch knots. "I can show you all the organs I've collected. I've kept them in special oils so they don't deteriorate."

"What are you doing with them?"

"I was going to bury them with my daughter, but I don't think that's going to be possible now."

"Why did you want them buried with her?"

"Because she's not whole. Her body has been left empty. Robbed of the very things that made her flesh and blood." She slammed his hands to the floor and stomped on them.

He winced, then groaned in pain, feeling one of his fingers snap as she pulled the rope tighter, gun still steady on Kevin.

"So, let me get this straight," he said. "You're going to kill Kara. Then Kevin. Then yourself. But not me." He didn't frame it as a question.

"Yes," she said, still standing on his hands. "I'm going to be reunited with my daughter while you're left here to suffer."

"I can't live with that."

"You're not going to have a choice," she said. "But I left out the most important part."

"What's that?"

"You're going to watch me tear open your son's chest so we can watch my daughter's heart stop beating...so she can move on to her rebirth."

A sharp pain ripped through Shane's temples. His own heart slowed, then raced wildly out of control. "That's not going to happen."

Tina laughed as she removed her foot from his hands, and bent forward, her face just inches from his. Her gun pointed toward Kara, but he noticed her aim was off just a tad.

"And," she whispered, "Kevin is going to be alive when I do it."

Kara gave Shane a quick nod, showing both her hands were free.

"You got that wrong." He raised his fists with brute force, landing squarely on Tina's nose as Kara threw herself in Kevin's direction.

Bang!

Vallen flipped back, holding her nose, blood oozing between her fingers.

He scrambled to get to his feet, looking toward Kevin, praying neither he nor Kara had been shot. Kara had snagged the gun and then slammed Vallen up against the wall, the barrel of the weapon pressed into Tina's temple. Blood continued to roll down Vallen's face and neck. Dark circles under her eyes already forming from the broken nose. "This is for hitting me over the head with my weapon." Kara smacked Vallen with the butt of the gun and she groaned, falling to her knees. "This is for threatening to kill the people I love." She kicked Vallen in the gut.

"I think that's enough," Shane said while he watched his son cut through Shane's restraints. As soon as his hands were free, he wrapped his arms around Kevin, holding him tight. "Are you hurt?"

"No," Kevin said quietly, his shoulders shaking. His face buried in Shane's neck. His fingers digging into Shane's shoulders. "I was so scared."

"We all were," Shane said, squeezing his son, trying desperately to stop the trembling fear that still rippled from Kevin's body. "You were very brave."

"I thought Kara was dead when she got hit over the head," Kevin said through sobs. "She laid on the floor for a long time, not waking up."

"She's awake now," Shane said. "I think we're all going to be okay."

The house filled with SWAT as well as Foster and Jones. It was Foster who handcuffed Vallen and escorted her out. Shane sat on the floor, holding his son, hand pressed against his chest, feeling the pounding of *his* heart.

"Hey." Kara sat down next to him. "You've got quite a kid. He literally saved us," she said.

"How did he do that?"

"Well, that's up to him to tell you."

Shane looked at his son. "What is she talking about?"

"Don't be mad, but I accidentally brought my pocketknife to school again, so I had it with me."

"Had he not been able to get me that pocketknife, we'd all be dead," Kara said.

"How'd you manage that?" Shane asked as he cupped his son's face, checking for damage that Tina might have inflicted as he wiped his son's tears away.

"I was able to free my hands from the rope."

"Using the knife that you're not supposed to take with you to school?" Shane asked.

"No." Kevin shook his head. "I've been practicing escape tricks for the school talent show. Gina's been helping me. I hadn't been able to do it until today."

"Without using the knife? That's amazing," Shane said. "How did you get the knife to Kara?"

"When Nurse Vallen left the room."

"I was quite shocked to see him reach into his pocket and hand it to me," Kara said. "Then it just became a waiting game. Took me nearly twenty minutes to free my hand and I think he did it in five minutes."

"A little longer than that," Kevin said. "I almost didn't try it because I was afraid she'd hurt Kara more if she found out."

"It was a brave move." Shane kissed the top of his son's head. "Smart to keep the rope around your wrists like that."

"Kara told me to do that."

He reached out and traced his finger along Kara's chin, pulling her toward him. He kissed her temple. "I'm sorry that lunatic hurt you."

"It's not your—"

He pressed his finger against her lips. "Thank you for taking care of my son."

"I think he took care of me." She leaned her head against his shoulder. "I've got a killer headache and that bitch shot me."

"What?" Shane lifted her head. "When I hit her?"

Kara held up her arm.

Gently, he tugged at her shirt, noting a small amount of blood. The bullet had sliced through the top part of her bicep. It wasn't a hole, but it wasn't a graze either. Shane waved the EMTs over, pointing to Kara's arm. Then he tilted her head from side to side. A lump the size of a golf ball formed just above her right ear, along with a cut that looked as though it was still bleeding. Her black eye grew darker, along with a nasty bruise on her swollen cheek.

"I'm tired," she whispered. Leaning against his shoulder. "I don't feel too well either."

"You probably have a concussion," he said. "We'll get you to the hospital."

"Okay," she said. "I think I'll put in for a few days off starting now."

"I think I'll join you."

25

SHANE STARED AT HIS TWO fingers taped together with a splint while he sat in the emergency waiting room with his son, who was sound asleep, his head resting on his grandmother's lap. His niece had been released, but he didn't want to leave until after Kara had been checked out and released. His parents had also refused to leave. His mother sat next to him, gently stroking Kevin's hair. His father and Theresa sat across from him. Theresa had her nose in a textbook, while his father read a book on his Kindle.

"You sure you don't want one of us to take him home?" His father peered over his electronic device.

"I promised him he could stay."

"I can't believe that nurse killed all those people," his mother said in a soft tone.

Foster entered the waiting room from the main

corridor. His usual cool demeanor had disappeared and was replaced with disheveled hair and dark circles around his eyes.

"Excuse me." Shane rose and met Foster near the doors. He didn't want his family to hear this conversation.

"Any news on Kara?" Foster asked.

"Half a dozen stitches in her arm, another three in her head. They kicked me out when they took her down for a CT scan. Doctor said he'd come get me when she's back in the ER. They might admit her for the night. Being thorough and making sure there's no bleeding in the brain or abnormal swelling. When I left, she was protesting and wanted to go home."

"Sounds like her," Foster said. "I've got some information for you about your niece's accident. The driver of the car that T-Boned her was paid a hefty sum to do so by Vallen."

"I suspected she had orchestrated it," Shane said.

"You also might like to know there wasn't another victim. Turns out a donor had their organs harvested last night and Vallen somehow managed to walk off with the thymus."

While Shane was glad no one else had died at the hands of that woman, a wave of sadness sent a cold shiver across his neck. Kevin hadn't asked about her daughter and his heart. His only concern seemed to be Kara, but Shane knew the conversation was coming. He wasn't sure who would have a harder time: him or his son. "Did you call Cleary? Any of the other victims' families?"

"They were all notified before the story broke," Foster said. "Cleary pleaded his DUI down to a drunk and disorderly. Not sure what will happen to his career, but he's going to make a public apology."

"What about the criminal sexual assault charges against the McCauley boy?"

"He was given a plea bargain for a misdemeanor, so no felony charges. Cleary said he was going to speak to the judge on behalf of the boy, asking for leniency."

"That's a tough one," Shane said. "But it sounds like some healing is starting to take place."

The doors into the ER buzzed before swinging open. Kara's doctor stepped through. "Agent Martin is back in her room," he said. "All the scans are normal. No reason to keep her overnight, but she was knocked out. Complications from concussions can present hours, even days later, so I'm sending her home with some strict orders. It will take about an hour to process the paperwork and get you all the information you need regarding her condition."

"Can my son and I see her now?" Shane asked.

"She's been asking for the both of you," the doctor said before turning and heading back through the electronic doors.

"Tell Kara I'll see her back at the office," Foster said.

"You're going back to D.C. now?"

Foster nodded. "Our team leader gave her a week's leave, but not me; I've been assigned another case."

Shane held out his hand. "It really was a pleasure working with you."

"You changed my mind about locals." He took Shane's hand and gave a long, firm handshake. "I know she's in good hands. Make sure you tell her I said goodbye and I'll call her tomorrow."

"Will do." Shane waited a moment before waking his son. He gently prodded his shoulder.

"Let him sleep," his mother protested.

"I promised him I'd bring him to see Kara as soon as possible."

"He'll understand," she said.

"No, he won't. He's formed a strong attachment to Kara, and considering what just happened, and relating it to his mother's death, he needs to *see* she's okay, not hear it." He shook Kevin's arm again.

"What?" Kevin sat up and wiped his eyes.

"Kara's back in the room and we can go see her." Shane took his son's hand. "And they're letting her come home tonight." He took small steps as they made their way across the waiting room and through the ER doors. His parents and niece all yelled to give Kara their best and that they would wait. He knew it was futile to tell them otherwise. Just like Kevin needed to see her, his parents needed to be there for him.

"I read with concussions you have to have brain

rest, and we should wake her every so often. You can have bad symptoms even days after."

"Where'd you read that?"

"On the internet on Theresa's phone. She agrees I'm old enough for a smartphone."

"Of course she does." Shane drew back the curtain, taking a quick peek in before pulling it back all the way. "Up for a couple of visitors?"

"Oh yeah." Kara was propped up in the hospital bed, wearing a set of scrubs since her blood-stained clothes were not fit to be worn. White gauze covered much of her bicep and a patch of hair just above her ear had been shaved, showing off a few stitches.

"How do you feel?" Kevin asked, taking a tentative step toward the bed.

She held out her hand. "Come sit."

"You sure it's okay?" Kevin said. "I don't want to hurt you."

"I'll be fine," Kara said. "I know I don't look that way, but the headache isn't as bad as what the side of my head looks like."

"Well, I read up on concussions and was just telling Dad about them, so we'll take good care of you."

"I know you will." She smiled.

Shane sat down in the ugly green chair that was supposed to be a recliner, but was more like a metal bench. His bones ached. He shifted a few times, unable to get comfortable. Kevin had climbed up on the bed, and sat at Kara's side, holding her hand.

"I'm sorry I went with her," Kevin said.

"Don't be." Shane shifted again. "She was someone you knew and trusted. But from now on we're going to have a safe word. If anyone but me or Kara or someone in our family comes to pick you up, they'll have to give you our secret safe word before you go with them."

"I'm very grateful," Kara said, "that your mother got you into magic. That's what saved us. I wish I could have met your mom. I bet she was something special."

"She was," Kevin said softly. "Dad?"

"What is it?" Shane leaned forward.

"Do you really think I have Nurse Vallen's daughter's heart?"

"I told you I'd never lie about stuff like this," Shane said. "It's possible, but that doesn't mean she was anything like Nurse Vallen."

Kevin nodded. "I thought I would feel different when I had the transplant, but I never did. Even now that we sort of know, I still don't feel different."

"Because you're not different." Kara tapped his chest. "You are who you are because you're part your father, part your mother, and part everyone who loves you."

Shane had to turn away and wipe his eyes.

"But I hear things like, *you've got to have heart*, or *you've got a kind heart*, like it's the heart that makes you who you are."

Shane squeezed his son's thigh. "Those are expressions and they come from years ago, before man really understood the human body. Our hearts sustain us. We can't live without one, but it doesn't make up our conscience." He tapped his own head. "What's up here. Our past experiences, our knowledge of right and wrong, that's who we are."

Kevin turned and hugged Kara. By the scrunched look on her face, he'd hit her bullet wound.

"Give her some room," Shane said, tugging at his son's arm. "I think you're hurting—"

"Oh, sorry." Kevin bolted upright. "I'm really glad you're okay...that your head is okay and I...well...I love you."

"I love you right back."

Kara held up the empty pitcher. "Will you get me some water?"

"Sure," Shane said.

"I'll get it." Kevin grabbed the pitcher. "I saw the ice and water machine on the way in."

"Come right back." Shane leaned back on the hard chair, letting out a long sigh. "You look like shit," Shane said to Kara after his son had left.

"You don't look that hot yourself," Kara said with a weak smile.

"I feel worse than you look."

"I seriously doubt that. You didn't get shot or knocked out."

"True, but the ache in my heart, knowing you're returning to D.C. in a week, is worse than any physical pain I can think of."

352

"I've been thinking about that." She patted the side of the bed. "Sit with me."

He pressed his hands on the armrests, wincing in pain from his broken finger.

"Worse than physical pain?" She laughed. "You're pathetic."

He sat on the edge of the bed, leaned over, and gently kissed her check. "I wish I had broken more than her nose for doing that to you."

She looped her good arm around his shoulder, sliding her hand up his neck, tugging at his hair. "I love you," she whispered as she drew him closer, her warm lips against his. Her soft tongue darted into his mouth in a slow, sensual dance that promised him the world.

He pulled back a little, keeping his lips close to hers. "I love you, too. I want to make this work. I don't want to lose you again."

"I'm not going to let that happen," she said. "I have a job opportunity and I want to take it, but I need to talk with you before making that decision."

"This isn't helping my discomfort regarding you leaving..." he let the words trail off.

She let out a small chuckle.

"I don't see what's so funny."

"I'm not leaving you. The Agent in Charge in the Rochester office is leaving and I was offered his job."

"Excuse me?" He stuck his finger in his ear. He couldn't have possibly heard her correctly. "You're moving back to Rochester?"

"I want to," she said, cupping his face. "Nothing is more important to me than you and Kevin."

"Wow." It wasn't often that he was speechless, but he opened his mouth and nothing came out. He cleared his throat and tried again. "Are you sure this is what you want? I can't ask you to give up something you've—"

"You haven't asked me. It's what I want," she said. "The job offer is a promotion for me. A good one. It starts in two weeks. I wouldn't have to travel like I do now and...we can be together if that's what—"

He didn't let her finish her statement as his mouth took hers in a lip lock that was messy and wet. There was nothing romantic about the kiss. It was pure passion and power, only he didn't know where to put his hands so as not to hurt her, so he settled for the pillow next to her head as he pressed his chest against hers. His tongue on a search and rescue mission.

She broke the kiss way too soon. "So, you're good with me moving here?"

"You really have to ask?" He kissed her nose. "I love you. I want to meet you in my dreams every night."

Thank you for taking the time to read *The Butterfly Murders*. Please feel free to leave an honest review. If you enjoyed this book, please consider checking out ***Investigate Away.***

Grab a glass of vino, kick back, relax, and let the romance roll in…

Sign up for my Newsletter (https://dl.bookfunnel.com/ 82gm8b9k4y) where I often give away free books before publication.

Join my private Facebook group (https://www.facebook.com/ groups/191706547909047/) where I post exclusive excerpts and discuss all things murder and love!

Never miss a new release. Follow me on Amazon:amazon.com/author/jentalty
And on Bookbub: bookbub.com/authors/jen-talty

ABOUT THE AUTHOR

Jen Talty is the *USA Today* Bestselling Author of Contemporary Romance, Romantic Suspense, and Paranormal Romance. In the fall of 2020, her short story was selected and featured in a 1001 Dark Nights Anthology.

Regardless of the genre, her goal is to take you on a ride that will leave you floating under the sun with warmth in your heart. She writes stories about broken heroes and heroines who aren't necessarily looking for romance, but in the end, they find the kind of love books are written about :).

She first started writing while carting her kids to one hockey rink after the other, averaging 170 games per year between 3 kids in 2 countries and 5 states. Her first book, IN TWO WEEKS was originally published in 2007. In 2010 she helped form a publishing company (Cool Gus Publishing) with *NY Times* Bestselling Author Bob Mayer where she ran the technical side of the business through 2016.

Jen is currently enjoying the next phase of her life…the empty nester! She and her husband reside in Jupiter, Florida.

Grab a glass of vino, kick back, relax, and let the romance roll in…

Sign up for my _Newsletter (https://dl.bookfunnel.com/82gm8b9k4y)_ where I often give away free books before publication.

Join my private _Facebook group_ (https://www.facebook.com/groups/191706547909047/) where I post exclusive excerpts and discuss all things murder and love!

Never miss a new release. Follow me on Amazon:amazon.com/author/jentalty

And on Bookbub: bookbub.com/authors/jen-talty

ALSO BY JEN TALTY

Brand new series: SAFE HARBOR!

Mine To Keep

Mine To Save

Mine To Protect

Mine to Hold

Mine to Love

Check out LOVE IN THE ADIRONDACKS!

Shattered Dreams

An Inconvenient Flame

The Wedding Driver

Clear Blue Sky

Blue Moon

Before the Storm

NY STATE TROOPER SERIES (also set in the Adirondacks!)

In Two Weeks

Dark Water

Deadly Secrets

Murder in Paradise Bay

To Protect His own

Deadly Seduction

When A Stranger Calls

His Deadly Past

The Corkscrew Killer

First Responders: A spin-off from the NY State Troopers series

Playing With Fire

Private Conversation

The Right Groom

After The Fire

Caught In The Flames

Chasing The Fire

Legacy Series

Dark Legacy

Legacy of Lies

Secret Legacy

Emerald City

Investigate Away

Sail Away

Fly Away

Flirt Away

Hawaii Brotherhood Protectors

Waylen Unleashed

Bowie's Battle

Colorado Brotherhood Protectors

Fighting For Esme

Defending Raven

Fay's Six

Darius' Promise

Yellowstone Brotherhood Protectors

Guarding Payton

Wyatt's Mission

Corbin's Mission

Candlewood Falls

Rivers Edge

The Buried Secret

Its In His Kiss

Lips Of An Angel

Kisses Sweeter than Wine

A Little Bit Whiskey

It's all in the Whiskey

Johnnie Walker

Georgia Moon

Jack Daniels

Jim Beam

DELTA FORCE-NEXT GENERATION

Shielding Jolene

Shielding Aalyiah

Shielding Laine

Shielding Talullah

Shielding Maribel

Shielding Daisy

The Men of Thief Lake

Rekindled

Destiny's Dream

Federal Investigators

Jane Doe's Return

The Butterfly Murders

THE AEGIS NETWORK

The Sarich Brother

The Lighthouse

Her Last Hope

The Last Flight

The Return Home

The Matriarch

Aegis Network: Jacksonville Division

A SEAL's Honor

Talon's Honor

Arthur's Honor

Rex's Honor

Kent's Honor

Buddy's Honor

Aegis Network Short Stories

Max & Milian

A Christmas Miracle

Spinning Wheels

Holiday's Vacation

The Brotherhood Protectors

Out of the Wild

Rough Justice

Rough Around The Edges

Rough Ride

Rough Edge

Rough Beauty

The Brotherhood Protectors

The Saving Series

Saving Love

Saving Magnolia

Saving Leather

www.ingramcontent.com/pod-product-compliance
Lightning Source LLC
Chambersburg PA
CBHW011144100726
47899CB00010B/3165